PINK CARNATIONS

A journey on Racism, his Pride, her Lust and joint Pain...

BY

NUALA URAIH

Harmony Publishing

Plot 1 Emmanuel Anabor, Off Mopo Road, United Estate, Sangotedo, Lagos, Nigeria

publish@harmonypublishing.com.ng

ISBN: 978-1-00569-524-8

Printed in Nigeria

Declaration

This book contains some fictional names, places, tribes and characters. South Ciskei is a fictional country and Xhosatan a fictional tribe. The story is set in a period where oppressed Africans are seen as fighters trying to sustain their heritage, which the western world colonized. However, some of the events portrayed in this story are based on both historical and real-life events from South Africa and Nigeria.

DEDICATION

I dedicate this book to my dad and mom, who taught me all I know about the benefit of inscribing words on paper. It is also dedicated to my baby brothers, Ekenem and Junboy, who saw the beauty in my storytelling even when I could not see it.

PROLOGUE

South Ciskei Uprising, The 1976 Massacre

The howl of the failed revolution could easily be heard through the walls of my mud house that windy morning. It was a concoction of the vibrating noise from the muzzle of the firing of guns, accompanied by the screams of the brave local students as they succumbed to their deaths. The screams were distant, yet sharp, piercing into the thickness of my sleep and jolting me to life. I can recollect the events of that morning with clarity, how my heart beat faster than my native drums. I can recall the expression on Papa's aged face that very day, a harvest of pride, victory and fulfilment.

Papa was an upright man, tall and handsome, with a bronze skin that made him the toast of young and old ladies alike, despite his age. He was also a respected teacher and village activist who would always be found wearing thick reading glasses and a short sleeve shirt, complete with a bow tie over worn-out trousers.

Earlier that morning, Papa had suddenly fallen sick with a bout of fever, and Mama had persuaded him to stay back home instead of going to school to join the demonstration while she mopped his hot body with a piece of cloth soaked in cold water. The fight was initiated by Papa, as South Ciskei locals were trying to preserve their African heritage; the western world had invaded their space for years and mistreated the native people. The word on the street was that the neighbouring countries had lost their heritage, their ancestral land replaced with taller buildings, their names westernized, and their folk songs replaced with the western blues. Papa hated the blues.

Around noon that day, while having a brunch of cocoyam and palm oil, we had unexpected visitors. Initially, I had frowned at the interruption because, you see, we always ate twice daily: brunch and dinner, with no in-betweens. That was how we survived on Papa's meagre salary. My train of thought was cut short when a white man with a long unkempt beard stormed into our house in the company of two white police officers and with an air of assured authority. I glanced at Papa's face. As usual, he looked composed, but I remember seeing a flicker of fear in his eyes. This was so strange to me because I had never seen a white man come into our quarters. You see, back then, white people were seen as mini gods who did not mix with coloured people, especially in their homes.

'This is Sheldrake's home, isn't it?' the white man asked aloud. He had a mean appearance; he was about 6 feet tall, broad-shouldered and with a memorable moustache that curled up at each edge.

'If it is Sheldrake, the head teacher, then it is,' Papa replied, as he laboured to his feet, with Mama supporting him.

'Don't transfer any disease to us boy,' the leader warned as he menacingly moved toward Papa. 'We heard you are the audacious teacher who is leading those fools out there to make this village ungovernable.'

'I would ask that you do not disrespect my home if you come into it uninvited!' Papa challenged him.

'Really?' he asked with a smirk. 'So, it is true. In that case, perhaps I should show you what it means to be disrespected. Arrest him,' he ordered.

As if that was an opportunity to teach Papa a lesson, the police officers descended on him with sturdy slaps, then violently handcuffed him. Papa cut the picture of the meek Jesus that I often heard about in our Sunday school classes at Savior's Baptist Church, which was often described as 'a lamb led to Golgotha'. I remember he didn't fight back as they dragged him out of the house, hands chained, pride drained. But Mama wailed and wailed. She struggled with the officers. Papa softly spoke to her to reassure her that he would return home soon. They attempted to take Papa to their car, but Mama blocked their way. She tried to grab the white man by his neck collar and scratched his face. He let out a cry of pain as Mama's fingernails dug into the flesh on his face.

'My eyes!' he screamed and tried to grab onto Mama's neck, with his eyes shut. I saw Papa struggle to break free from the police officer's grips and chains, but it was to no avail. They held him tightly and then shoved him to the back of the car seat.

'You bastard! God will punish you,' Mama screamed at the white man in our local Xhosatan lingo as he tried to push her away from him. But Mama seemed determined. There was venom in her eyes, a look I had never seen before. Was the demon in her, which she had carefully tamed, let loose? Was it a woman's love? Or unbridled hatred for her husband's traducers? It was a new mama we saw that morning.

'Enough! Let that woman go.' A deep baritone voice with unmistakable superiority suddenly halted the chaos. It was a white man with a fiercer look and a more commanding tone. He was dressed up in a brown English suit and held a gold-plated walking stick. I thought at that moment that he must be important, because, as soon as he came, the other white man let Mama go.

'This little bitch tried to kill me, Brother,' the cruel bearded white man screamed in anger as he let Mama go. I realised that the white man with the authoritative tone was indeed related to the other angry white man, because they had similar facial features.

'Interesting that you let a little negro woman overpower you, Jefferson.' He continued without a smile, 'The English and the bloody American press have flooded the whole area. We can't risk more negative publicity. I am running for office soon. So, release the man.'

The policemen and the angry bearded white man looked defeated; Mama rushed to the car door and quickly opened the door for Papa. When Papa got out of the car, with Mama holding onto his arm in tears, he looked up at the white man and murmured a thank you. But the white man didn't reply. He took a few steps towards Mama and Papa, with his gaze on her face.

'We are so very grateful...' Mama stammered.

'You are the head teacher?' he asked, without shifting his gaze from Mama. Papa didn't like his look towards Mama, but he was helpless. Mama spoke up for him while still in shock. 'Ermm....no sir...I....'

'I wasn't asking you, madam.' He was still looking at her.

Papa got the clue and, in a subdued voice, spoke. 'I am the science teacher.'

'The school is burnt down. You and your people would need work to feed your family soon...'

'I do not understand?'

'I am opening a coal and gold mine soon. I need all the hands I can get. Though you are a teacher, your knowledge and the respect you have garnered among the people will come in handy. So, you can come and work for me as a manager.'

'Are you trying to bribe me?' Papa growled.

'He will come,' Mama immediately interrupted Papa, as she took the white envelope from the man's outstretched hand.

'Let's say I am trying to provide good employment for the minority. Isn't good employment one of the causes for your fight?' he asked firmly. Papa nodded.

'What the hell! He can't be a manager, Brother,' the other white man, Jefferson, tried to protest, but his brother shut him up with a wave of his hand.

'Let's go,' he commanded.

And just like that, they left our home.

Papa died a few months after he took up the job at the gold mine.

CHAPTER ONE

THE YEAR 1995, ST DOMINIC CATHOLIC CHURCH, NIGERIA

Their angelic voices could be heard from miles away. It was the familiar worship song from the choir of the magnificent St. Dominic's Catholic Church. Correspondents from all broadcasting networks in the world focused their cameras on the face of an aged soloist who treated the solemn congregation to 'Ave Maria'. She was clad in a black choir robe alongside the rest of her choral group members.

The church was packed with a congregation of both black and white men and women. They were mostly clothed in chic black outfits and head fascinators. The cameras gradually trailed the faces of the crowd. Some were captured sniffing their noses with handkerchiefs while others were seen wiping the tears from the corners of their eyes.

Soon, the tenor of the choir decreased, which indicated that the song was coming to an end. The camera rested on an attractive black lady in her teens, who was sitting in the front row of the church. She put on a large, dark Oliver Goldsmith Manhattan's sunglasses that concealed the unique features of her tired eyes and neatly powdered cheek bone. A simple lace scarf wrapped around her head concealed her skinny neck line. Her gaze was transfixed on a closed gold-plated coffin covered with dozens of pink carnations flowers that were placed ahead of her. She began to slowly and painfully clutch her plain twenty-karat gold necklace for emotional support. A frail hand reached out to her left hand for solace. She then let go of her necklace. The face of a black man in his sixties, who sat next to her, was now the attention of the television network. He was dressed in a black two-piece French suit. He whispered in her ears and at the same time, the soloist finished her song. The man got up and slowly walked to the front of the church. He was accompanied by a white elderly man, who took the microphone and spoke to the silent crowd.

'Thank you all for being here today. It sure has been a long journey for us all...'

***

SHELDRAKE

South Ciskei, Southern Africa, Shweta Township, 1984

The scenario of the slums in Shweta township, which was under the control of the city council at that time, during the apartheid, could easily be envisaged based on the prominent tales of the contentious lives of its inhabitants. The rows of tiny shanties or small brown houses were commonly called 'matchbox' houses for the Negros. These matchbox houses were built on piles of garbage near rustic streams with abandoned broken bottles. The withered leaves from the Eucalyptus trees mostly bore conspicuous sign posts, scribbled with racial restrictions, which could easily be seen from afar. These signages would read 'the entrance of the South Ciskei', 'Private road' or 'Negros entering this area must have a permit'. Also, desolate little Negros, who mostly appeared unkempt, scantily clothed and atrophied could be pictured taking their daily naps in front of their parasite-infested homes. Their domestic pets ran around the frightening streets. The images of the firing of open missiles by white policemen and the thunderous voices from black revolutionaries were still heard as they irately matched along the dodgy streets of the district in search of autonomy, after the abrupt South Ciskei uprising and massacre.

However, most children could be spotted playing 'football' with empty Coca-Cola and milk cans, despite the scary uprising. Also, older men contentedly smoked cheap tobacco with broken pipes while they drank their local whisky – what do they call that drink now? Fuga, yes, I think they call it Fuga – as they drown their worries in a game of draft. They did not know a better way to escape the racial struggles than with the intoxication of strong liquor. After all, as the saying goes, what you don't know won't harm you.

In my yard, before the cock would crow, most middle-aged women dressed up in their neatly sewn housemaids' uniforms can be seen rushing out of their quarters to catch the early morning train to their work stations. That picture of strong and inspired women was the most memorable picture of my neighbourhood at that time. Mama, a beautiful, petite, bronze-skinned, middle-aged woman with a stunning afro hairdo was constantly the object of attention in my small neighbourhood. In the mornings, she struggled with the door as she tried to lock up our ramshackle front door. That morning, as usual, she was cursing noisily in our native Xhosatan tongue, as if the poor thing could hear her. Her profanities were mostly caused by my baby sister, a six-year-old pain in the arse who always cried out aloud as soon as she tried to hinder the front door from shutting when Mama was late for work.

My sister always reminded me that Mama would often yell behind the shut doors:

'Stay in the house and wait for your brother, Martha! Oh good Lord, I will kill him when I get a hold of him.'

You see, I was hardly ever around.

But wait. Before I start telling my story, let me introduce myself. I am Mandiva Sheldrake, a proud South Ciskei African native from the Xhosatan Clan. I lived with my mother, Miriam, and little sister, Martha, in the Shweta ghetto, Old Panaville, which was beside the popular borders of Danaloof and Meadowstick, to be exact.

The series of events that transformed me from a timid young man to an iron-willed adult started in April 1984. This date was also memorable, as it was one of the hottest days in Shweta. The leaves from the oak trees were withering, and the humidity in the air was unbearable. Sweat oiled by the blazing sun rolled down my temple into my misty eyes. I was exhausted from the day's work. The work is called *black man's work of shame*. For it was what the majority of coloured men from South Ciskei did for survival back in the day. This meant that every elderly Negro was working their arse off in

4

the coal and gold mine alongside their underage sons. It was a case of slave fathers and slave sons. The little ones would run errands in the same mine like getting a bottle of milk and pastries for their white masters for breakfast or shining their dusty shoes. Failure to do these could result in the harsh exercising of the fucking apartheid rule. This was because back then, the Xhosatans tribe in Shweta were governed by the toothless Urban Bantutu Council, which had no executive power and could only act in the advisory capacity to the white authorities. For this reason, we often referred to this council as the '*useless Boys Club*'.

The white Superintendent who indirectly called all the shots for the eleven administrative offices, by which the Shweta Township was controlled, was a ruthless man feared and hated at the same time. I was amongst the victims of his terror reign. On the local television, his justification for engaging in any inhumane acts was that as the mayor, he understands that to rule such a community, force is needed and that he must exact such a force. Most Africans are animals, he reasoned, and he would not hesitate to treat them as such. For example, he preferred giving white-collar jobs to the white minority and the odd jobs to the Negros because 'he needed blacks to take responsibility and go to school'. Worse still, any Negro caught stealing even a piece of bread was served the maximum sentence. They hardly ever get an opportunity for any proper hearings or appeals from the court. Rumours had it that these cases were intentionally lost in transit. The superintendent was popularly known as 'The Mad Mayor' amongst my peers, which was translated as a white extremist by most black locals.

Papa had died slaving in the mine when I was only seven years old, after he had taken the job offer from the Mayor back then. The memories of Papa's death still tortured me in my dreams. We received no apologies or compensation, which justified his nickname. It was typical of the regime; we were to lick our wounds in silence and without complaints. So, my mother had to work extra hard to put some food on our table. Unfortunately, she ended up working for the mayor. The horrible mayor owned everything in South Ciskei.

Eight years later, as I had reached the age of fifteen, I had become a tall, slim young man with a muscular physique. I frequently dressed up in my favourite blue khaki shorts and brown worn-out singlet, which had the South Ciskei flag boldly printed on it. I loved my homeland despite our state of poverty.

I stood over the hilltop with a broad grin on my face as I watched two middle-aged black men wrestle. One of the fighters was Papa's brother and the other was a stranger to me. I swung my fist in the air to imitate my uncle, the bald fighter, as he pummelled his opponent into submission. The fight was soon over. I began to clap as the winner of the fight approached me. I ran to meet him with a warm embrace, not minding the sweat all over his muscular body. My uncle, who was nicknamed Jide Sheldrake, was victorious once again. Papa had explained to me years ago that uncle was nicknamed Jide because he took after his favourite boxer, a Nigerian, named Jide who came to South Ciske to fight a long time ago. However, Uncle Jide was like a dreamer to Mama, which irritated her. She believed he had no savings as he invested his little income from the bar he worked in buying lots of books, which he then somehow used in preaching to the villagers about subversion.

I moved towards him screaming in excitement, 'That was brilliant, Uncle!'

But his response was a cold rebuke.

'My boy, you can't be showing up here every day to watch old men fight. Aren't you meant to be in school, Mandiva?'

'I don't want to go to school. I want to be a fighter like you.' I replied in Xhosatan 'Besides, I have been out of school for a while because Mother couldn't pay the fees for my exams.'

'But your mother goes to work. Don't they pay her?' he asked.

'She has been going, Uncle. I think she is even doing extra shifts at the MDS boy's residence now. She said she hasn't been able to raise the money completely.'

I remember Uncle frowning at me before giving me a nudge, 'Don't let them white folks hear you calling the mayor 'The Mad Mayor' boy. You would be out of school for life; you will be bunkmates with the real Mandela in prison at Robin Island.' He gave me a gentle smack on the head and wimped as he watched me flinch. As we walked home, he continued 'Is the rumour true? Heard mayor's wife is returning today with her son from England.'

Suddenly it hit me. 'Oh my God, I forgot to deliver the milk for Mother to make pastries.'

I picked up the bucket filled up with bottles of freshly extracted milk from the cows in the dairy farm and raced down the hills with it. After a few seconds, I came within touching distance of a large estate that had an astonishing grey mansion in its centre. I searched my pocket to show my pass to the security guard at the gate so that they would let me go to the house. But it seemed I had lost it during my run.

'I can't find my interior passport sir,' I pleaded to the two black security guards outside the gate.

'Then you can't enter, son. we are expecting special guests today, so they told us to beef up security.'

You see, the interior passports were used to control black settlement and it was called the Pass Laws. Black people of colour used the identification passport to enter the cities during work hours, because the rest of the time, coloured people were not allowed in the cities at that time. The Pass Laws represented a lucrative opportunity for white-owned mining companies to employ and exploit the coloured workers while enjoying their massive wealth. In a nutshell, it was illegal for a black person not to carry a passbook.

'He is with me. Let him in.'

I heard a voice from behind. I turned around to see Mr Minschini. He was the oldest butler on the premises and Mama's good friend. He always looked frail when he stood at the front door of his station, but he always had a big smile on his face as he did his job serving the white man. He showed them his pass. The security guards nodded and let me in.

'Oh thank you, Mr Minschini. Mama would have killed me if I didn't show up.'

'I know, son. Now hurry to the kitchen. She has been waiting,' he smiled, as he rushed me into the house through the backdoor to enter the kitchen.

The kitchen was a vast space; it was appropriately fitted with modern kitchen utensils that were orderly arranged above the kitchen cabinet. The room was filled with black men and women of various heights, shapes and sizes. The most striking thing that they shared in common was the colour of their skin: black, and that of their aprons: white. Some were cutting vegetables on chopping boards, while others were pulling out freshly baked cornbread and cheese soufflé for desserts out of the oven. Meanwhile, the coloured valet, butler and footmen were being ordered by the older kitchen hands in the native language to assist in carrying the desserts to the dining hall. I browsed around the kitchen in search of Mama, trying my best not to be carried away by the sweet aroma of freshly baked cornbread that filled the room. Eventually, I located her in a corner rolling out dough on a wooden pan.

When I finally approached her, she looked up at me and pulled a face. I recalled her saying 'I can as well give you a good knock on the head, Maddy. You know you are late and I waited in the house all day for you to get back with the milk. I had to leave your sister home alone; you know I can't afford to lose this job.'

I stammered an apology. I knew Mama's knocks could make a grown man cry.

'I am so sorry Mama it won't happen again.' I put the milk down on the table in front of her.

'I guess you stopped by the hills again to watch that brainless uncle of yours fight. You better wake up Mandiva from your trance and work hard, and make some money or go to school. Do you want to end up like Jide – a broke man who can't afford to keep a wife or help his sister-in-law, nephew or niece in any positive way? And stop looking at the damn floor because I have told you this one-million times before. Look at me when I talk,' she warned, loud enough for me to feel threatened, but I remained silent not to provoke her further or attract the attention of her co-workers.

'Sorry Mama,' I apologised again.

'You would be sorrier if I lost this job, boy.'

I was thankful when the head cook, an elderly woman in uniform, came in and interrupted the discussion. She was Aunty Rose, Mama's best mate. She had apparently watched the drama between the mother and son and knew something was wrong.

'It's okay Miriam, stop scolding the boy. The mayor's wife will arrive in two minutes. We all have to be outside to welcome them—' She turned to the chefs and announced, 'we are wrapping up our cooking now. The mayor and his guests are received in two minutes. We have to be of our finest behaviour. That is if you still want your jobs, I am damn sure I want to keep mine. So, we wait outside to welcome them.'

Within a few seconds, the kitchen was magically tidied up by the workers. They all took off their aprons and made their way to the mansion frontage.

'Mama, can I come?' I asked.

'Yes, but be on your best behaviour. That is, your mouth shut at all times.' She agreed, rushing to the entrance door at the same time, grabbing hold of my hand. That is one thing about my mother. She forgave you as quickly as she rebuked you.

Soon all the coloured staff members of the Mayor's residence had filed out like primary school pupils on a Monday morning assembly to the front of the house. We were left standing outside under the burning sun for a few minutes. Most of us began to sweat as the flies settled on our foreheads. We couldn't have stood for more than five minutes, but it seemed like an hour to me. I began to grumble. A middle-aged limping white man soon approached us. Everyone immediately fell silent as they heard the firm sound of his limp on one leg, aided by a wooden cane. He was known as Mr Jefferson Van. I recalled that the white Dutch man was the same person that intruded on our home years ago and tried to arrest Father. I frowned. The only difference between him then and now was his limp. He was dressed in a white plain shirt, a grey tuxedo with Cowboy boots and a grey western hat to match. As he approached the servants, I could see the fear on everyone's faces. He was accompanied by five white bodyguards with guns. Jefferson was feared by most people in town. He was known to be ruthless and egotistic in his belief in white supremacy and the open oppression of Negros. He was the voice and the right-hand man of his brother, the mayor.

'When are they coming Mama, I am hungry?' I asked to the chagrin of my mother.

'Hush your mouth, Mandiva.' Mama pulled my ears. You better learn how to control your mouth, boy. She hissed.

Jefferson made a croaking cough for attention, and he watched every servant present adjust their bodies. They tried to stand alert like soldiers. To me, it seemed we were still in the 18th century at the time of slavery, as the staff acted like the captured slave called Chicken George or Kunta Kinte from my favourite novel, *Roots*. Jefferson then read out loud the telegram from his brother, the mayor. When he finished, he added as a footnote, 'The mayor would be here in the next 3 minutes. At least that leaves sufficient time to get you niggas to tidy up your mess and look presentable for the mayor and his company.'

He turned to Mr Minschini, the short beefy butler standing directly opposite him, who had helped me at the gate earlier. He walked closer to him. Sweat dripped down his temple. Jefferson pulled out a handkerchief from his left breast pocket and covered his nose.

'Hey boy, why are you sweating like a pig? You have a distasteful body odour and are killing the buzz here. What's your name, boy?'

I recall the Butler replying, 'Minschini, Sir'. As he began to tremble with fear, the sweat on his temple dropped on his white-collar shirt. The buzzing of flies seemed to increase at that moment. He looked stupid.

'You don't look clean enough, besides you are too old for this job. Your appearance would jolt my little nephew and his Mama. You are fired, Minschini boy.' The servants began to mumble amongst themselves as Minschini immediately prostrated on the floor, crying for mercy. He grasped Jefferson's one good leg as he cried for mercy. Miffed, Jefferson used his walking stick to hit the butler's hand. Minschini was at the same time screaming in his native tongue to the murmuring workers.

'Silence!'

All the servants became quiet.

'Please sir, if you sack me, I am finished,' he pleaded in laboured English. 'I have worked here for a long time, master. I need to pay my children's school fees. Sir, my wife is sick!' Minschini's grip tightened on Jefferson's legs. Jefferson took off his hat at the same time he looked down at Minschini in disgruntlement.

'Education is not meant for your kind. Your body odour soils the floor on this land boy. Don't let me repeat myself. I said you are fired.' As soon as he said that, his bodyguards cocked their guns and pointed them at Minschini's face.

'You are trying to harass a white official. That's clearly against the law. Now let go of my leg,' Jefferson calmly commanded him.

Minschini slowly pulled his hands off Jefferson's leg and remained on the ground with his face down and started sobbing. Jefferson kicked the stone in front of him. A cloud of dust and sand from his boots covered Minschini's face. Minschini remained on the ground, sobbing and coughing from the dust he just inhaled. Poor Minschini, nobody was brave enough to plead on his behalf. It appeared that everyone knew that trying to plead on his behalf would amount to signing off on their own jobs. They could only give him a sorry look from their positions. He could not pick himself up, and it was only Mama who was brave enough to walk up to him and she assisted him to stand up on his feet.

'Go home, Brother, it's okay.' She consoled him, bending down to pick up his cap, which lay on the floor, and handed it over to him.

We all watched him leave the mansion of the white man that day. I remember the painful leap he took as he dragged himself out of that mansion. He was a shattered old man. That was the last time we saw Minschini at work. As we would later learn, Minschini got home that night, and seeing his five children and a sick wife and with no hope of ever being able to take care of them, he turned to the street for help. When money wasn't forthcoming, he tried to steal from the mayor's mine. He was caught and killed like every other African man that crossed the governor's path.

Once he left, the mayor arrived in a convoy of two glossy blue Volkswagens and pulled up in front of the house, as if he was waiting for Minschini to exit the compound. The door of the first car opened and a tall white man stepped out; he was grey-haired with a black moustache. He was clad in a two-piece grey French suit with black leather shoes. I realised that he was the same man that saved Papa from being arrested years ago by his obnoxious brother. The other vehicle was accompanied by a young sophisticated lady and a white dark-haired boy of my age. The lady was nicely dressed in a grey floral dress and a nude straw hat. She stepped out of the car and took off her sunglasses. Her deep blue eyes briefly scanned the place. Her perfume enchanted the place better than the stench of the native leaves I usually picked up for Mama in the fields. She was the most beautiful creature I had ever set my eyes on. Even as a child, I was struck by her sheer class and beauty. She looked so poised and sophisticated, like the models I saw on the cover of magazines whenever I went to the mayor's house. Her red short curly hair fell neatly at her cheekbone, which reminded me of the coral beads worn by the great kings of the Xhosatan tribe. Her perfume and the aura around her captivated and intimidated every poor folk that stood in front of the mansion that day, at least, the looks on their faces gave away that much.

Now as I recollect, I understand what I saw that day that made me alter my entire perspective on life. It was a rare combination of poise, grace and elegance, and I wanted them all. I had come to terms with reality, there was a social stratum that my family and I didn't belong to, and it was glaring down at us in our black faces.

For the first time in my life as a boy, I wondered why Mama or any of the African women didn't look like the lady of the house. I later learnt that she was from a royal family in Britain, with the title 'Duchess of York'. My undying fascination was agreeable with her British accent. At that time, as a little boy, I thought she spoke funny. My thoughts were suddenly interrupted by the husky voice of her husband, Mayor Stan Van.

'I hope the house is clean enough for my wife and my son. They haven't been to Africa before, and I am sure you will make them comfortable.'

As he spoke, his son, Abednego, a skinny white boy of my height, in grey shorts, a white collar shirt and a bow tie, stepped out of the vehicle. We all turned to see his face, only for him to take cover behind his mother's skirt. He looked frightened, as he gazed at the crowd of black servants before him. I felt it was awkward for a boy of his age to hide behind his mother's skirt. But I also felt sorry for him. He looked lost and frightened with the amount of negros forcefully smiling at him. Now, I know this 'sorry feeling' was ironic because the people that should be pitied were 'us', the labourers.

Soon, we were all instructed to proceed to our territory, the kitchen. A welcome cocktail party was to take place in a few hours. As it turned out, that was the social gathering that would determine my fate.

CHAPTER TWO

FIVE HOURS LATER AT THE MAYOR'S MANOR

I was all alone with Mama in the vast kitchen, at the receiving end of her scolding as usual. 'You better behave yourself Mandiva Sheldrake... I am going to attend to the guests,' Mama cautioned me, grabbing a dessert tray filled with cream caramel and apples. She soon left me grumbling to myself in the empty kitchen.

I didn't want to linger in the damn kitchen alone. But acquiescently, I sat down on the wooden arm chair in the kitchen and waited. I hung around for over 30 minutes. I had become famished, thirsty and frantic.

In a little while, I became overwhelmed by the echo of jazz from the party. I had always been curious about the real picture of a gramophone. I recalled the headmaster at school once saying that it looked like a magical box that produced blissful sounds. Then I thought to myself that this was an opportunity to actually see one. I felt the urge to go back to school because I could then brag to my peers that I had seen the magical box at last. Mama had said that the *mad Mayor* has a record player in every room, when I enquired about the existence of the box one hot Sunday afternoon after lunch. On an impulse, I made my way out of the kitchen and slowly, I crept up the stairs. I could hear the melodious laughter of the elites coming from their parlour. It was not like the laughter I was used to, but a mixture of unknown groaning and giggling. If you are rich, everything about you will be just different. Even your laugh. The music became louder as I drew closer to the hallway upstairs. Impulsively, I stopped in front of the first door I saw. This time, the music had become softer; I hesitated for a second, then with an itch, I gently pushed the door open and looked into the vast room. Then I saw something. Something I should never have seen.

Initially, it seemed like Mama was standing too close to the mister, and he was grabbing her arm tightly. I froze as I soon saw pain and tears pouring down her eyes.

'We can't, please. Your wife and my family are outside, sir.' She whispered in a pleading tone and tried to pull back but he yanked her to his lap. Soon, her hands were trembling as they went around his thin neck, kissing him passionately, as he was smooching her. His one hand was working wonders inside her skirt, and the other was holding a cocktail glass half filled with a martini. Soon, they were making deep guttural sounds. His shirt was half unbuttoned, and his knotted tie was half loosened. They didn't notice I was standing there. They seemed consumed in the ecstasy of their absurdity. I watched him slowly slip her black panties down her knee, while she now provocatively unbuttoned her black brassiere, exposing her firm breasts. His eyes were beaming with delight as he emptied the glass of martini on her nipples. Mama moaned aloud when she felt the chill of the drink on her flesh. He grabbed her breast with one hand and sucked hungrily at her nipple. He let the cocktail glass fall on the floor and shattered on the red woollen carpet but the broken glass didn't stop their ecstasy. I could not remember how long I stood there while I watched my mother in disbelief. All I recall now was that I stood there long enough to watch his long red cock slide in between my mother's widely opened legs. He started thrusting in and out slowly and then faster. Soon, it seemed she was coming to her senses and she tried to struggle to break free from his grasp, but he wasn't having it because he was pinning her down. Suddenly, there was a scream that echoed around the room, and the trance I initially thought I was in, vanished in a split second. Just then, the mayor saw me. My mother jumped up and broke away from his grip as her gaze fell on my horrified face. The mayor didn't flinch. He simply sat down with his trouser unzipped and his erect cock exposed.

I turned around to see who had screamed, and I saw the mayor's brother and young master standing behind me. They had witnessed the same incident, but Abednego couldn't bear the shock and he screamed. Unfortunately, I was the victim who was mute but got caught. I heard the mayor speak harshly to his brother, commanding him to restrain me. I raced down the stairs and ran out of the mansion without looking back. I had run for over thirty minutes before I eventually stopped in front of the Carnation Bar to catch my breath. I sat on the floor and began to pant heavily. Then I walked to the side of the bar and sat on the floor, still in shock. I could not comprehend what I had seen or heard. My mother always spoke of the church and God. She had etched meticulously into my consciousness the picture of a tough, hard-working black woman who was religiously empowered to provide for her family irrespective of all obstacles, such as the death of her husband. I was mystified. I lost respect for Mama all at once. I wondered like the typical African male how Mother could give into him without a good fight. Yet, I was confused because I expected her to murder him, even if she was forced to sleep with him. The thought of her sleeping with him disgusted me.

My thoughts soon became distracted by the sudden loud music coming from the club. It was worsened by the loud laughter coming from old black men as they exited the club hand in hand with young half naked black women. Suddenly, I had mixed emotions, which were mostly powered by fear and consumed with rage within me. I covered my face with shame to stop the tears of anger and repulsion from falling down my cheeks. I began punching the tree stub outside of Carnation Bar out of frustration. I stopped when I saw blood dripping from the back of my hands. My skin had peeled off but I felt no pain at that moment because I was still consumed with rage. I began to use the blood on my hand to wipe away my eyes, I thought this would wipe off the memory in my head. When I realised it wasn't working in about 5 minutes, I touched my nose and saw blood trickling down my nostrils. *I must have hit my nose somewhere.*

I stooped down and picked up a stone that lay beneath my shoes. I threw it at the window of the club out of frustration. I watched the glass window shatter. Immediately, there was a commotion in the bar as people started screaming. They might have thought it was the white police men from the district who normally came around to arrest and torture them at every given opportunity.

I realised what I had done and ducked immediately. I felt this creeping fear of being caught by the angry and drunken black men that rushed out of the club house with old machete and knives. *It's best to let them think it was the white folks coming to make trouble.*

'You are really silly throwing that stone, you know,' I heard a small voice from behind me call out. This startled me and at the same time, interrupted my thoughts of an escape from the bizarre situation I found myself in. I turned around to see Abednego standing behind me with folded arms and a frown on his face.

'What the hell are you doing here? Are you following me?' I blurted out in annoyance.

'Not really. There is a big fight at home because my uncle and father are having a go at each other over your mother. My uncle believes your mother did some African voodoo on my dad and should be arrested.'

'Arrested?'

'Your mother took off crying. So, I was curious to know about the family of the maid that is fucking my dad. My uncle once told me coloured people are quick to sell their brothers just for a bottle of coca cola. So, I bribed the cook's son with my father's cheapest wine and funny enough, it worked because he brought me here to you.' I gazed over his shoulder and saw Aunty Rose's son standing a distance away from both of us. It seems he caught the frown and recognised the anger on my face for bringing Abednego to me, so he quickly turned around and ran away.

I initially was perplexed by his vocabulary. He spoke English with an air of authority and arrogance for a boy of his age and fragile looks.

'You white bastard, don't you dare speak about my mother like that! Your father raped her! You are his blood and I will kill you for that.'

'Sure, didn't look like rape to me.... she seemed quite pleased,' he grinned mischievously and then added 'She seemed she had fun just like the negro whores my father had fun with in London, you sure ended that fine party.'

I was shocked by his carelessness. He appeared so fragile; his skin was as pale as a ghost, and I never thought he could utter such words about his father in a nonchalant way. His father was used to sleeping with black maids too in Europe? But he seemed not to care about possible gossip that could arise and affect his own mother.

'May your eyes and your father's never see daylight!' I cursed him from the top of my lungs in my dialect. I rushed towards him and knocked him down. It satisfied me that I had pulled him down to fall on the muddy earth on which he once stood like an emperor. I grabbed his right arm and dug my teeth into it, biting with fearless rage like a mad man. He screamed out aloud in shock and pain. Soon, we were wrestling like cats and rats on the ground. Soon, all the people from the club came out and surrounded us, cheering for the fight.

'Come on, you beast! Are you tired already? Give it to me boy!' He got up and challenged me, landing a weak punch on my face. I remember stumbling and falling on the floor as I missed my steps. I experienced flashes of light and dizziness as my face hit a stone on the floor. I pulled myself up and felt blood dripping out of my nose. My head felt heavy, but I still felt enraged to teach this insolent white boy a lesson. He would pay for the sin of his father. I could hear footsteps approaching from behind. I could also hear the voices of the men from the club urging me not to disappoint them.

'Get up and fight boy, lash that white trash!'

'Kill that white boy!'

But the ovation was of little use. I felt a throbbing headache in the frontal region of my head. My vision was blurred, but I could still figure out that the wild crowd were cheering in delight. The crowd had grown considerably larger now. It seemed there was more to this fight than a fight between two random boys. I understood I was their hero then. I felt that I must not let them down. I became reinvigorated. Immediately, I swung around and threw a punch at his jaw. He fell and hit his head on the ground. I heard the crowd cheer behind me again. I landed three solid punches on his stomach and face. I writhed in pain but I felt fulfilled. I was momentarily distracted by the shouts that came from the rapidly growing open space. Abednego saw his opportunity. He swept out his leg in a wide graceful art, connecting with my ankles and throwing me off balance. Before I realised what had happened, I was flat on my back, taking in deep breaths of dusty air that seemed devoid of oxygen. The consequent tunnel vision that threatened to take my sight cleared, with just enough time to roll away from an impending kick to my ribs. This motion made Abednego land again on the floor and then I attacked. I threw him a punch on his jaw.

'You little fool.' I heard an angry voice yell from behind me. I recognised the voice as I tried to make a run. But I was caught by my shirt collar. It was my dad's brother, Uncle Jide. He managed the Carnations Bar. Soon, he held onto my shoulders and shook me ferociously in rage.

'Do you know who you are fighting with? Mandiva!' he turned to the crowd and announced angrily, 'Entertainment is over, everybody. Go home. The club is closed today.'

'Why!' the crowd chorused in anger and disappointment.

'That's the mayor's son you shit heads, I bet the police would be here any second and all of you would be shot dead, or if you are lucky, you would be sitting next to that protester Mandela in the Robben Island cell.' As soon as he said that, everyone began to turn around and soon, the sound of hurried steps replaced the cheers. Uncle Jide pushed me into the safety of the deserted bar before going back to assist the mayor's son on his feet.

'Are you okay, son?' he asked in a concerned tone.

'Did you bite him? Are you now an animal too?' he enquired to the red-faced boy.

'I'm okay, his blows are not too bad' Abednego replied in a cheerful tone and a grin. I watched Uncle Jide smile back at him. I frowned in annoyance. I didn't understand where the sudden rage came from when I bit him. I only knew I had a goddamn banging headache.

'Come with me son,' he led him to the bar. 'I need to dress that bite and put some ice on your cheek and then we will figure out a way to take you home. As for you, Mandiva...' he turned around to face me, 'go home and lock up. You are a disappointment. Thank God your father is not here to see this. Anger should be controlled. You have to think before acting boy. That's what a Sheldrake does. Now, what separates you from all the other black people the whites call savages?' he spoke harshly to me in my native dialect.

As I made my way home later that night, I remembered his stern look as his voice lingered on. The white always had to be right, I thought in anger. My cheeks were hurting too but the white boy got the ice on his instead. Soon, I was running down the hill in anger. Then, I didn't understand the words *'anger... control... or how to act like a Sheldrake'* to me at that place in time, those were empty words from a frightened Negro.

CHAPTER THREE

ABEDNEGO, 1984, A DAY LATER

I sauntered up the hill, whistling and sweating at the same time. I whistled because I was captivated by the beautiful scene of the slums of my newly found South Ciskei home. I had heard so much about how dangerous the place was, before my mom and I moved a day before. I remember being warned by my maternal granddad that I should always take the security guards with me and never try to walk on the street unaccompanied because black people were bad. But I realised that the natives weren't bad at all after the incident the previous day.

I recall sitting down with Mr Jide in his bar while he magnanimously dressed my wounds. I flinched and gave a cry of pain every time he placed herbal leaves on the wound. Finally, he handed over to me a piece of dressing filled with ice blocks to place on my bruised temple.

'Thank you, you are most kind,' I uttered.

Without responding, he moved towards his bar and poured himself a glass of whiskey into a half-chipped glass.

'You better run along before your folks start looking for you.'

I nodded as I made my way to the door silently. I was about to pull the handle of the door when he said, 'We don't want any trouble from your father and uncle, son. As you see, this bar is the only thing that I have got, and so do those black people out there. The music and all the activities that go on here are the only things that keep us going. That kid you fought with is a good boy, he is my nephew. I practically raised him after the tragic death of his father.'

'His dad is dead?' I murmured in pity. 'Hmmm...What happened to him?'

'You don't want to know, son.'

'But I want to,' I persisted.

'His father died working in your father's mine. My nephew was just a child when this happened. He witnessed the death of his father at the mine, the collapsing of the mine still wakes him up at night.'

He gulped the whiskey and continued, 'It's funny the white doctors shut the hospital door on our faces that night, and tried to save only your father. I watched how they only wheeled your dad into the hospital and left his father unattended outside. I tried to force the door open that night and I pleaded to no avail. Then I saw Mister Jefferson, your uncle, arrive at the hospital. He ignored my plea and did absolutely nothing to help, while the white practitioner just looked at us from the windows of the emergency room. I heard the screaming and tears from my poor nephew, as he held onto his wounded father. At that point, I summoned courage, with my brother on my back. I took him to this very place you stand right now. I tried to stop the bleeding but couldn't...'

I watched him relieve the past as he drifted away. I saw the agony in his eyes, which I had never witnessed before from anyone.

'Your dad is alive and well, but he never compensated my family; he only offered a job to Mandiva's mother as a maid. She can't even afford to keep Mandiva and his sister, Martha, in school with her meagre wages.' I watched him pour himself another glass of local whiskey. He gulped down the drink with his eyes shut. He got up from the wooden stool he sat on.

'You are a kid, and you might not understand this world. But I want you to see something.' He led me to a door and soon, we were descending the stairs of the basement. I reached the bottom of the stairs and was frozen by what I encountered. It was a transformed white room, which had large oil paintings on the opposite wall; there were paintings of black revolutionaries and a boxing ring in the middle. Two pairs of dirty boxing gloves were lying on the floor of the ring. I stared at the ceiling and saw a lot of names scribbled on the ceiling and next to the hanging light bulb, the name 'Sheldrake' was boldly written.

'Wow, this is cool...' I climbed into the ring and picked up the gloves. I watched him get into the ring too. He took one of the gloves from me and slipped it into his right hand.

'That's why all these people were so excited to see a fight, because this is their fighting sanctuary. We call it our Pink Carnations. It is named after the beautiful flower that represents death. It means we believe we will fight for our freedom till we die. Black men come here to practice, bet on fights and learn to defend themselves. It's a form of therapy where they transfer aggression to other fighters here. Every name on this ceiling, both male and female, died because they were helpless and unable to do anything to stay alive. So did my brother... Sheldrake,' he lifted his head and pointed to the inscribed name on the ceiling.

I saw tears finally drop from his eyes. He wiped his face before he added 'you strike me as a good kid and I am never wrong with my instinct. You never judge people by their race but by their personality. That is why I am going to ask you, please don't tell the boss or Mister Jefferson about what happened here tonight.' He continued, 'My nephew has been through a lot, which accounts for his aggression. He watched his father die while trying to save yours a long time ago at the mining site.'

'You have my word, Mr Jide,' I uttered. I walked towards him and stretched my gloved hand for a hand shake.

'One question sir, why did your brother try to save my dad? It seems my dad isn't a good man; no coloured person likes him here.'

'Your father gave my brother a job at the mine. He was grateful. That job changed his perception of life, and he stopped being a rebel. He tried to beat the white man by employing black people for white-collar jobs, which he

29

assumed we needed the most. I remember him telling me that if we could get our black people off the streets and make money through this mine, we could learn the white man's ways through the mining trade and pay for our education and then defeat them in their own game…. My brother was a good man, just like his son.'

I nodded in agreement and was sorrowful to learn how a good man died. That was the beginning of my friendship with Jide.

***

Soon, I was standing in front of a dilapidated house. I was shocked by the state of poverty that surrounded me. However, Mandiva's house was quite neat and impressive for a house in the suburb of South Ciskei. It was a brown bungalow. The wooden windows were wide open, telling a visitor that there was someone in the house. Directly in front of the house was a long rope suspended by two iron poles for hanging clothes. On the rope were faded brown drapes and linen, and worn-out stockings. I turned to assess my side view and saw some black children dressed only in washed-out pants; they were looking at me with suspicion, as I made my way to the door of the matchbox house. I hastily placed a knock at the door and waited for an answer. In a few seconds, the door swung open and Mandiva was standing in front, with an inquisitive frown on his face.

He spoke in his native dialect.

'Don't speak Xhosatan, I'm still trying to learn the language.'

'What are you doing here?' He translated it into English. Before I could utter a word, he shoved me inside the house in anger.

'What the hell are you doing?' I mumbled in confusion.

'You want to get killed here, right? Your daddy wouldn't know you brought your skinny white arse to this neighbourhood to be purposely slaughtered. What is wrong with you?'

'Didn't know things were so bad down here... Relax, my friend,' I stammered, as I was apprehensive by the look in his eyes. I tried straightening my crumpled shirt.

'If you call me friend once again, I will knock you out and kick you outside for my real friends in the compound outside to eat you for dinner,' he burst out in anger.

'What's going on, Mandiva?' It was a tiny voice from the room. I turned around and saw a skinny little girl in dreadlocks. She was dressed in a purple shirt and grey blouse. She was rubbing her large brown eyes with her little finger; apparently, she had just woken up from sleep.

'How is that your business? By the way, where's your sweater, Martha? Haven't I told you to always button up and wear your sweater in this weather?' Mandiva scolded the little girl.

'My sweater is torn, Brother...' She replied sadly. She then looked up at me with a sparkle in her big brown eyes and continued in a whisper '...you are white.'

I burst out laughing; she looked as adorable as her dirty-looking, sewn-up black doll, which she held close to her chest.

'What's so funny?' Mandiva grumbled behind me. I watched him move a sack of rumbled clothes on the table next to him. He pulled out a torn pink sweater and walked up to his sister. He began to dress her in it. Immediately, I realised this was the kind of family I had always dreamt of, instead of an only child whose parents hardly realised was in existence.

My family was a charade in the public eye. My mother was born into a wealthy and royal family in England, while my father was an ambitious son of a failed aristocrat from Holland, who was determined to redeem the family name at all costs when they arrived in England. My father had wooed my mother with his charm and grace and succeeded in marrying her under a false claim to wealth and prestige in Holland. Her parents had initially objected because he was neither British nor from a prominent aristocratic background. They had to give up when my mom was pregnant. However, in their second year of marriage, my mother found out that my dad's family was broke and had no royal ties in Holland as he claimed. By that time, he had successfully used her money to run for congress and won a seat in the parliament. He became 'busy' and therefore, distant. Having got what he wanted from her, he became his own man with little regard for her. The once-loving man became a shadow of his old self. Mother turned to drinking for comfort. He had the money now but he could never divorce her because he needed her family name to climb the ladder of political success. My father later moved to

Southern Africa as an Ambassador. My mother had chosen to stay back in England because she felt the distance would suit her fine to which my father readily agreed. We returned to South Ciskei to visit my father because now, after twelve solid years of political sojourn, he wanted to run for prime minister in England. He, therefore, needed to present a picture of the perfect family man to the British press.

'Why don't you take my sweater, it's cashmere, it would keep the cold away.' I offered, removing the black sweater I was wearing.

'Hippy!' she ran towards me in pure puerile delight and grabbed the sweater from my hand.

'Return the sweater, Martha. We don't need his handouts.'

'Come on, your sister is cold... besides, that sweater can't even keep an ant warm.'

'Please, Brother...' she pleaded in a tiny tone as she tightened her grip on the sweater.

'Look, even if I decide she keeps the sweater, Mama would never allow it. Besides, I don't want the white man bursting inside here saying we stole your sweater.' He protested, as he passed his gaze from his sister to me.

'My parents would never notice, I have more than a hundred of those. I could talk to your mother if she's the problem....'

'And why in God's name would she listen to the son that got her fired in the first place?'

'I can as well try. I might have a way with words.' I winked, delighted that I was beginning to calm this very stubborn boy down. I had expected him to be outraged when I said that but instead, he burst into horrendous laughter.

'Okay, what's so funny?' I asked, puzzled.

'You little skinny motherfucker... You are your father's child. No one would ever think these words can come out from you. You appear so lost.'

I knew he was spot on about my appearance, so I only grinned at him and replied, 'I know, it's hereditary.'

'So honestly, tell me what brings you here?' he asked curiously. 'I know you didn't just come all the way to bring us a sweater.'

'I want to learn how to fight,' I replied with a serious look. I always looked pale and fragile and needed to change that. I was always bullied at school in England. I had no friends and there was always the rumour that my father enjoyed the company of servant girls more than my mother.

'What?'

'Being white doesn't make you have everything sometimes. Maybe I might have everything here but not back home. I want to learn how to defend myself and I know you can teach me. I am always bullied in boarding school because my father was always absent and my mother prefers the company of bottles. I know one day we will return home.'

I calmly muttered. 'You did fight remarkably well, and I still need to defend myself out here, besides, if you agree to teach me how to fight, the sweater will be your payment. So technically, it's not free.'

He studied me for a few seconds and I guessed he saw my honesty, so he smiled back at me as he turned to his sister, 'You can keep the jacket Martha... got to hide it from Mama regardless.... I will teach you.' It was right there I knew that this was the beginning of a new and everlasting friendship.

CHAPTER FOUR

MARTHA, JULY 1985

I rushed into the Pink Carnation Bar downtown, in apprehension, and looked around the unfamiliar room in anxiety. The room was crammed with people in different states of drunkenness. Nonetheless, they seemed to be enjoying the live music adroitly delivered by two Skwentna women. The women, Chaka and Makeba, were dressed in skimpy navy blue ties and dye printed trousers and petite tops. I thought they looked like sluts for the occasion, with bloody red lipsticks and loud adornments. It's such an irony because later on in life people would gladly call these lipstick colours *Ruby Woo by Mac!*

The smell of the room was filled with the choking combination of cheap perfumes, the unfamiliar stench of human bodies and local tobacco, with soft music. This was accompanied by some dry laughter from women as the men whispered into their ears. I knew I would be dead if my mother or brother saw me come to this bar. But then, I assured myself that it was for a good cause, because Mama was looking for Mandiva, and she wouldn't hesitate to whip his butt if she found he had been messing around in this sort of place. She had gone to his school and was told that he wasn't there. She had come home fuming and screaming that she was going to kill Brother before he killed her with high blood pressure. I had crept out of the house while she was in the kitchen, to look for him; but there was more: I also wanted to see Abednego.

Abednego, Mandiva and I had become best of friends. He always came to visit us when Mama wasn't around bearing a box of assorted pastries packed in wooden brown boxes. I could swear I had begun to grow taller since he started bringing those delicious freshly baked chocolate bread, macaroons and apple pies to the house. He had also become friends with the black boys in the neighbourhood because of Mandiva. The boys soon got fond of him because he was witty and always came with presents for every one of them. I remember the football he gave Kesta, a notorious black thug who lived next to us and frequently called us 'Uncle Tom'. This meant 'white lover' at that time. That wasn't a good name to be called back in the days, because of the apartheid and it also meant that any black man was a sell-out to his race. He never called us that again since he was given the football. That day, I thought that Abednego was clever, amusing and sweet.

I had hardly seen him for a week because he and Mandiva had started going out to the bar more regularly than usual. When I asked Mandiva what they always do at the bar, he ignored me and said, 'What we do is not your business.'

'Where are Mandiva and Abednego?' I stopped to ask a plump waitress at the bar. She nodded in the direction of the door behind me and looked at me in disagreement when she added that I shouldn't be in the bar. I murmured my thanks and walked towards the door. The door was shut when I tried to open it. What could they be doing that warranted locking the door? I wondered. Getting impatient, I began to hit the door with my clenched fist. *Someone open up, goddamn it!*, I thought to myself. A few seconds later, a huge bald-man with a pot belly appeared in front of the door. He stared down at me with a frown as he opened the door, with a bottle of gin in one hand. Clearly, I felt intimidated by his size. Undeterred, I stared up at him and then stammered.

'I am looking for my brother... Mandiva?'

'Who sent you here? You are too little?' He responded as if that was the answer to my question. 'I want to see my brother,' I persisted. He sized me from head to toe with his blood shot eyes.

'Follow me.'

I was led into an inner room filled with a large male crowd accompanied by lots of drumming, cheering and clapping. I was puzzled. Later, I spotted a boxing ring in the middle of the room. After I succeeded in squeezing my way through the mad crowd, I missed the big black man. No one seemed to notice me because they were so engrossed by the show in the centre of the ring. Lo and behold, it was Mandiva in the ring, battering an opponent. The referee had enough and counted out aloud '*ONE! TWO! THREE!*' as Mandiva prance about the ring. Abednego, standing close to the ring, could not contain his joy at the victory of his friend.

Initially, the whole show confused me. Soon everyone was cheering for my brother. Abednego jumped into the ring and took hold of his hand and raised it after Uncle Jide had come into the ring and raised Mandiva's other hand as a sign of victory. In a few seconds, my eyes caught Abednego's and he saw the terror in my eyes and the tears that fell down my cheeks. *Brother has killed a man and Abednego is cheering him on.*

I watched him tap Mandiva on his shoulder as his smile gradually vanished from his face. Mandiva turned to look at me. I didn't wait to see his reaction as I raced out of the room. I heard footsteps behind me as I rushed out of the salon. I could hear Mandiva and Abednego scream my name as I increased my pace.

I pulled open the exit door of the bar and stumbled on Mama. She stared straight at me and then at Abednego and Mandiva, who had caught up with me by now. Mother grabbed me by the arm with blood shot eyes and furiously said to Mandiva, 'What the hell are you doing in here with your sister?'

'Let me explain, Mama,' Mandiva tried to explain as he stammered.

'Don't you dare interrupt me when I talk...' she turned to Abednego, venom in her eyes '...you want to get my children into trouble!'

'I'm sorry.' Abednego blurted.

'Don't you think your father has done enough?' she cut in. 'Do you also want to hurt my children the way your father's kind killed their father?' She asked, tears beginning to well up in her eyes. With a now shaky voice, she continued, all attempts to conceal her broken emotion seemed futile, 'I heard the rumours, about how you boys have become famous as you come here to fight. You are now the bloody buffoon of the village.'

She turned towards me and asked, 'By the time the mayor finds out about this circus, don't you know that you would be inviting a fate like your father's? She wasn't expecting an answer. Mandiva did not answer. Then she added with a note of finality, 'Now get your things and come home. Abednego, you would stay away from my family and find yourself suitable white friends from your class,' she pulled me out of the bar. Soon, we had left Abednego at the door of Carnations, his face a caricature of gloom and regret.

I remember this incident so vividly because I had never seen Mama that furious. That day it drizzled as we made our way back to the house.

We arrived home, way past the time it usually would take us because Mama kept on pulling me by my sweater as she stamped her feet all the way home. Brother followed a little distance behind us, looking sober now. He had cause to be worried. Indeed, we both did, as neither of us had seen Mama exhibit this kind of rage before. We finally arrived home as the rain began to pour heavily accompanied by bolts of angry thunder and lightning. Mama shoved me into the house, at the same time tried to drag Mandiva to come in. We both stood motionless as we watched Mama swiftly move towards the half-broken windows to close them as the rain began to pour into the house.

'Fetch me the wrapper!' she screamed at Mandiva. He hurriedly picked up Mama's wrapper, which was located on the wooden bench behind him. Mama draped the wrapper over the half-opened window. Having taken care of that more urgent matter, she now turned her attention to us.

'I went to your school today and I heard you haven't been attending classes.'

'I can explain.'

'Be quiet, I don't want to hear a word from you,' she sternly but calmly interrupted my brother. She continued. 'Your teacher says you haven't attended classes for over a month. In addition, the last time you showed up at her class, a white boy – who I believe is Abednego – came into the school and threw a note over the windowpane to you. You were going to be punished for disrupting the class but instead, you insulted the principal and walked out of the class to meet your white friend.'

'Mama...'

'Shut up!' I watched my mother walk towards Mandiva and struck him on the cheek. He held his check, a look of horror on his face. Mama had never slapped him before. Mandiva did not cry, however. What he did next shocked Mama, and me. He started laughing hysterically, shouting and cursing in our native dialect.

'You dare hit me, because I left school to try and make money to feed this family, to prevent you from whoring and ruining my father's good name.' I watched Mama's countenance change at that point, from that of anger to horror. She looked pale, like she had just seen a ghost. She placed a hand on her chest as she gripped her sweater at the same time, she closed her eyes in pain.

'W...wh...what did you say?' she stammered in shock, unable to believe she was hearing right.

'You heard me right. Who did you think stopped the landlord from throwing us out of the house after you were fired? Did you think it was by your false prayers that the landlord hasn't shown up for over a month to collect his money? Of course, you didn't think about it. All you want is for your children to have western education. Why? Because it strokes your pride to know that your children are also learning the white man's way. Didn't Papa have that education and what good did that bring him? But still, you want me and my sister to have the white man's education after they brutally murdered children like me in cold blood. Do you know what those teachers you speak so highly of say behind you... about my so-called mother! Don't you know the whole neighbourhood knows that you were fucking the enemy?'

Like a hungry lioness, Mama pounced on Mandiva and began to rain heavy blows and slaps on his face. She didn't stop until Brother fell. I rushed to hold Mama's hand. Unable to placate her, I began to cry out in fear. Mama realised that she had petrified me. She stopped hitting my brother. Panting, she paused to catch her breath and collect herself. She moved forward to pick me up but I shoved her away while my sobbing increased. Mandiva picked himself up slowly from the ground leaning on me for support as we both got on our feet. In a show of camaraderie, he wrapped his arms around me to console me.

'You know nothing of the sacrifices I have made for this family,' She spoke in a subdued voice. 'It's a pity your sister worships you. Your father always wanted you to be educated. You are leading your sister through a dark hole with all this hate inside you. Her progress in school suffers because she has missed school twice because of you. If you think street fighting and making friends with a rich white boy is the answer to your problem, then you are a damn fool.'

'If you want to have a sensible future out of this ghetto, it is that white man's education that would give it to you and not becoming a thug. But if you insist on going through that path of self-destruction that you have chosen for yourself, there won't be room for you under my roof. So go, and don't come back.' She spoke in Xhosatan. She shook her head as a sign of disappointment and then dragged me from Brother's embrace.

'Your roof was last paid for by the street fight and not the language that the school teaches. Remember that.' He calmly spoke back at Mama with blazing anger in his eyes.

Mama carried me to the small room I shared with her – a room that consisted of a wooden stool, a blue mat and a cheap lantern, placed close to the cracked wall. The dim light reflected on Mama's uniform from her late employer and on her only favourite dress, a white cotton pleated dress that Papa bought for her on her birthday some years ago. She placed me on the large mat that took up all leg space in the room. I coiled up on the cold ground. I remember Mama stroking my hair and humming a Xhosatan song as I lay down to sleep.

Soon I slept off, totally oblivious to the tension in the house. I didn't hear my brother step out of the house. He had turned off the lantern in the sitting room, put on a rain coat and made his way out of the house; he was heading towards the mansion. I was not awake to see the tears that poured down Mama's eyes when she heard Mandiva open and shut the door.

CHAPTER FIVE

SHELDRAKE

I had passed the night at the stable after my fight with Mama. Filled with rage, I braved the stormy weather as I made my way there. It was unbelievable that Mama had kicked me out. *How ungrateful!* I joined the fight at the Pink Carnations because I needed to make enough money to pay for the rent as soon as I discovered that I could make money from people placing bets on wrestlers in a ring fight. Abednego had only encouraged me to go because I didn't want to take any money from him and we had both come to love the idea of wrestling. With much practice with Uncle Jide, we both discovered that I had a spectacular gift of wrestling at my age and that I was as good as any great fighter uncle had encountered. I made my way to the barn that day to find any used material for the horses to keep warm. I was dripping wet from the storm. Luckily for me, I found some towels there. I dried myself and soon, I lay down on the straws on the floor and fell asleep.

I recall having a dream that night, for the first time since my childhood, about the specific incident surrounding the death of Papa. I was sitting with Mama and Papa in the dream, watching the news on our black-and-white TV set. We heard a knock on the door, and Papa opened it. He returned to Mama with a letter in his hand. Mama asked him who it was as she got up from her seat to meet him.

'The black revolutionary groups I teach have revolted and set the mine with explosives because they misunderstand that I have turned on them to work for the White men here.'

'This is madness. You have been using the opportunity to help our people to get better-paying jobs. How can they possibly think the white man can buy you?' Mama blurted out.

'Yes it is, my love, but I have to go and stop them. The mayor is going to be at the mine tonight. I need to inform him.'

'You aren't going anywhere, that mine can be collapsing any minute from now.'

'The mayor has a wife and son. Just like I do. I need to save him regardless of his colour.'

'No, you don't... aren't you done saving the world? You could die there.'

'I need to go.'

'But...'

Father had dismissed Mother just like that, and he was swiftly heading towards the door of the house, ignoring the panic and fear that crippled Mama's eyes. Hearing the conversation and seeing tears trickle from Mama's eyes, I rushed out of the house, calling out Papa's name. I wanted to follow him because I had sensed that unexplained fear. But it was too late because Papa had entered his deadbeat motorcycle and driven off, not hearing me call after him. I ran after the motorcycle and ignored Mama calling out my name. I ran towards Uncle Jide's house and found him sitting outside smoking his pipe. He seemed confused to see me all alone that night. I told him about the conversation I heard with Mama and Papa. He immediately stood up from the stool and with one hand, carried me on his shoulder as he ran towards the mine.

But by the time Uncle Jide and I got into the mine to stop Papa from proceeding, the mine had collapsed already. There was commotion everywhere that day as people surrounded the collapsed mine and pointed to Papa's leg, which was trapped between the rocks. His famous reading glasses and boots were lying down next to him. His face was unrecognisable with the smoke that overwhelmed the surrounding, but it was obvious it was him because Uncle Jide tried to cover my face from seeing the lifeless body with a missing arm. It seemed to be too late already. I fell on the fall and began to weep. The siren of the ambulance could be heard as soon as we had gotten to the scene, and we watched the half-conscious mayor being taken to the hospital by the Dutch ambulance as the white-dominated paramedic left us to defend for ourselves.

I watched Uncle Jide call for help as he tried to pull some of the scattered rock off Papa's leg. Only the coloured people at the scene that night rushed to assist Uncle Jide. I lay on the floor crying as Papa's body was lifted from the rocks, but at the same time, I could see the face of the mayor's brother watching us from afar. He was sitting in his pickup truck with a toothpick in his mouth, as he was watching the scene quietly. I recognised his face as the first white man who came to my house, and I ran towards his vehicle. I thought maybe he could save Papa as he was a white man, which represented Power.

'We need to get my papa to a hospital sir, please help us.'

I noticed that he seemed shocked for a split second. He removed his toothpick as he sat down in his car, not making an effort to come out. He shockingly spat on my face and he immediately drove off.

I suddenly woke up gasping for breath as sweat covered my whole body. I was The dream worried me, because I had subconsciously blocked the incidence of Papa's death out of my mind.

I pulled myself up from the floor and made my way to the mayor's house. I decided that I was going to see Abednego and ask him for a sweater and some food. I was still mad at Mama and the dream I had, added to my fury because Papa had always tried to use education to assist the black community. But some of our people had misunderstood his intention for a sell-out because he worked for the mayor and did not appreciate him for that. He only got appreciated after his death when Uncle Jide made it a ritual to tell Papa's story after every boxing match at the Pink Carnation bar. This was another reason I was adamant about not learning the white man's curriculum such as the mandatory English language at school.

I entered the kitchen where I spotted Madam Rose, Mama's good old friend. I heard her instructing a maid to take a bottle of whiskey to the mayor.

'Madam Rose, is Abednego in the house?' I enquired without greeting her. Recognising my voice, she turned around to me with a frown. She began speaking in Xhosatan.

'Abednego is gone. What have you done, Sheldrake? You little rascal. Don't you ever get tired of hurting your Mama or anyone near you? You would have to leave this house before anyone sees you.' She began to shoo me like a fowl towards the exit door of the mansion, giving me no room to talk.

'I don't understand what you are saying, ma. Where is Abednego...?' I stepped out of the house and turned around to face her in confusion.

She suddenly stood still. There were looks of confusion on her face too. 'Didn't you fight with Abednego?'

'I don't understand?'

'You didn't ...? Now I'm confused. He staggered to the house last night drenched in blood. The poor boy fainted at the doorstep without being able to speak with anyone. Word going around says he was attacked by a black man. The Lady has packed Abednego's things and hers; she's taking him back to England. She says she is done with Africa and never coming back. The mayor was mad. Mr Jefferson said it was you that beat him because you have been seen hanging around. The mayor has sent Jefferson to take care of it...' she added sadly.

'I don't understand... I didn't do anything Madam Rose, I swear.' I added. 'But... what do you mean take care of it?'

'Boy, been trying to get to your Mama since I overheard them talking. I sent my boy over to your place. You have to go home, child. I don't know what's going to happen but I bet it would be ugly. You need to get your Mama and sister out of that house.' I didn't wait for her to finish before I began to run out of the mayor's estate. The rain increased and, this time, was accompanied by an angry storm. I missed my steps and slipped on the wet ground as I got close to the mountain that linked to my house. I got up immediately as the memory of Madam Rose's voice lingered in my head.

'You need to get your Mama and sister out of that house.'

I continued to race down the sloppy hill. Finally, I could see my house from a distance. The front door was wide open. This alarmed me. I had shut the front door when I left the house, and Mama would never leave the door open. Slowly, I walked into the opened door, an eerie feeling pervading the wet atmosphere. On the hard cold floor lay a familiar black male body. Hesitantly, I turned him around and found that it was Isaiah, Mrs Rose's son. Blood was drooling from his mouth. Weakly, he opened his eyes as I held onto him.

'What happened? Where are Mama and sister? Who did this to you? There was a rope lying beside him and a red strangulated mark crested around his neck line.

'Help your mother, she's been taken to the barn,' he said, coughing. It immediately occurred to me in a flash because I held tightly unto him as if my embrace would keep him. I watched helplessly as life slowly slipped out of his body. He died in my arms. I put his head away from my lap as hot tears dripped down my eyes. Out of the blue, I heard imminent screams from the back of the house. I quickly made it to the doormat lying next to the lit lantern and pulled out a cutlass from beneath it. Out of the door, I headed towards the barn behind my house. Mama was lying in the dirt, half-naked. Jefferson was on top of her while he pinned her to the ground. He was muttering something incoherently, as he heartlessly molested her. As I approached, I could hear the words, *'Come on bitch, is it only my brother you can satisfy?'* Her nightgown was torn into shreds. She was screaming and struggling beneath him. He had his pants down. As if weeping for my mother, thunder gave a deafening roar as I rushed behind him and with one stroke of the machete, I slashed his back. He cried like a wounded animal and fell in pain. I helped my mom stand up as she tried to pull her shredded clothes to cover her exposed breasts and groin. I pulled her closer to my bosom and I whispered in her ears:

'It's not your fault Mama, I know....'

'You killed him?' Mama asked in horror.

'I don't think he has died,' I replied. We watched Jefferson stagger on his feet, his white shirt turned red.

'You little son of a bitch,' he pulled up a cutlass next to him and tried to attack me. He only ended up giving me a surface cut on my face. I didn't flinch. The cutlass fell from his hand

and he began to tremble as he saw the demon in my eyes. 'The police are coming soon to get you and your whore of a mother. I came here to spare you from the torture they would inflict on you, but you repay me with this shit!'

'We did nothing wrong! And you have no right to touch my mother.'

As if on a cue, heavy coordinated steps were heard running towards us. I trembled and so did Mama.

'They are here... the police.' He grinned wickedly. 'Of course, you did nothing wrong. I always wanted your mother, but she chose to fuck my brother instead. So, so I asked some niggars to beat up my nephew. He is a disgrace. Now boy... you and your mother are dead meat, just like your dead father.'

'My father?' I stammered.

'Do you think I would have allowed any good hospital to treat your father after the explosion at the mine? Your daddy was attracting too much attention at the mine... fighting for equal pay for monkeys. It was time for him to go, boy.' I realised that he had taken my father's and my mother's pride at the same time. I had a sudden headache. I immediately staggered, and it looked like he realised I was unbalanced so he tried to approach me. I felt a sudden rage that came over me at that instance, as I charged at him with the machete, and ran the blade through his neckline. I watched his half-decapitated body fall to the floor.

'What have I done?' I asked myself as the machete dropped from my hand. I begin to shiver and wail. I turned around to face Mama for comfort. But the reaction I got from her was rather unexpected. She stood unmoved and slapped me hard on the face. She pulled my fallen chin up with her fingers and spoke to me emotionlessly.

'He killed your father and many good black men. Remember that. You are a Sheldrake and we don't cry. So, the next time I see you shed a tear I will hunt you down for the rest of your life. You are going to get your sister; she's hiding in the dairy farm in the dry well behind the oak tree. Keep her alive and get her a good education. Now go...' she commanded firmly.

'I don't understand, Mama; I can't leave you?' I stammered in confusion.

'Yes, you can! I need to distract them and now you run away from here and don't look back' she said, as we heard the approaching footsteps from the soldiers growing louder. They were now closer to the barn. I grabbed Mama's hand, squeezed it, and reluctantly let go. I began to run, leaving it all behind – my tattered house, loving mother and life. What was ahead, I didn't know. I convinced myself that the future would take care of itself.

Less than five yards out, I heard a gunshot. I stopped running. I froze. Then there was a second gun shot. And a third. I knew they had shot Mama. I felt a sudden sharp pain in my heart. I placed my hand on my chest, to stop the excruciating pain that penetrated through it. But it was to no avail. I suddenly heard the barking of dogs. I knew the dogs were normally used to track down thieves by the superintendent.

I began to run again, as Mama's voice kept on ringing in my head. *You are going to get your sister; she's hiding in the dry well behind the oak tree on the farm. You are going to keep her alive.* I ran faster as these words repeatedly sounded in my head. Soon, I was sprinting down the woods towards the oak tree. I approached the well and looked down inside. I saw Martha coiled inside the well. I exhaled with relief and whispered her name. She looked up to see me with tears in her big brown eyes. She was about to call my name when I hushed her with a finger placed across my lips.

'Shhhhhh! I am coming.' I looked around and saw some fallen timbers lying on the ground. I hurriedly covered the surface of the well with the wooden timbers. When the well was fully covered, satisfied that she was safe, I climbed up the oak tree to hide. I rested uncomfortably on the tree branch, where I could observe the five guards with the two Alsatian dogs. One of the dogs had a piece of Mama's robe in its mouth. I watched as the team approached the well with my heart in my mouth. I began to whisper a prayer. And just as suddenly as they appeared, they began to make a detour in the wrong direction, which was at the opposite side of the well.

Soon, my eyes were closing, and I drifted away, to an unknown place, where I could neither hear the chirping of the birds nor the splash of the flying vulture faeces that soon fell on the back of my shirt.

CHAPTER SIX

MARTHA

I may well commit to memory, the moments of my sitting down frightened in the dry well with my hand rested on my knees, while I whispered a prayer. Tears rolled down my cheeks. I couldn't comprehend what was going on. Mama had woken me up in the dead of the night and handed me over to a strange boy who took me to the well on Papa's farm. She had instructed me to do as he said. The strange boy had warned me to keep still until Mama came back to fetch me. Then he disappeared. My young mind told me Mama was in trouble. Brother appeared after I had waited for an hour in the well. Then he was soon gone after he covered the well with wood and dry leaves. My body began to quiver as I heard the faint barking of the dogs above. The well was dark so I couldn't see anything, not even the tiny ants and other insects that crawled into the wall of the well and on my skin. I panicked as my bladder gave way and I experienced the uncontrollable passage of my urine in my pants. Soon, everywhere fell silent and in the shivering cold I drifted off to sleep.

I was woken by the bright ray of light that fell on me inside the well the next morning. I opened my eyes and looked up.

It was my brother. He had taken off the leaves and the wood. He handed me a rope, which I gratefully grabbed, and I gradually climbed out of the well. He held me close as I began to sob. He whispered soothingly into my ears that all will be fine. And I believed him.

'I wet my pants, Brother... Mama always told me not to. Where is Mama? And Abednego?' I sobbed harder as reality dawned on me that we were all alone. He wiped away my tears with his mud-stained hand and answered:

'Mama has gone to heaven, little one. And Abednego, he went on a long trip.'

'They all travelled and didn't say goodbye?' I asked, confused.

'They did, Mama says she had to go away to watch over us and she loves you. She will visit us soon.'

That seemed comforting enough. I smiled back at him and asked about Abednego.

'He said he would come back soon,'

'Ok... I am cold'

I watched him take off his rain coat and wrap me round the cheap piece of cloth. He held my hand and said, 'Let's go, we are going to Pink carnations to see Uncle.'

We soon began to travel the long, lonely and menacing road out of Papa's farm towards Carnations.

***

Pink Carnation Tavern

We approached Pink Carnations, but the building was nowhere to be seen. What was only visible was the burnt-down foundation of the building and its hovering smoke that rose into the thin air. We saw thousands of natives standing in front of the burning building with horror written on their faces. Some were trying to stop the fire with buckets of water and blankets, but it was futile. Ironically, the sun that day shone so brightly with no sign that it had rained earlier that morning. It appeared like the natives were praying for the rain to pour again, but no luck. *Some Apartheid!* We smuggled through the crowd and caught a glimpse of Uncle Jide who had his hands placed on his hips looking jaded and sad. Brother tapped Uncle on his shoulder. He turned around and saw us.

'Thank God,' there was a look of relief on his face.

'You shouldn't be here,' he whispered. The mayor has sent word that you should be arrested as soon as you are seen. Now, go to my house and wait for me. The key is hidden under my canoe by the water side. Do you understand me?'

Brother nodded.

He immediately pulled my hand firmly as we again struggled through the crowd. We hurried to Uncle Jide's residence, which was located near the bank of the river. Brother collected the key and let us into Uncle's house. The house was small, dusty and stuffy. Dilapidated furniture took up the available spaces just as darkness settled contentedly in the crib. We made our way into the kitchen in search of a comfortable place to rest our tired legs. Old pictures of Uncle Jide and of Mama and Papa hung casually on the wall.

'I am thirsty,' I mumbled to my brother. I watched him open the clay pot next to him after dusting off the dirt on the cover of the pot. He used his hand and scooped some water from the large terracotta container and tasted it.

'You can drink it. I bent near the pot and scooped some water from the cup provided by Mandiva. Filled, I passed the cup back to him for his own drink. Soon, we were interrupted by the clatter of the gliding of a door. Brother quickly pulled me by the hand. He shoved me behind a little cabinet and then turned back to pick up a dagger laying on the kitchen cupboard.

'Who's there?' Brother called out bravely. His voice had the reverberation of a harsh, loud and strong tone. From behind the cupboard, I could see his determined face. It was like he had aged in a second. He suddenly looked like Papa... Like a man.

'It's me, Mandiva. Where are you guys?' We heard Uncle Jide's voice.

'In here,' Mandiva replied. I could hear the relief in his voice. My brother assisted me out of my hiding as Uncle Jide cupped me in his warm embrace. He sighed once more.

'Was worried sick... The mayor went mad. We have to get out of town.'

'They burnt the club... what would you do?' Brother asked in hesitation.

'Luckily for us, we got some free tickets to West Africa – Nigeria, through some friends who owe me. We can work on the deck as seamen... We have limited cash.'

'Nigeria?' I murmured.

'That's where your great-grandmother originally came from. She got married to a Xhosatan tribe man after the slave trade when she found herself in South Ciskei.'

'How about you?' Brother asked.

'I will come with you. Try to start a new life too. I will teach you how to defend yourselves and get a job at the bar. Besides, your friend sent a letter to us through a maid in the mansion before he was shipped off. He put in some money. Don't know where he got the money but thank God, he sent it, because, I swear, we need it. A beggar can't be a chooser now. He's a good kid... hope to God we see again someday,' Uncle said after he pulled the letter from his pocket. He handed it over to Brother.

Uncle continued, 'We don't have time for you to read that now... the boat sails in a few minutes, let's go.' We watched him grab a light bag and tossed in a pack of sliced bread, two shirts, a wrapper and a sweater.

We shortly left the house and after several minutes of walking we approached a jetty with a ship. Uncle Jide suddenly turned to Brother and whispered, 'The mayor might be looking for you on the ship, so from now on you answer your surname. Your name is now Sheldrake Mbutho and not Mandiva Sheldrake. You got that boy?' Brother

nodded and looked down at me and asked gently, 'And you?'
I nodded in agreement. 'That's just Papa's name, it's easy to
remember.' I added. He smiled down at me and patted my
head. 'Smart girl,' he said.

Soon, we were exiting through the back door and heading
towards a large brown boat at the shipyard. We joined the
crowd of dirty, hungry-looking fishermen, who were heading
towards the boat with their nets. The narrow slab that led to
the boat was rowdy and noisy. Brother held firmly onto my
right hand and Uncle Jide onto my left, we joined the others
to enter the fishermen's vessel. At the entrance of the ship,
we came across two huge white men, dressed up in navy
uniforms. They asked Uncle for the boat fare, which Uncle
Jide paid. They handed us three tickets. As we were about to
go through the ship, we heard a voice from behind.

'Hey, stop, what are your names again?' I think my heart
stopped beating for a second as we all turned around. I felt
the sweat on Uncle Jide's palm.

'My name is Sheldrake Mbutho, this is my father John and
my sister Martha,' I heard my brother confidently respond.

The speaker, the supervisor of the naval officers, gave us a
cursory look and seemed satisfied. 'Oh okay, move along,'
he commanded. Uncle gave a deep sigh of relief as we
proceeded into the boat.

As soon as we got in, Uncle murmured to Brother 'John?'. I
heard Brother reply in a calm, collected and confident tone,
'I don't get to be the only one with a different name, Father.'
He replied sarcastically with a grin. And from that day on,

my brother was called Sheldrake and Uncle Jide ceased to be
called Uncle and became Papa John to me.

CHAPTER SEVEN

SHELDRAKE, 6 MONTHS LATER

You are a Sheldrake and we don't cry... so the next time I see you shed a tear I will hunt you down for the rest of your life. You are going to get your sister...you are going to keep her alive... and get her a damn good education and make her grow into a fine lady like your father always wanted...'

The voice of Mama could be heard from my sleep. I woke up gasping for air and soaked in sweat. It was a dream about that night again. About Mama's death and her words, which seemed to be haunting me for no reason. I sat up on the deck of the cargo vessel as my gaze fell on the waves of the sea. I shivered in the darkness because of the chill of the night. Moreover, the smell of dead Sea fish and cheap cigarettes nauseated me and with the feeling of loneliness, I felt sick at the life of a penniless fugitive. I felt pity for myself. We had been sailing for over five months and docking at strange and unfriendly places to offload certain cargoes. To release my frustration, I mostly got up at night when all the crew members were asleep and freed my aggression by throwing punches at an imaginary opponent and butchering raw meats in the cold room.

As soon as we went onboard, I had started working towards making all the money I could. My job description entailed working in the kitchen as a cleaner and scrubbing the deck of the ship, and I sometimes assisted the cook in scaling fish to earn extra. Uncle Jide had developed sea sickness, making him cough, vomit and complain bitterly of abdominal pains. I had to take up his duties in the interim, in addition to mine. Through this difficult period, I had rapidly grown up from a boy to a man as I had to earn enough to look after my uncle and my baby sister to remain on that ship. I noticed that I had gradually outgrown my clothes; my shirt felt tighter and my voice became deeper. Also, I started developing facial hair; it seemed my hairline was receding, which made me look bald and hardened. However, I always made out time to teach Martha how to read using old newspapers from the ship. Soon, I had started smoking cheap cigarettes, too, with other seafarers. Smoking gave me a sort of relief from the cold and my nightmares. Martha was growing fast too. Her clothes appeared small for her and her hair had started growing longer. It seemed she was beginning to look like Mama every day. Most of the time, I wondered if I was taking care of her as much as Mama had instructed me to.

I made my way to check on her as she slept serenely on the arctic wooden floor alongside thousands of crew members. I covered her with a small tattered wrapper and later, turned to cover up Uncle Jide, who snored noisily beside her. His face was stony, a motif of endless suffering. Even in sleep, he looked combative. His hair was greying, much faster than it should, I think. But behind that mask of a hard man, Uncle Jide had a good heart.

After six months of hard labour on the boat, I had time to look at Abednego's letter. Somehow, I seemed to have blocked his memory or his letter from my mind. The white captains on the vessel are harsh, unfriendly and unkind to most black crew members. Honestly, just a day on that South Ciskei vessel could make a Xhosatan man or any nigger turn on a white man forever. I pulled the letter from my pocket, lighting a cigarette.

Dear Mandiva,

I apologise for all the grievances that knowing me may have caused you and your family. If this letter got to you then it means that you are alive and well. Then I am happy. You may have heard I was beaten to a pulp by two black men from the club. Taking advantage of my supposed unconsciousness, I learnt that my uncle told my father that you were the one who ordered the hit on me. I don't know why he would do such an ugly thing. I have always known him to be a racist and dishonest man, but I never thought he would be this beastly. I gathered this information from the kitchen maid, Rose. I apologise because I couldn't correct this injustice, given that my mother has refused my father from seeing me again. She also discovered my father's affairs with other women, she heard that he had slept with your mother from my uncle. We will soon be on our way to England shortly after I have written this letter.

My mother plans to divorce my father after this incident. She blames your mother and my father for my battering. As for me, I don't blame your Mama because this separation was a long time coming; I honestly don't know why she has to be held accountable for my father's misconduct. He is a man I never want to be compared to when I become my own man in future. You see, it's public knowledge that he married

Mother for her wealth and not for love. I look at Mother in her distress sometimes and pray she doesn't depart this life because of alcohol or a broken heart. My heart aches when she cries.

I hope my little angel Martha is well, I will miss her dearly. I put in all my savings to help you all get away to a safer place. I express some regret because I didn't have time to raise more funds. I would continue boxing to remember you all. It has taught me to be confident in the outside world and I pray we meet again in the nearest future. Goodbye, Brother.

Yours sincerely,

Your brother, Abednego

I smiled. Such an intelligent friend. I did admire him and somehow, I knew I would miss him. He was like a brother I never had. But he belongs to my past. I must move on. I folded the letter and threw it into the sea.

CHAPTER EIGHT

ABEDNEGO, ENGLAND 1993

The 90s fashion was the bridge to the 21st century, which brought a great change in my taste for fashion, women and my fast lifestyle. You see, I was Britain's golden boy to the people and they believed that I and my wife could do no wrong. We were publicised, loved and worshipped as royalty, just like the Prince and the Princess of Wales. However, I would say the public's love for us was comparable to the monarch before Prince Charles fucked up with the ugly duckling, Camilla.

That very day in London, I gazed at the camera in front of me and gave my usual killer smile. I knew I looked spot on, as usual, dressed in my cream, loose baggy suit with a solid black tucked-in crewneck t-shirt. I tried to concentrate on the interview questions the British brunette was throwing at me, but was distracted by her cleavage. It is such a pity that most men lose concentration when they are being interviewed by beautiful journalists. You see, I was now the undefeated world heavyweight champion for three consecutive years and was standing before a multitude of these provocatively dressed female reporters with my wife standing next to me. As for any accusations of my filthy thoughts, the answer is I don't give a damn! I just love women.

I ran my fingers through my short dark hair restlessly as I stared at another Chinese female correspondent in front of me. I was knackered. The forum was becoming too long and boring. The reporters were everywhere in the room. Today was my final press conference as Britain's heavyweight boxing champion, but nobody knew it yet. *But in a few seconds, they sure will.*

'*...So* Abednego, *after winning the match three nights ago... That is the third Britain and world championships belt in a row for you... What is the next step and why did you refuse to make the press conference two days ago after the match? And why the sudden conference call? Does your wife have anything to do with this sudden turn of events? Because as they say, you guys are Britain's golden couple.*'

'Woo... slow down, Mrs Cruise... is it Miss or Mrs?' I asked her. I watched her blush before correcting me. 'It's Mrs,' she almost sounded disappointed that it was a '*Mrs*'. I continued with my public display of charm. '...I called this press meeting because I have an important announcement to make. I decided to keep it till the end, but now that you have asked, I will make it. I am retiring as the world boxing champion....' An uproar greeted this announcement. Flashes from the camera followed in quick succession. Every reporter was speaking at the same time. The look on my manager's face was that of an indescribable shock. My wife's facial expression was blank as usual. She gave a quick smile to the camera.

I met Shelly back at the University of Oxford. She was an *A* student in sharp contrast to the *F* grade I maintained. Her father, Lord Richard Abbey of Yorkshire, was a wealthy Duke. He had wanted to marry Mother when she was much younger, but she turned him down to marry Father, which I believe was the greatest mistake of her life. My grandmother had explained to me one sunny afternoon, after I got back from school, that Mother had fallen ill and died. She had died of complicated malaria. This was shortly after we returned to England. I knew she lied to me. Mother's actual cause of death would have been a blow to the family name if the news got out in public. Grandmother thought I couldn't understand Mother's circumstances at my age, so she tried to protect me, but I knew Mother had died out of the emotional trauma she passed through at the hands of Father. She simply had nothing more to live for. After her death, I was sent to live with my grandparents. After that, I learnt my father had turned into a drunk and committed suicide after he lost the election in South Ciskei. This election was shortly after my mother's death. My grandparents had made sure he lost the race. I grew up in boarding school and had to make out life on my own. I learnt my father had squandered his fortune and that of my mother on the electoral campaign. The only inheritance I got from him was his good looks and a goddamn gramophone box, which was imported to me from his bankrupt estate in Africa. As I grew up, I realised that my grandparents could only offer me a fundamental education. My extravagant lifestyle couldn't continue. In the university, I could easily get a free pass into the magnificent clubs and gala because of my 6-feet height, dashing aristocratic looks and charisma. The ladies loved me, and I took all the advantages that came with it. When I met Shelly, she had no wit, beauty or sexual appeal, but she had a dominating and debonair personality, so my grandparents encouraged me to court her since her father was running for parliament at that time. He had won the election and so I proposed.

We got married at the cathedral by York Minster. The wedding was grand. A few days after the honeymoon, I enrolled in the British lightweight boxing championship competition despite Shelly and her father's disapproval. I won the tournament and from then on, I went on to become the heavyweight boxing champion of the world.

'Hey, if you could be quiet, you guys could make a lot of money capturing my last public speech....' That did the magic. I observed the noise in the room gradually subside before I continued. 'I am about to commence a new programme that focuses on how to enlist new boxers and I would groom them to become world champions like me. I have won a lot of medals in the past few years, and it's becoming boring. I need a new challenge in life. That's why I am going to focus on helping young boys.' I turned around and winked at my wife, who returned my wink with a fake broadened smile and cold stare. *Damn, ice queen*, I said to myself.

'So, where is this programme going to take place?' two reporters asked simultaneously. I began to tap my fingers on the table in frustration. I was becoming restless and claustrophobic. *I need to get away from England.* The whole media, publicity on my marriage, my wife's family and having

a career as a hugely successful boxer was choking me.
Sometimes I yearned for the freedom I once had as a child
in South Ciskei. I knew that would never happen again.
Maybe when I finally die. I looked directly into the camera
and gave my reformed Monalisa smile before replying,
'Africa, Nigeria. That is all. Thank you.'

Straight away, I walked out of the room ignoring the frantic
attempts by the reporters to get more comments out of me.

'Why Africa?'

*Why Nigeria of all places? Does that mean you are relocating to
Africa? And why would you want to move back to Africa after the
story of your horrible childhood?'*

*'Don't you think that this decision would mean a great loss to our
country Britain?'*

*'Does this decision have anything to do with your late father, Lord
Abednego?'*

My bodyguards stopped the reporters from following me as
I exited the room with my entourage in tow, my wife Shelly,
my manager Jimmy, and my personal Assistant, Christopher.
I was escorted to my Limousine. As if on a cue, Shelly and
Jimmy verbally descended on me all at once.

'What the hell was that?' they yelled.

'Good lord, Abednego, I have managed you for over five
years, and you couldn't tell me of this preposterous decision!'

'For heaven's sake, go to Nigeria?'

'Hey! Chill, you guys. Let me explain...' I interrupted them both harshly. I turned to my wife and explained, 'Hey baby... you and your dad have always been on my neck about leaving boxing. Now, I have accepted that, and I intend to recruit young boxers and train them. It's a passion you know I have and it would generate funds worldwide.' I knew I got her there. The mention of money brought fire to her eyes. I had nailed a point that she wouldn't dare to overlook. I knew her too damn well. *She was a spoilt, money-conscious bitch.*

'Yeah, I can't lie that I am not elated about this retirement. If this decision would generate funds for the family... boxing has always been quite tacky to me but the thought of Africa?' She shrugged.

'Well, I don't expect you to go with me if you don't want to... You can stay in England and go ahead with your charity and gala nights as you have always done.'

'Of course, you know I am not going to move to Africa. You know that. For Daddy's election, we need to keep up appearances...' she snapped, rolling her eye balls.

'I will come in every two months and be present for the primaries, while you come for a day or two to AFRICA' I stressed the word Africa because I knew it would irritate her.

'It seemed you got this impulsive decision all sorted out. Then that's brilliant. We have to talk this over with Daddy first.'

'Sure baby.' I nodded in concordance, while I watched her slip on her pink Chanel silk gloves.

As for Jimmy, I gave him a meaningful wink that made him relax. He knew we had a lot to thrash out...behind Shelly.

The car pulled up in front of my magnificent mansion. The chauffeur opened the door, and my wife stepped out of the car. I sighed a sigh of relief as soon as she was out and slipped a cigarette in my mouth and lit it.

'We are home...Are you coming down, sir?' the driver asked as he realised I had not moved an inch from my sitting position.

'No Daniel, I need a minute. Shut the door.' He nodded and shut the car door. I turned to my manager who calmly sat opposite me.

He didn't wait for me to start. 'What's this all about, this sudden resignation and relocation to Africa? I have been with you for 5 years Abednego, and for once, you couldn't mention it. I am disappointed.'

'Relax Jim, I understand your fear. But there is no need for it. You are still not out of a job, you still have to train young athletes.'

'That is beside the point. If you are trying to get away from your wife and her family, try America or the South of France for God's sake. Africa has a lot of bad roads, poor people and bad governments.' He was frantic. I giggled. He had figured me out.

'I know you think I am throwing my career away at this age. But I need you to be positive. We are going to make history in Africa, Jimmy. And just maybe I would find that inner peace you keep preaching about.'

'What you are looking for I hope you find it in Nigeria. You have to learn to be content with life sometimes.' He replied with deep concern.

'I will find it, lad.'

CHAPTER NINE

MARTHA, NIGERIA

I pulled my natural, tough hair backwards into a knot as I stared at my reflection in the half-cracked mirror on the wall. I frowned as usual. I am all grown up now, 16 years old, about 5.9 feet tall, skinny and lanky with prominent check bones, big eye balls and hips. My breasts were firm, protruding prominently in my overused school uniform. People said I was maturing rapidly for my age and class. I seemed to agree with them. I was attending the local Secondary grammar school, St Patrick's Grammar School, at Yaba settlement in Lagos. I hated the smell of the school and my classmates. I had no friends. I was teased all day because of my height. My classmates also constantly mocked me because of my undersized uniform. They called me a giraffe and the worst part of it all, I had to sit at the back roll of the classroom because the school teacher felt I was going to hinder the short pupils from seeing the blackboard. My poor eyesight would later be diagnosed as myopia by the doctors in my adulthood. This sort of bullying by my peers and enabling by my teachers made me timid, so I didn't keep any friends or enemies. It compounded my low self-esteem and self-hatred. I felt ugly.

It was hard to talk to Brother about my feelings most times because he was always busy. He worked at least two jobs. He was a butcher in the meat shop in Ilupeju and a waiter in a fancy restaurant on Victoria Island. He often came back late and exhausted, making him sleep all day. I complained to Father, who told me that rather than complain, I should be grateful because my brother was working hard to send me to school; he wanted the best for me. I remembered saying that I wanted to work too to reduce the burden on his shoulders, but Brother scolded me that night after Father mentioned our discussion to him. He warned me never to bring it up again and I never did. Sometimes, I couldn't help but have a heart ache as I watched Brother work his arse off for me and he had aged so much. Like me, he didn't have friends. Most of the time, he appeared withdrawn and quiet too. However, he had a companion – his boxing bag and gloves. He was consistent in his daily boxing exercise and prayers. We had a big sack filled with cotton hanging from the ceiling in our one-room apartment, which he practised religiously. Father and Brother normally jogged up the jagged road of Apapa and Ajegunle for training. I think that was what still gave him solace in his thoughts because after a run with Father, he always came back with hot roasted corn and pear for me from the lady down the street, especially during its season. It always made me happy.

As for Father, he was a newspaper vendor in the mornings and worked part-time in the same local bar with Brother during the day. I remember how they came home dancing the day they got the job at the bar, after months of an endless search for a job in Lagos. That day was one of the most memorable days of our lives. Sadly, such days don't come often for us.

That morning, I was distracted from my thoughts when my eyes fell on the calendar on the wall. As if hit by a lightening, it suddenly occurred to me that it was Brother's birthday that very day. I had circled the date with a big red biro to remember. I sighed because I was supposed to go to school in a few seconds. I already planned on making a delicacy for him on his birthday. At that instant, I decided I would make him a pudding basin of fried akara and roasted cocoyam. He had fallen in love with this Nigerian delicacy. I planned to go to the restaurant and give it to him. I smiled at my brilliant plan. *Only if I knew better...*

CHAPTER TEN

SHELDRAKE

Zen Chinese Restaurant, Victoria Island, Nigeria

I collected the tray of king-fried prawns, Singapore noodles, spring rolls and samosa from the kitchen chef and made my way out of the kitchen to the dining hall. I hated the whole buzz of the festive seasons, especially Christmas. I was still silently battling with my inner demons as I hadn't come to terms with what Jesus had done to me, Mama or dead Papa. I tried to ignore the Elvis Presley version of '*I am dreaming of a white Christmas*', which played in the background of the restaurant. I forced a smile as I saw a crowd of new faces that day at the restaurant. I spotted the couple that placed an order and I made my way to their table.

I assumed that the unusual appearance of the overzealous crowd at the brasserie was due to the expected presence of the international superstar who was coming to the restaurant that afternoon. The Chinese manager had announced to us during an emergency staff meeting that morning that a celebrity from England was coming in that day. He had further warned that employees should be on their best professional behaviour. He also said that he needed us to work overtime. *I was rather irritated by this overtime news since I hadn't been granted my entitled leave and I had to work this extra shift for free.* I couldn't care less about the rich celebrity that was showing up. However, I couldn't afford to lose the job since it was the closest I had come to smelling wealth. It paid my rent and granted me the liberty to take home leftover Singapore noodles for Martha once a month. She could take the bowls to school and show them off in front of her school mates. She was a smart kid. Her results from school showed her grades were brilliant and that was all that kept me going. One day, she would end up in a fantastic college and be a fancy lady like Mrs Mayor. I often told myself. That was the kind of education that Mama had always wanted for her.

I placed the orders on the table for the customer and gave a professional smile. I repeated each of their orders to the guest while serving them.

'King fried prawns, Singapore noodles, vegetable spring rolls and samosa.'

'Thank you,' the lady murmured without glancing up at me. I nodded after placing the plate on the table and I began to head back to the kitchen. As I was about to pass through the revolving door of the dinner hall which led to the kitchen, my attention was drawn to the cheers from the customers at the dining hall and a series of camera flashes across the room. I paused to catch a glimpse of the celebrity that was spoken so highly about and attracted this much attention. Soon my concentration was interrupted by the loud announcement from Mr Yans across the kitchen, 'Abednego has arrived; we must have all our delicacies on point. This publicity is what we need in this restaurant.'

I slowly turned around, but amid all the flashes from the cameras in the dining hall, I could still recognise him. He was walking majestically like a superstar towards a reserved table, an elderly man by his side and two huge-looking bodyguards. He looked totally different. Confident, tall, huge, dressed in a body-fitted grey Prada suit and cream tie. He was a carbon copy of his father. I could almost swear I was seeing MDS, except that Abednego cultivated a well-shaped moustache, unlike his clean-shaven father. He seemed amused by a comment made by the elderly man that accompanied him. MDS never laughed, especially in public. Suddenly a rush of blocked-up memory came flowing back to me. Here was my childhood friend. But all I could see was MDS, the author of my miserable life. I jolted as I heard the manager screaming my name. I swiftly closed the door and moved towards him.

'Hope you are not day dreaming, Sheldrake... Today we need all the attention necessary.'

'Yes, sir,' I replied. I watched him move over to the head chef to chat with him and then later take his exit. Uncle Jide, now called Father, came, rushing excitedly into the room with an open newspaper in his hands. He was showing me something. 'Guess who is coming to Nigeria! Abednego! The world champion in boxing, son!'

'Who?' I replied nonchalantly to the news. Since Uncle Jide and I loved boxing, we had independently followed the career of Abednego in the newspapers once in a while. We never spoke about him since it only generated bad memories and we decided to bury the past.

'Abednego!' He repeated. 'He retired a few weeks ago from England and now he is in Nigeria searching for new talents to recruit young boxers.' He screamed excitedly.

'Wetin dey make you shout, biko? That one na new gist? No, be the man wey dey inside the dining hall now? Abeg person go think say una know am.' The head chef, totally uninvited, cut in, in broken English, which was popularly called pidgin English, spoken by the commoners in Nigeria.

'Abi oh. You think say because you come from the same country that celebrity grow up, you wan come lie to us.'

'We sure say you even come from that side?' another waiter chipped in.

I understood their aggression. Everyone was grumbling because they had to work over time for the new celebrity that suddenly appeared in the restaurant.

'Of course, we know him. He was best friends with this chap here during childhood.' Father proudly said, tapping my shoulders with a grin. As soon as he said that, all the kitchen staff burst out laughing.

'Abeg, do you think I would lie about my son and Abednego being best friends in South Ciskei? Sheldrake and I taught him how to fight.' Father protested in annoyance. They responded by laughing harder.

'Come on, Father, that's a long time ago. Besides, things change,' I nudged him with my elbow, embarrassed.

'I know that you will go and meet him, son.' He continued in determination.

'So, Mr Jide, if you are so convinced that you know him, you will be the one to serve the starter they just ordered.... abi?' The head cook loudly interjected.

'I don't think that is necessary...' I immediately said.

'Yes, you would.' Father sternly interrupted me. 'That's a chance to get enrolled in a boxing tournament, reunite with that kid.'

Reluctantly, I collected the tray of pecking soup and samosa from the head chef, Mr Olatunde. He gave me a sarcastic smile as he handed the tray over to me. I made my way to the dining hall, trying to forget the number of penetrating eyes that stared behind me. The entire kitchen staff were watching me intently from behind; I imagined them hurrying to the kitchen window to peep. I exhaled while I slowly made my way to the table. Suddenly, I was standing in front of Abednego and his crew. I cleared my throat out loud. He was engrossed in a discussion with the elderly man.

'Your order sir, peking soup and samosa for starters.' I placed the dishes on the table. For whatever reason, He didn't raise his head to look at me. He was deeply engrossed in his conversation. Soon, I was standing by the table embarrassed, because I could see the other staff watching me expectantly through the window across the room. I turned around and was about to leave when he called me.

'Excuse me waiter, where is your drink menu?' He called out to me. I turned around and slowly walked up to him. I handed him the drink menu. He collected the menu from me without any hesitation. I watched him flip through the pages of the menu; he then lifted his head and read the name on my name tag.

'Sheldrake... that's the name, isn't it? Please get me a bottle of Limca, I want to taste the Nigerian brand before the vodka sets in,' he turned his attention back to the elderly man and continued his conversation. I turned around and walked briskly outside the dining hall. I ignored the excruciating laughter that greeted me as soon as I got to the kitchen exit door. I made my way to the blind alley to seize a smoke. I could hear Father's limping footsteps following me, but I ignored him.

'You know you shouldn't take things too seriously. It honestly has been a while, I am sure we just have to find another way for him to remember.'

'You know you should stop it right there because you are right, it's been ten years. In god's fucking name, he wouldn't remember shit because he's now a splitting image of his father. And you should have known better instead of telling the goddamn world, and now I just made a fool of myself.' I turned around to face him. The pain in my heart was obvious. He shook his head and handed me a stick of cigarettes. He lit it up for me, from a match box he took from his pocket before he spoke up.

'Those people in the kitchen are not the whole world, son; they are a bunch of people confined in a little kitchen doing hard labour just like you and me. If you have forgotten, we are all called *servants*.' He stressed the word before calmly lightening his stick of cigarette. He continued '...I read in the papers that he is searching for recruits, and we both know you are good; you should be looking for a way to better yourself and not dwell on the scorn of haters. Nothing good comes easy for Sheldrakes, boy. I'm sure you should know that by now.'

'Know what?' We heard Martha's tiny voice from behind us. We turned around and saw her smiling broadly while she stood in her school uniform; from the distance, we could perceive the sweet-smelling akara (bean cake). A wrapper was tied around the ribbon that covered it. A large tacky '*happy birthday*' was boldly written on the ribbon with a red marker. I frowned.

CHAPTER ELEVEN

MARTHA

I had never seen Brother so livid with me before that memorable day. I had only intended on surprising him on his birthday and not freak him out. However, I didn't feel as hurt as I should have expected when he screamed at me to return to school. I was perplexed. Was this because I had overheard his discussion with Father? *Abednego was here. It couldn't be!*

'You hear me, you will return to school at once and stop any further birthday surprises. You can surprise me when you get to the university by winning honours!'

'Abednego is here?' I asked stammering, in a rush of emotions: joy, anger, ambivalence.

'Goddamn it, Martha. Didn't you hear what I said? Father, please take this child away from here and back to school before I lose my cool!' He flared up in anger.

'What the hell are you all doing here?' I heard a voice and sprung around to see the manager of the restaurant standing behind us with an angry face. 'Do you know that Mister Abednego hasn't gotten his drink served because the damn waiter that took his order forgot to hand over the bloody request?' His face was turning red like flames, as he fumed.

'I'm so sorry sir. It's a grave mistake on my part....' Brother apologized.

'How does sorry compensate for the negative reviews by an international food critic... and what the hell am I hearing? You are claiming you know the world boxing champion and implying that you stupidly forgot to take his order because of a bet by your peers? And on top of it all, you got your sister bringing a bag of offensive-smelling stuff to the restaurant. Jesus Christ, you are fired, Sheldrake!' he sniffed as he suspiciously eyed the bag of food in my hands.

'Please, Mr Yan...' Brother pleaded with him, as Father hurriedly took my arms and led me out of the scene.

'I could help him beg Mr Yan...' I struggled with Father as I wanted to go back to help my brother. *He was going to be fired partly because of me.*

'I don't think that's such a good idea, Martha. You have done enough damage already, and I don't think that would help matters.' He explained to me as he continued pulling me by the arms towards the back exit gate of the restaurant. As we approached the exit gate, I remember we couldn't leave because there was security stationed there.

'What's going on here, Oga?' Father asked the uniformed police man confused. He explained that a lot of fans have tried to get inside the restaurant to see Abednego, so they had to beef up security. It was only the front gate that was the exit out of the restaurant. Father thanked him and continued leading me through a passage in the restaurant towards the main exit. Tears began to well up in my eyes, and the customers at the restaurant gave me funny looks. I passed them while holding onto the akara basket firmly. I must confess, as we slowly reached the front exit door, I began to hear the lively sound of the familiar laughter that lit up the room despite my tears and the suffocation of shame due to the looks of disgust given to me by some of the customers. Suddenly, I spotted Abednego sitting amongst some distinguished-looking men.

'That's Abendego...' I told Papa, barely able to contain myself. I dropped the bowl of akara on the floor unintentionally, sending the food flying around the room.

'Yeah, it is, child, but it would be difficult to reach him... Damn it you can't drop this on the floor! I would be the next person losing my job,' he growled as he limped and quickly bent down to pick up the balls of akara on the floor.

In a few seconds, we heard the quick footsteps of the ugly, grumpy, stout sadist of a manager approaching us. He had a murderous look on his face. I realised that if the manager came in contact with me, I would be thrown out of the restaurant and never have the opportunity to see Abednego again. Impulsively, I began to run towards Abednego, ignoring Papa who had started calling out my name. The mean-looking security men watching him now turned to me. I avoided them and ran to him, but it was too late. I reached his table but unfortunately for me, the two guards had caught up with me. They held me by my shoulder and hands.

'Miss... you have to leave.'

'Abednego!' I screamed his name aloud as the security started pulling me away. I watched him look up and stare at me for a second. He then frowned and turned his head away and continued talking to the other gentleman, who was introducing him to an elegantly dressed lady. I continued screaming out his name for attention.

'Don't you remember me?' I called out in tears in Xhosatan. Soon, I was exhausted; the security man carried me outside the restaurant. Papa rushed to my side as the security guard tossed me aside on the pavement.

'She's just a child,' he yelled at the guard. I sat on the stairs crying my eyes out. I remember Papa trying to calm me down.

'Hush child, you know if your brother hears about this embarrassment there would be a big fight in this place, and there wouldn't be any possible way for getting his or my job back. You have to keep quiet and be calm.' He tried to calm me in Xhosatan. It had been a while since I had heard Papa speak Xhosatan. It was like he and Brother tried very hard to block out our South Ciskein roots.

'But he didn't remember me? Why Papa? I hate myself and school and now I made my brother lose his job. Why can't he remember us, Papa? 'I wailed like a bride jilted by a randy groom on her wedding day. He tried to console me by patting me on my head. I clutched onto his chest as minutes ticked away. After two minutes of snoring, I heard the familiar voice once more, which immediately stopped my tears.

'Martha' I heard him call from behind me. I lifted my head from Papa's bosom in shock and slowly turned around. There he was, strikingly tall like a white Xhosatan God, with wavy dark hair, wearing a white, half-open buttoned silk cotton shirt with rolled-up sleeves. I slowly stood up, with all my attention on him. It felt like it was only us two that stood on the pavement of the restaurant that day. His bodyguards stood behind him, along with the restaurant Manager, Mr Yan, and the customers from the restaurant that had come outside to witness the commotion. Papa stood beside me with a grin on his face, and the whole world suddenly seemed to stand still.

'Is that really you?' he spoke in a familiar British accent, a broad smile on his chiselled face. That seemed like the most beautiful smile I had ever seen. I tried to speak but I couldn't. I just stood motionlessly in front of him and nodded my head. He walked closer to me and opened up his arms. I ran into his open arms. He held me close to his chest. I began to snub again. Soon, he was carrying me up in the air and laughing, and the images of Abednego carrying me and swinging me around as a little girl in the valley in South Ciskei came rushing back to me. I remember giggling out loud as I did that very moment.

'My little rascal Martha,' he laughed out loud. Soon, I too was giggling. He dropped me down, planted kisses on my forehead and then as usual, patted my hair. He gently pushed me backwards to access me as he said 'you haven't changed kid, still look the same but taller.'

'You too, but you are soooooo tall and handsome,' I whispered shyly to him. He soon turned towards Papa and smiled. He stretched out his hand for a hand shake. Papa nodded and shook his outstretched hand with a huge grin.

'Good day, Uncle. It's been ages,' he said.

'Ages? It's an understatement. Mandiva can't wait to see you.' Papa replied.

'Where's Mandiva? Take me to him,' he asked, searching the crowd with his eye.

'He works in the kitchen. We call him Sheldrake now.' Papa said.

'Brother would be most delighted.' I spoke out loud. He held my hand as I led him to the kitchen where Sheldrake was packing his belongings.

CHAPTER TWELVE

ABEDNEGO

I walked down the neat passageway of the kitchen, holding Martha by the hand. Mr Jide was telling me about their journey to Nigeria. I listened attentively and laughed at his funny exclamations. I recalled chatting with my manager when he introduced me to two Moroccan female fans. They were twins, tall, elegant and sexy with beautiful brunette hair. The cliché was that they were girls that I could easily have a quickie with, meaning quick sex in the restaurant bathroom. I was that spontaneous in my sexual inclinations but at that point, I was distracted by the sudden offensive smell that filled the air in the restaurant. I became more enamoured by screams coming my way. I thought it might have been another sick fan. Until I got to Nigeria, I hadn't realised that my popularity was next to God's in Africa. I was as popular in Nigeria as I was in most developed countries. I was more than flattered, especially by the open admiration shown to me by the ladies. I stopped to think that maybe that same desire from women was similar to the attraction shown to my father by African women in his time. As the scream from the fans grew further away because the security had taken control of the situation, I asked the ladies what was going on.

'Did she just speak in Xhosatan?' I asked the ladies in my sexy baritone voice.

'Yeah, she was saying you couldn't remember her; how can you when she's wearing a damn ugly uniform?' One of the girls said. 'Crazy peasant fan,' she giggled and winked at me.

'A uniform.' I looked up at the screaming lady and then I recalled the voice. Her tiny little voice was still the same. I stood up immediately. It couldn't be, I told myself. *Could this be Martha?*

'What's the problem?' my manager asked, alarmed. I stood up and called one of my security guards.

'Take me to the screaming girl.'

'Are you crazy, Abednego? Do you want to be mobbed?'

I ignored Jimmy and made my way towards the exit door with the security in tow. I studied the back profile of the girl sitting on the stairway sobbing, with an elderly man consoling her. They spoke in Xhosatan, and immediately I was reassured by the hard tone of Jide and Martha's little voice as she sobbed. *I finally found them.* I told myself. It was like a heavy load had been lifted off my shoulder. *I found my real family.* They didn't hear me when I walked behind them. After listening to them for a few seconds, I called out her name. It was the happiest moment in my life when she slowly turned around and shyly smiled up at me with her huge teary eyeballs. *My little Martha...*

Soon, we reached the kitchen and there, I spotted him. It appeared that he was packing his belongings in a small brown carton. He had his usual frown on his face. He had changed so much over the years. He appeared much older and different. I would never have recognised him if had I met him on the roadside; he was heavily built, taller, with a skinned haircut and was much darker in complexion than I remembered.

'Sheldrake!' Jide called out. He looked up at him with a frown. That frown made it evident that it was really him. He suddenly caught sight of me. However, he pretended he did not see me, and went back to doing what he was doing until I was directly in front of him and called his name.

'Mandiva.'

He looked up at me and frowned again.

'What can I do for you, Abednego? As you can see, I just got fired. And if I may ask, where have you been?' he said nonchalantly.

'Being the fucking world boxing champion, and of course, with the ladies, I heard you have been suffering in this shithole.' I replied with a broad grin. Mandiva burst out laughing. That laughter was such a relief!

'You haven't changed,' he said.

'You neither.' We hugged each other.

I saw the look of confusion and admiration on the faces of the staff in the kitchen and my manager. The Chinese manager of the restaurant who earlier had introduced himself to me came forward.

'Mr Abednego, it's so nice to see you in our kitchen, Sheldrake has been a wonderful staff here.'

'You just fired him, from what I heard.' I interrupted him.

'Well, that was a misunderstanding; he has his job back...'

'Really?' Sheldrake and Jide asked sarcastically.

'Of course, a nice misunderstanding. Get your stuff. We are out of here buddy.' I said, and then turned around to my assistant and instructed that his things were to be taken to my limousine.

'Uncle Jide, you too, let's leave this shithole,' I ran my fingers through Martha's hair and scattered it as usual. She kept on giggling.

'Where are we off to, Abednego?' she asked in her cute tone.

'To my house,' I replied. Soon, we were leaving the fucked-up restaurant, leaving the whole kitchen staff staring, beaming and dumbfounded, as we headed towards my limo.

CHAPTER THIRTEEN

SHELDRAKE

For the first time in my life, I felt euphoric from the sensation of the warm water from the tap in my bathroom running down my body. I stepped out of the shower and stared thoughtfully at my reflection in the French designed wall mirror in front of me. The splashes of fresh water on my face immediately took my memory to South Ciske. I had turned on the tap in Mister Jefferson's room when Mama had sent me to put some towels on his bed. For the first time, I walked into a luxurious bedroom. The faucet was made of gold. I was fascinated by the colour of its handle and curiously, I turned it open and watched the water come out of the tap. I had only ever experienced water from the old and rusty well at my house.

'Wow!' I said. 'We must be really poor,' I murmured to myself. Suddenly, I heard footsteps in the bedroom and I panicked and headed behind the half-opened door of the bathroom. I could hear Jefferson's husky voice. He was speaking to Abednego's mother. She was sobbing, and he tried to console her.

'She has bewitched him. We need to get rid of her,' he told her.

'Your brother has been sleeping with negro women before he came to her. She is not the problem, he is,' she cried more.

'Since he met that maid, he has lost his head.'

I froze. It seems that they were talking about Mama.

'I am so embarrassed,' she snapped. 'How long would your brother humiliate me? I heard the servants whispering this morning about both of them.'

'Don't worry, I will take care of it. He assured her. Another person's footsteps were heard approaching, which belonged to the lady's maid.

'The minister and the mayor call for you, sir.'

'I need to leave now. Promise me you will speak with him,' she was wiping her tears with her handkerchief as she pleaded. I then heard her footsteps receding. It seemed only Jefferson was left alone now. I watched him pour himself a drink. Then, he started to make his way to the bathroom, as I felt my heart beat. He approached the door that I was behind, but I was saved by a sudden knock on the door. He turned around to open the door. It was Mama's voice I heard at the doorway. It seemed she was looking for him.

'I apologize, sir. I wanted to make sure your bathroom had the hand towel I sent.'

'You can come in and check,' I heard his alluring tone. I watched Mama walk into the room and to the bathroom. She looked behind the door and saw me. Our eyes met each other, I could see the critical eyes she gave me and immediately, she closed the door. I heard her say 'the towels are there, sir. The mayor is calling you, sir.'

'Why don't we have some wild sex first before visiting the mayor?' I heard him tell Mama. I felt anger inside me as I peeped through the keyhole. He had grabbed Mama's hand.

'Let go of me, sir,' Mama firmly told him as she pulled her hands away from him.

'Seems this nigga here likes only powerful men.' He pulled her arms again but this time, in aggression.

I heard Mama speak up to him firmly.

'If you don't leave my arm in two seconds and come with me like a gentleman down stairs, I promise you I will scream my lungs out. The British press are downstairs, sir. I believe we don't want that attention, do we?' I watched him as he let go of Mama's arms in reluctance.

He spat on Mama's face in response to her comment before adding, 'Just an appetizer for you to feel my taste before the main course.' He adjusted his buckle as he left the room. I watched Mama use her petticoat to wipe her face, still composed. She turned around and followed him out of the room.

I walked up to the sink in the bathroom and inhaled. I opened the tap in front of me and splashed water on my face with my hands. I tried to scoop some water to drink. The heat from the hot water from the tap burnt my skin, which juggled me to my new reality. It took a reality check to believe that I was living now in such luxury, that I could bathe with warm water without having to first boil cold water with firewood. I blinked again. I was standing in the middle of my gigantic bathroom. The bathroom was double the size of the room where Papa, Martha and I used to live. Abednego had moved us into his luxurious quarters in Victoria Island, Lagos. It felt like paradise on earth. I walked out of the bathroom into my huge bedroom and then towards the patio that was connected to my room. I thought to myself *could this be real?* As I pinched myself, I heard Abednego's voice from behind me.

'You are alive, Brother!' I turned around and heartily laughed at his joke.

'What is that supposed to mean, man?'

'I remember you, any time I brought lunch for you, you would have to pinch yourself to check if the food was real.' He laughed.

'True.' I agreed with him. I walked over to him as he handed me a glass of whisky. He continued, 'I just checked on Martha. She's sleeping like a baby. She still grabs onto her pillow. Why she still does that, I will never understand.'

'Because she's a kid, white boy,' I replied. It seemed we had never departed from him. He still sounded and acted the same.

'You are still full of yourself, I understand,' he replied with a grin. We both laughed.

'So, tell me about you... I read in the papers that you got married to some queen of England. You should be happy, where is she?'

'In England where she belongs, my friend...' He replied with a smirk.

'I don't understand?'

'Don't believe everything you read in the papers... My marriage is the biggest and saddest charade you can ever be in. I married my wife because it was convenient for me to do so. My fucked-up father squandered all my inheritance on women and his electoral campaign.' He talked about it with sadness in his eyes while he drifted away. 'You know me; I was used to and still needed the extravagant lifestyle. I could never cope with being poor...' He laughed. 'My marriage set the foundation for me to box without wondering about the financial implication to it, that is if I failed or not. Just as Jide once taught us all, through boxing, we learn to get our frustration out. It was my sanctuary. And funny enough, I became one of the luckiest sonsofbitches... the world champion.'

'So you married for money? Just like your old man.'

That seemed to hurt him. 'Fuck you. I will never be like him.'

'I didn't mean that,' I apologised. 'Life has been so hard, Abednego, trying to put Martha through school and paying Uncle Jide's medical bills. I don't think I would have ever married someone just to get out of my present misery.'

'Medical bills?' he murmured, ignoring the marriage part.

'He has hypertension and diabetes.'

'Before ranting about what medical condition I am in, why don't you leave trivial matters and start discussing important issues such as enrolling you in the amateur boxing competition next week?' Uncle Jide interjected from the door.

'Amateur boxing competition?' I was confused.

'Well, your health is of utmost importance too, Uncle, and I am sorry about the news.' Abednego sounded truly worried.

'We'll discuss it with your manager Jimmy. He says if we win the amateur competition, then we could try the heavyweight championship, depending on how good you are.'

'You are already talking business but...'

'Well, I am, and that is what we should be doing. You dreamt of boxing your whole life since you were a kid. So, no buts...' he interrupted me with a serious look.

'I am not as young and as fast as when I once was, Uncle. Trying to go professional is a big deal. I don't want Abednego investing money in me or a failed adventure.' I interrupted.

'I don't invest stupidly, my friend. That is one trait I didn't inherit from my father. If you enrol in this competition and show that you can engage in professional boxing instead of street fighting then I promise to take you to the top of your career, bro. And as for you, Uncle Jide, tomorrow you are going to see my personal doctor, Nina, and that's settled.' Abednego added.

'K, kiddo.' Uncle Jide agreed. He leapt towards me and collected my glass of whisky. He gulped it all at once and said, 'And finally, life begins...'

***

A week later......

I was in another dream land again but as usual, it was about my past. I was a little boy all over again, and Mama had sent me to the barn to check on the mayor's horses when I returned from school. I grumbled, but couldn't disobey her. I had my school books in one hand and roasted corn in the other. As I approached the barn, I heard screams. I quickened my pace so that I could try and help the person, as he sounded like he was pleading. But I froze on the spot as I saw Jefferson flogging a black man with wires with the mayor sitting down as he watched calmly like a spectator. The black man was tied to a pole like an animal.

'So why did you steal from the mine?' Jefferson asked as he kept on whipping the man. I saw blood pour out of the man's body as he screamed. Saliva dribbled from his mouth.

Immediately, my books fell from my hand. Jefferson's eyes and the mayor's caught up with mine. My legs were weak, so I didn't dare try to run.

'Bring him here,' the mayor commanded. I began to sweat profusely. I watched Jefferson walk up to me with his limp. He stooped down and frowned.

'You look just like your mother.'

'I...' I was very frightened to reply. He looked up to his white bodyguards, and they came up to me and pulled me towards the tied-up man. I realised he was the old butler, Minschini. It seemed the rumour was true; he had tried to steal from the mine to pay his children's fees a few days after he was fired.

'Pull a chair for him,' the mayor ordered, and the bodyguard handed me a seat to sit. I was still trembling.

'You would watch and learn. No one takes what's ours.' Jefferson then moved closer to me and whispered in my ear so the mayor couldn't hear. 'Send that message to your mother.'

The mayor handed Jefferson two boxing gloves and he started throwing punches at Minschini's face. I heard Minschini's scream again. Tears poured down my eyes. I watched his body become lifeless. I tried to look away and my eyes caught the shadow of a black young woman hiding behind the barn as tears poured down her eyes. She was covering her mouth with her hands as if preventing herself from screaming out loud. I wondered who she was. Our eyes caught each other, but she immediately turned around and disappeared.

The knock on my bedroom door jolted me back to reality. It was time for my first big fight. I was glad to see that it was Uncle Jide who entered my room. He came to give me his first motivational speech that stayed with me throughout my boxing career.

'You have to rise and shine, son, and remember that every fight you face can be a win if you channel it to every event in your life.' I nodded and made my way to the ring that day and waited patiently for my opponent, ignoring the discouraging cheering from the crowd when they called his name.

I recall my opponent's trainer walking into the arena with so much confidence at the beginning of the game, while I waited for him in the ring. The manager caught my attention and I frowned. He was a white man, he had a walking stick and he limped. He reminded me of Jefferson. I felt a sudden rage as Jefferson came into my memory. And just like that, I couldn't see the face of my opponent's coach anymore, and in my mind, it got replaced by the image of Jefferson walking into that arena instead with his lap dog to fight me. I then knew that I was going to win. I was going for the kill. The referee and commentator announced the commencement of the fight, and I knocked my contender down in less than fifteen minutes. The audience went crazy when this occurred as they had never seen such a quick fight and the arena was in an uproar. Uncle Jide, Jimmy and Abednego got into the ring to congratulate me with a mixture of shock and joy.

As I stared at my opponent on the floor of the boxing arena while my hand was being lifted by the referee as a winner, I knew that Uncle Jide was right. My win was propagated by the punches from memories of Jefferson. Every punch I gave my opponent was weighed with the memories of Jefferson.

Soon, I heard Abednego, Papa and Jimmy clapping. I had won the amateur boxing competition.

'I have to admit you are good.' Jimmy finally said. Ever since I started boxing, Jimmy had been unnecessarily tough on me. It was obvious he didn't like or want to accept, Papa, Martha or me. He had welcomed us with suspicion. I remember having a conversation with him before the first match started while I was in the locker room. Abednego and Papa had just stepped out of the room to answer phone calls from his wife and Martha at school. Jimmy had made an announcement in front of all the amateur competitors that day. The locker room was filled with twenty young men who remained quiet while he spoke.

'Today is the first day of the boxing tournament, and it could be the start of a major career for whoever makes it at the end. So, it is a life changer. You eventually get to mingle with the pros at the world championship. So, take this fight damn seriously! The whole world is watching! So, move it to your individual changing rooms and good luck boys! Give SPN T.V a show!' As I was leaving, he stopped me.

'Hey, Sheldrake, a minute.'

He had a frown and then a smirk on his face.

'I am a good reader of people, and I hate this because I seem not to be able to read you...'

'What are you getting at?' I asked with a bland look.

'It simply means I don't like you. Abednego is putting a lot down for you and your family. He is already ordering an expansion of his crib to accommodate you guys and planning on changing your sister's school and opening a trust fund for her education in Harvard.'

I flinched.

'Harvard?'

'Yeah, Harvard university, and of course, you won't have a clue what or where that is, knowing where you are coming from.'

'I had no clue.' I said truthfully.

'I don't give a damn if you do or do not. I firmly believe in hard work. It's been less than two weeks since you guys arrived, and he is spending a lot on you. I am an economist, and I have managed his funds for years and I don't like this because you haven't earned a damn thing. So, an advice for you, young man... you better earn every penny on this game.'

He left the room.

I stared at Jimmy now in the arena and gave a half frown. He nodded and turned around.

'What's his problem?' Papa asked me. 'Don't like that guy.'

'Me neither.'

The day was a good day, I had won. I realised that my road to victory had just begun.

CHAPTER FOURTEEN

MaRthA, Abednego's residence

I peeped outside my window and studied the number of local reporters outside our apartment building. They had been outside for two days and Brother had been granting interviews. Abednego and Jimmy said that publicity was a good strategy for Brother's image but to me, this was not the kind of publicity I wanted, because it was taking Brother further away from me. I couldn't remember when last we had breakfast as a family, and moreover, he hadn't noticed that Abednego had helped me change my school. The new school was prestigious but I felt insecure amongst my peers because they all had foreign accents and carried nice designer bags and fancy jewels. I hadn't made any friends, and this was my second week. I felt more alone than ever.

'How long have you been staring out that window?' Abednego's voice interrupted my thoughts. I turned around and smiled at him.

'How long have you been watching me?' I asked him shyly.

'Ten minutes or more, kiddo.... got this for you.' He handed me a cup of hot chocolate.

'Thanks...' I collected it. I moved to my bed with-a sad face.

'So, shoot... Talk to me, smallie.'

'I have observed that ever since my brother started professional boxing, he has forgotten about me. I can't remember when we had breakfast together... and I don't have friends in my new school. I think they look at me funny. They must think I am ugly.'

'You ugly? You are nuts and they are crazy too. You are the most adorable kid I have ever seen and you know I don't like children,' he winked at me.

'I am going to be 17 next week. I am no child, Abednego.' I snapped

'Ok, kid...'

'Kid?' I stamped my feet in frustration.

'Yep. Come on, kiddo, before you know it all the boys in school will be hitting on you when you turn 18 and besides, you need to understand that your brother is busy... He's not doing it intentionally; he needs to create fame for his career growth. He wants the best for you and you know that.'

'Why 18?' I asked. 'I don't think I like that fame you are trying to let him acquire, Abednego.' I sulked. 'He's slipping away from me, and so is Papa.'

'Then, my angel, you would officially be a lady. Come here...' he pulled me close to his chest and patted my head. 'I don't want you distracting Sheldrake with your complaints because

I know you are his world. You are his Achilles heel too. You have me here, and that's all that matters.'

'Is it?' I lifted my head from his chest and embraced him tighter. I looked up shyly at him and stared into his beautiful eyes. Then I realised. I was in love with him. *I have always been.*

'Of course, kiddo,' he began to tickle me and then he picked me up from the floor and lifted me in the air. He began to giggle as I laughed out aloud.

'Put me down. I mean it, Abednego!' I struggled.

'Well, I am taking you downstairs.' Soon he was carrying me down the stairs as I gleefully struggled with him, kicking my skinny legs in the air. As he ran down the stairs with me in his arms, the domestic staff in the house stopped to look at us as we passed them and some shook their heads in disapproval while others giggled too. Soon, we were racing past Papa, Jimmy and Brother, who had just come into the house.

'Help me, Brother! Abednego is crazy.' I called out, as we brushed past him.

'Hey, you rascal, where are you taking my sister to?' Brother called out in jest.

'I am stealing her,' he replied. He carried me out of the house and threw me into the pool.

'My hair… oh God!' I felt the cold splash of water come over my body as I landed in the pool. I lifted my head from the pool with a fake frown as Brother and Abednego laughed at me. I swam to the edge of the pool and got a hold of my brother's trousers and pulled him in unexpectedly. He fell into the pool and before I knew it, Abednego had dived into the pool too. Soon, we were all gleefully playing in the pool. Brother pulled my ponytail, while Abednego playfully held onto my waist.

'Let go of me, you rascals.'

For a while, I wished that those few seconds would never end. I wanted all of us to stay in that happy place forever. I was seeing my brother being playful and less uptight for the first time in years, and Abednego was close to me. This made me feel all grown up, just like a lady. I loved that feeling. But I was naïve, as usual, because that joyous moment came to an abrupt end when Jimmy and Papa came into the pool house.

'What the hell do they think they are doing? Acting like a bunch of puppets.' Jimmy frowned, sipping a glass of Jack Daniels.

'It's called playing,' Papa replied sarcastically.

'There is so much publicity and money to be made at this point, and playing like little goddamn children is not part of the agenda!' Jimmy snapped, obviously getting the sarcasm. Before Papa could respond, the housekeeper walked in and announced to Papa that he had a telephone call. Papa exited to receive the call and, in a few seconds, he returned to join us with a huge grin on his face. He turned to Jimmy.

'You won't believe this.'

'Believe what? Speak up, man. Why the smirk?' Jimmy asked with a frown.

'Talk of the devil… A BBC representative just called. They want an exclusive interview with Sheldrake before he turns pro. He says there is speculation that the Minister of Sports and the Nigerian president want to set up a match with Sheldrake and the current Nigerian heavyweight champion.'

'Holy shit! That's what I am talking about… One brilliant goddamn right publicity!'

We heard Jimmy calling out Brother's name.

'Sheldrake, you need to come out of the pool right now.'

'Give the man some breathing space, Jimmy.' Abednego called out.

'No time for that man. There's good news.' Brother anxiously swam out of the pool while Abednego followed lazily to the edge of the pool. I suddenly felt invisible in the pool when they started talking about the upcoming championship game. They totally forgot about me.

'What is it, man?' Brother asked.

'BBC wants rights to an exclusive interview with you tonight. Rumours have it that the Minister of Sports and the President might want to make a surprise visit at the interview. You know the C-IN-C is a big fan of boxing. They are blown away by your fights, it seems.'

'No fucking way!' Brother exclaimed.

'So let's get ready, man...' Jimmy tossed a bathing robe to Sheldrake as he continued '...Abednego, you need to prep him for the interview because that is going to be your international debut, so you need to get your butt out of that water. Come on, Sheldrake, we are going to the mall. We need to get you flossed, see the stylist and a barber for a complete makeover...'

I watched Brother exiting, talking to Jimmy. Abednego got out of the swimming pool, while Papa handed him a towel.

'Jimmy is a nutcase, really. One minute, it's obvious he can't stand Sheldrake, and the next, he's attached to him like glue.' Papa blurted out. I heard Abednego laugh out loud in response to Papa's comment.

'When it comes to money, he can do anything. Just let him do his thing that makes us money. Then he is happy, and we are all happy. There is nothing personal, believe me. He was a pain in my ass for years before I could understand him.' While he spoke, I watched him unbutton and slowly take off his soaked white linen shirt that clung to his body. His body was perfect. His chest was perfectly V-shaped, with eight packs and prominent biceps and triceps to die for.

'Well, you have to admit it, Jide. He's a fucking good manager and PR consultant. He won't rest until he makes all the money for Sheldrake.'

'True. Well, we have to respect him for that.' Papa agreed with him, albeit reluctantly. Abednego soon turned around and looked at me in the pool.

'Are you okay, kid? You look flushed.'

'Hmmmm,' I nodded.

'We need to prepare your brother for some stuff; I promise we will be back in no time, kid. Don't look so moody.' He sounded sympathetic. *Moody, my ass. Only if you know what you are making me feel down here.* He put on his robe and unconsciously gave me his killer smile. My heart stopped beating for a moment. His attention was immediately diverted by a slender female that walked in. She wore a figure-hugging silk dress with a deep V-neck line, which emphasised her huge breasts and figure. She had wavy, brown hair, which was nicely let open on her shoulder.

'Hilda, what are you doing here?' he casually asked her with a smile.

'Came to accompany you to the conference room,' she smiled back at him, after they both exchanged pleasantries with kisses placed on their cheeks.

'Jimmy called you,' he murmured.

'Well, you know Jimmy. He said that you would be late as always. Came to hurry you and one Mr Jide up.' She turned around to face Papa, 'I believe that is you.'

'Well, you would distract me, not hurry me, love,' Abednego teased her. He slipped his hand around her waist. Instantly I felt my blood rush. I never had realised I had so much anger or jealousy within me. I was confused about the mixed feelings I was developing all of a sudden.

'I am a professional stylist, darling,' she flirted with him.

'Me too,' he replied. I watched his hands slip down her butt. She let his hand remain there as she bit the bottom of her Ruby Woo red-painted lip. My heart screamed out loud. *Bitch*.

'Get a room, son.' I heard Papa say with a hiss. 'It's late so move it, would you?'

CHAPTER FIFTEEN

ABEDNEGO

I picked up my plain, white sleeveless Renzo Rosso shirt from Hilda's bed sheet and slipped it on. I went to the open windowpane, stared at the magnificent view and lit a cigarette. I ignored Hilda's seductive voice, which suddenly interrupted my thoughts.

'Come back to bed, darling.'

I winked at her but didn't return till I had finished my cigarette.

'Bring me my jeans, babe.' I watched her slowly slip out of bed. She was stark naked, her long wavy hair covering both her nipples. A few seconds ago, I was gravely aroused by her slender curve. But now, I was turned off. *I had tasted the cookie already. They all felt the same afterwards. Unsavoury.* She slowly picked up my dark blue vintage jeans on the floor and walked towards me. I gave her my usual charming smile. I took the jeans from her and slipped them on. She put her arms around my waist and whispered in my ears.

'Stay with me.'

'I'm married, love, so don't become too clingy. Duty calls.' I replied.

'But she's not here, she's not even in Nigeria.'

'No buts,' I interrupted her. 'Besides, I got to check up on my adopted kid, Martha.'

'Martha is a big girl,' she interjected.

'And you are a bigger girl.' I placed a kiss on her cheek and quickly shut her up with an additional long kiss on her soft lips. I then hurriedly walked out of her apartment. I felt her longing eyes stare at me from behind. *Women! They always want more than they can chew and can never get enough.*

Soon, I was seated on the back of my Mercedes as the driver drove me back to my crib. I got time to reflect on what took place yesterday. My business seemed to be going on well. Sheldrake had done a fantastic job at the amateur games. He was the talk of the whole country and also the world. The interview with the president and BBC correspondent was incredible. He was eloquent and showed so much composure that the BBC correspondent asked if he had a university degree. He just responded to that with a smile. Sheldrake was easy to teach. He was hungry to make the best out of life for his sister. He lived for her. But unfortunately, he was spending so much time with Jimmy and me for coaching lessons and didn't realise how lonely Martha felt. I had to fill in for him. I saw the sadness in her eyes sometimes. She was such a sweet and vulnerable child. I felt she needed a direction, and I always felt drawn to her ever since she came into my life. I couldn't understand why she didn't have friends. She was such an adorable child. She reminded me of myself as a child, lonely and depressed until I found her and her brother in South Ciskei. It was then I experienced what it was to have a real family. My cell phone rang. I looked at the number and frowned. It was my wife.

'Hello, sweetheart. Did you watch the news?'

'Of course, I did. Daddy is so proud of you. The campaign polls are increasing drastically because of your achievements in Africa...' she kept on as my mind travelled. I was thinking I needed to set up a bank account for Martha. She needs to occupy herself with some shopping.

'Darling... are you there? Babbbbby...'

'Yes honey, of course, I am here. Will talk to you soon. I need to sort a few things out.'

'Of course. Talk to you later sweetheart.'

I exhaled a sigh of relief.

In a few seconds, the car was pulling over in the garage of my mansion on the Island. I stepped out of the car and was on my way to my bedroom when I was distracted by the soft sweet melody of a song called '*angel*', which came from my study room. Suddenly, I experienced a flashback to my childhood home in South Ciskei, when I silently opened the door of my dad's studio. I was in my favourite khaki shorts and white T-shirt and behind me were Sheldrake and Martha. That was the first time they had ever seen the room. I recollected the light and excitement in their eyes when they were in the room. They stood staring at the magnificent renaissance paintings of Pablo Picasso and Leonardo de Vinci, which boldly covered the walls of the studio. Also, the marble walls and music box that stood at the corner of the room had fascinated them too.

'What's that?' Martha had asked, pointing to the musical box.

'It's a music box, right, Abednego?'

'Yeah.' I replied.

'I remember the music teacher in school talking about some magical box,' he added.

'Woahhh, it's lovely,' she said in her tiny voice.

'Don't worry, Martha. When I become rich, I will buy you thousands of these,' he said in a fair determination.

'Well, before you become rich, listen to my favourite song,' I sighed. I walked towards the musical box and turned it on. The song '*stupid cupid*' started playing. I started dancing.

'Funny white boy, you can't even dance.' Sheldrake laughed at me, as he watched me dance. Soon, he started dancing the Xhosatan dance as Martha followed in his footsteps. I watched them in astonishment. The dance was strange, but looked like fun.

I recalled that night so vividly as I pulled open the study door and switched on the light. I was taken aback, as I saw Martha curled up in an armchair, with a magazine on her lap as she slept sweetly. I moved up to her and picked up the opened vogue magazine on her lap and glanced at the page she was reading. It was an article titled '*how to make a man love you*'. I chuckled and quietly closed it. I walked up to the gramophone and decreased the volume of the music.

'Why did you reduce it?' Martha asked dreamily, to my surprise.

'Sleeping beauty wakes with a frown...' I teased her.

'School sucks.' She frowned back.

'At your age, kiddo, school is supposed to be fun... Rich young boys are supposed to chase after you. That's why I changed your school to a mixed school. Not the all-catholic girl school for peasants you were in.' I further teased her as I made my way towards her and sat down on the wooden armchair next to hers. I then grabbed her and tickled her. She laughed aloud with happy tears tucked in her eyes, before I released her.

'Well, I am too ugly for boys to look at me.' She looked down on the floor as she replied.

'Hey, look at me kid...' I said as I lifted her chin. 'I don't ever want to hear you talk such nonsense. You have a different kind of beauty and that's what's called an 'exotic black look'. The French would call it *belle*. You know if you were older, I would have wooed you to heaven and back for you to be my woman.' I teased as I watched her blush.

'Would you...? I would be 17 soon, so you could then,' she responded shyly.

'You are so innocent. I am your brother, silly. The difference between the two of us is that we just have different skin colours,' I chuckled. *Then, I didn't understand what those little brotherly words meant to her. If I knew, I wouldn't have said them. It was too late.*

'Yeah. So, don't you ever speak little of yourself. You got that?' I added firmly and watched her nod in response. 'Good. So tomorrow, you are going to go to school and invite everyone for a pool party at the mansion this weekend. I will send my secretary to make you a customised invitation card, and everyone is going to love you at school after that.'

'That's so cool.' she spread open her arms and hugged me and then she kissed my cheek. Right then, the door of the study opened, and Sheldrake strolled in.

'What's all the lovey-dovey for?' He asked. I watched him take off his jacket as he walked up to Martha who pulled away from me and turned to give him a kiss on his forehead.

'Abednego is going to allow me to throw a big party at the pool this Saturday,' she replied excitedly.

'Hmmm... Aren't you supposed to be studying for your examinations for university? I just paid for a tutor to coach you on Further Maths. I don't want any form of luxury to set you back. I didn't like the B you had on your last test results. You are an A student.' He frowned.

'Well... I would still study in the morning before the party.' She pleaded.

'B is a good score, man. Come on, dude. Let her have some fun, we are mostly away from her. She should make some friends.'

'She will make those friends when she gets into the university. She needs the grades for the scholarship,' he firmly replied.

'Look, you are going to be worth 100 million Naira in a few days after the fight. She doesn't need a scholarship to go to school now. Besides, what am I here for?' I intervened.

'I don't want Martha to forget where she is coming from, and you, Abednego, don't push it. We are not for a charity. If she can attain the scholarship, then she shouldn't miss the opportunity. Besides, I haven't won the match yet. No party, okay? You can have that on your birthday. That's next week. Mr Habib is coming to tutor you this weekend, and that's final.'

'Why, Brother? I remember where I am from always because you constantly remind me. Sometimes... don't you realise that I might just want to forget?' she replied with a sting in her voice.

'That's enough now. Go to your room.'

Martha ran out of the study sobbing.

'Come on, Jesus Christ. Let the kid breathe!' I exclaimed as I watched her run out of the study.

'She will when she gets into the university as I said. So, my brother, don't spoil her,' he replied. I watched him pour himself a glass of Jack Daniels and then tried to loosen his tie. I shook my head.

'You are too stuck up. You need to breathe yourself, and let me tell you one secret to winning.'

'Now what secret is that?'

'Letting go...'

'You mean letting go with sex.'

'Well, you need it. It's a form of hypnotherapy. It's proven.' I laughed.

'Says a married man with fifty whores.'

'Give me some credit... ladies just want me.' I poured myself a drink and soon we were both cracking up. Then we fell quiet unanimously, as we both sat down listening to the music from the gramophone while sipping our drinks slowly. At that moment, it was like we were both lost in our own thoughts.

CHAPTER SIXTEEN

SHELDRAKE

I looked intently at my contender, who was standing a few steps in front of me and for a few seconds, I experienced trepidation. We were finally in the boxing ring, and it was then reality dawned on me that I was going into a fight with the Nigerian heavyweight boxing champion. The event was covered live on every network in Africa and England because of Abednego's popularity and influence. I was 6.1 ft tall, but he was a towering 6.7 ft, with a menacing look. I presented to the world my usual inexpressive facial expression as I gaped above his shoulder and into the cheering crowd. The arena was filled up to the brim with spectators, and the camera could hardly let me see. It was the first time that a winner from an amateur boxing competition was going to fight a heavyweight champion, and this match was claimed to be ridiculous by every newspaper in Nigeria. The publicity of the match was so enormous that even the British government were covering the match live with their news correspondents from Nigeria. I got a glimpse of Abednego outside the boxing ring. He looked composed as usual in his sunglasses, classic Donatella Versace one-button suits, his strong V silhouette, with a silk shirt and slim fitted black pants. Papa was next to him with his walking stick and bowler hat. Jimmy, as usual, was tense and pacing up and down the ring before the fight began. *The bastard didn't know he agitated me more with his pacing all over the ring.* The Minister of Sports of Nigeria, his entourage and all other important delegates occupied the front roll, which was directly opposite me. I had an immediate flash back of the previous few minutes in the locker room before I had entered the ring. I felt a sudden chill and sudden panic when Jimmy appeared with the *Daily Sun* newspaper, which had the headline '*The end of the ex-Britain's world champion career with his puppy Sheldrake!*'

'Negative press is good. This newspaper here is going to be one that would give you that one-time fame and world recognition...' he said observing my horrified look after viewing the newspaper Jimmy had held.

'A puppy? Jesus Christ, how can you be certain?' I asked.

'Been in the business for damn too long not to know.'

'All you need, son, is a win.' Papa added.

'We have the publicity, the whole fucking world watching and all you need is to win this so-called impossible fight. We watched his moves on TV, remember? As we observed, we need a long game. You need to weigh him down and then go for the kill. Take him at least to round 12. Then you are good. That's what makes us different from the rest of the fighters. You need a brain not only the skill to fight hard and my brother that is what he lacks.' Abednego calmly said.

'Now let's go do this, boy.' Papa said as he helped me get into my robe.

We were about to leave the locker room when Jimmy's voice interrupted me.

'There is one more thing that you should know. If we lose this match, we are all screwed. Just wanted you to keep that in mind.'

I nodded and turned to exit the room as I heard the commentator announce my name.

'Is Jimmy supposed to make that frightening comment a few minutes before the man is supposed to fight?' I overheard an angry Papa tell Abednego.

'He's a stupid man,' Papa added.

'He says that to me all the time before a match. Believe me, it keeps you going,' Abednego replied in Xhosatan.

I heard the commentator say, 'the match begins', and I saw the referee nod. The fighting bell rang.

***

2:30 hours later

I stared at my opponent on the floor. The referee lifted my hand. I had won after the 8th round of boxing. The crowd was screaming with excitement. I remember Abednego jumping inside the ring, alongside Jimmy and Papa. He was raising my other hand and screaming.

'This is the real champ here! Fucking told you so!'

The next minute, I began to feel dizzy. The area around my orbital region was swollen, and I experienced a sudden sharp pain in my chest and a banging headache. At the same time, my nose began to bleed, and the room around me began to spin. I collapsed.

I woke up a few minutes later and found myself lying down on the couch of a hospital room. My vision was blurred and a sharp light from a pen touch was reflecting at the pupils of my eyes. This made me startle and impulsively I gripped a hand and at the same time tried to shove away the pen touch from the person that was bending over me, wearing a white overcoat.

'Mr Sheldrake, you are hurting me.' I heard a soft-spoken female voice say. At that instance, my vision became clearer and I realised that the person in the white coat was a doctor. Her face was the prettiest face I had seen in a long time. I could see her brown large eyes behind the large spectacles. Her brown hair was pulled back in a bun and I noticed her prominent cheekbone and slender neck. My gaze fell on her upper clavicle and perfectly sized breasts resting on my chest as I still held onto her wrist.

'Who are you?' I asked, confused.

'I am Doctor Nina Warmate, Abednego's personal physician and now your doctor,' she replied calmly.

As soon as I heard Abednego's 'personal physician', I frowned. *Damn, that means he has slept with her already.*

'You are still hurting me, Mr Sheldrake. You should let go of me.' But I didn't let go. I pulled her closer to my chest.

'How long are you going to be my doctor?' I asked with a grin.

'For as long as you keep boxing and as long as you want me too. Now, kindly let go,' she replied in a professional tone.

'So, sorry,' I said, finally letting go of her wrist. I watched her move to her desk, which was directly opposite the couch I lay on. I then got a better view of her long and perfect legs. She wore a plain white cotton blouse and flowery, printed navy blue pencil skirt which emphasised her tiny waist. I wished the ward coat she wore did not hide her perfect back side. *I knew the size of the buttock would be just right.*

'Ideally, you should have come for a routine medical check-up before that fight. But that was ignored by Mr Abednego, as usual.' She hissed as she turned through the pages of my case note on her desk, and she began to scribble something down. I watched her lips as she kept on speaking.

'From my examination, you just sustained a minor concussion due to the fight, but you would have to come for some routine check-up. That is an X-ray, and I will suggest an MRI. I would book you for next Monday....' She looked up at me. 'Hope that's okay?'

I nodded. Then she continued, 'Do you have any questions?'

'Have you slept with Abednego?' I couldn't help myself from asking.

I could see the shock on her face when I said this.

'I beg your pardon?'

'You heard me right. You asked if I have any questions and my question is have you been in bed with Abednego?'

'From your bio-data, it indicates that you lack substantial education. I see that's why your manners are flawed...' she replied with a calm and stern look. That comment obviously got to me. My ego was bruised.

'A doctor that says such nonsense to her patients should be as dumb as you think I am, so obviously, that education is a waste. Don't you think?'

I watched her angry eyes flare up but before she could respond Abednego and Papa Jide walked into the consulting room.

'Hey, son, I see that you are good to go.' Uncle Jide said with a smile.

'The Nigerian heavyweight Champ!' Abednego added. He was already collecting my sweater from the couch and handing me a pair of slippers to put on. I guess they didn't realise that there was tension in the room.

I gradually pulled myself together when I heard Doctor Nina say, 'Yeah, he should be leaving immediately because I have things to do.'

'You are always busy, Nina.' Abednego replied. He kept on chatting with her, while Jide helped me walk out of the room and into the elevator.

'So how do you feel?' Papa Jide asked me in the elevator. I frowned at his comment.

'What do you mean?'

'You are the Nigerian Champion now boy. You should feel something and not just frown all the way on an elevator ride.'

'I just need to get some sleep.' I replied. Suddenly, I wasn't feeling the thrill of winning the championship anymore.

'What's wrong with you this time?' Jide asked.

'Nothing.' I snapped.

The elevator finally stopped, and we both got out of it and made our exit through the back door of the hospital to avoid the press. We headed to the waiting Range Rover.

'Just out of curiosity. What do you know about Dr Nina?' I asked, feigning nonchalance.

'What do I know?'

'Yep. She is your doctor too.'

'She's a smart lady. That's what I know for her to be a doctor...'

'Yeah... I meant about her personal life,' I interrupted.

'Hmmm... I know you a lot, boy! Seems to me that you like the doctor.'

'Of course, not. I am just asking,' I denied. Abednego entered the car and the car started moving.

'Good God, Sheldrake I heard you asked Nina if we were fuck buddies. Nina is so furious with you,' Abednego began to giggle in the car.

'Oh my God, you do like this girl, don't you?' Uncle Jide added as he began to laugh along with Abednego.

I frowned at both of them as they got their amusement off me. I waited for their laughter to cease before I continued.

'So, are you sleeping with her?' I calmly asked again.

'Sorry to disappoint you, no, I'm not fucking her because I think she's a lesbian?' he replied, lighting a cigarette.

'No, she's not. She has a fiancé. I met him in her office last week. But he is white and my age.' Papa interjected.

'That's why she is gay... an old man? Who refuses me for an old man? She definitely has some issues.'

I began to laugh suddenly. I felt much better. Abednego had made a pass as suspected, and she had turned him down.

'So, because a girl isn't into you, she is definitely gay?' I burst out laughing.

CHAPTER SEVENTEEN

MARTHA

Today was Sheldrake's surprise victory party at the penthouse. The plan was that Papa and Abednego would pick Sheldrake up from the hospital and bring him to the event at the house. Jimmy and Abednego's PR firm had already sent out express invitation cards to some important dignitaries, and most of them had responded promptly and arrived in their elegant attires at the house. Also, the ballroom at the penthouse was stylishly decorated with a blend of some superb African and Chinese ornaments for the occasion. A diverse selection of African cuisine was gallantly displayed on the side banquet table. Jimmy had requested a buffet-style setting for the event.

I stared at my reflection in the mirror. As usual, I frowned at myself. I was dressed in a navy green and white pleated, polka-dotted, knee-length dress, which Abednego's stylist had picked out for me. And she had put some silly Alice band and some ribbons on my hair. I hated the dress. I looked like a neonate. Deep in my mind, I knew I looked adorable but I wanted to look as pretty and sexy as all the girls Abednego spent time with. *He would always see me as a little girl in this outfit.*

I pulled out my purse and took out the lipstick that I got from the mall when I went shopping with the stylist. I thought it was the same red lipstick that Abednego's women wore to attract his attention and my aim that night was to look like them to attract him. I applied it to my lip and then smiled at the reflection that I saw. *I look closer to a grown-up now.* I slipped on my light brown ballerina-like-shoes and made my way to the ballroom. I walked down the stairs and noticed Jimmy having a discussion with Silver, a famous journalist. I easily located her because she had a really weird hairdo and her face was always on the 9 pm network news. I walked towards them and greeted them.

'You look adorable in that dress, child.' He replied with a smirk.

'I will be seventeen this month, so I am no longer a child.' I replied in an irritated manner.

'Oh really...' I saw him observe me closely before he continued. 'Sliver, please can you excuse us...'

'Of course, let me make sure the cameras are rolling before the victorious man walks in. I would kill anyone that misses any significant detail; this is being covered live. And we still haven't finished our discussion Jimmy, we want to buy the exclusive rights for airing this party and the next interview.' She patted his face and left after Jimmy reassured her.

'Do tell me, how do you feel about your brother making a good history?'

'Of course, I am happy for my brother, but he seems far away.' I replied offhandedly. I hated his British accent and his demeanour.

'Pray do tell... I don't understand?'

'This boxing is taking him away from me; I can't remember when last we had breakfast together or ate at the same table. Sometimes, I don't see him for days. That's just it, and you seem to be the one wearing him out.'

'Child, I have watched you for the past few months, and I know what you mean. That's why you should listen to me carefully; I don't want any distractions from you. A few months ago, you had no food on that breakfast table, because you couldn't even afford a table. But right now, you are in a room filled with the élite, waiting to welcome your brother home. So, my candid advice to you is to keep being grateful to God. I might seem like a jerk, but I am only one when I need to be. You seem like a good kid... so read a book and make friends of your own age... Abendego is not your mate.'

'Sorry?' I stammered. *Did he know how I feel?*

'Yeah, I understand he is like a brother to you. You seem closer to him than Sheldrake now, because of the time he dedicates to you. But, believe me, kid, things always go wrong when you rely on someone that is not your real blood. You start seeing and feeling things that are not really there.'

'I don't understand.'

'Look, take my advice kid… go and make friends of your own age from school, especially lots of friends from the opposite sex.'

He knew.

Luckily, for me, he couldn't see my shocked expression, because we were interrupted by the sound of approaching footsteps from Silver, who mentioned to us that Brother was coming in. Soon the lights were turned off, and the entrance door was being opened and everyone in the room was yelling 'SURPRISE!' As soon as they stepped in, Nigerian artist Bobby Benson's *'okokoko'* began to play in the background. I saw the look in my brother's eyes when he realised that a multitude of guests in the room was waiting to see him. His eyes lit up with joy, and his lips gave away a smile of accomplishment. I began to cry with joy. It had been such a long time since I had seen such genuine happiness radiate from my brother effortlessly. Papa and Abednego stood next to him and they were laughing too, beaming with delight. The guests came forward to shake brother and Abednego's hands after they congratulated him. I walked up to my brother and Papa, but they hadn't noticed me, they were both engrossed in a discussion with Jimmy and Silver. I stood alone for about 30 minutes observing the sophisticated ambience of the room before I turned to glance at Abednego, who was chatting with the daughter of the Nigerian president, Aisha Banta. I still recognise her from the newspapers. She was flirting with him. He smiled sweetly as I approached them. Predictably, my heart melted. He was dashing in his simple brown blazer, white cotton shirt and half-knotted black tie.

'What's up, kid? You look adorable.' He pulled me closer. 'Aisha, this is my favourite kid sister.'

'He has no kid sister...' I said.

'Then forgive me, my favourite sister then.' He laughed. He was caressing my hair now, as he playfully put his arms around my neck.

'Let go of me,' I struggled in resentment as I heard Aisha giggle with him. He finally let go. I grumbled.

'You are definitely an adorable child.' Aisha smiled at me. *It was obvious that the bitch wanted him. Every woman in that room wanted him.*

'How can I possibly be an adorable sister? I am black and he is white. So, what you said actually makes no sense.' I innocently said. I recognised the annoyance that came on her face. I gave a vindictive smile in return while Abednego just kept on being amused. He was having a good time, which meant he didn't see the harm in my comment.

Brother and Papa finally caught up with us.

'So, what is my favourite girl doing here when she should be studying?' Brother asked, as he came to stand next to me.

'I just wanted to see how the party was going to be, besides...' I suddenly noticed the look on my brother's face, which startled me.

'What the hell is on your lip?' he asked with a frown.

'It's just red lipstick, Brother...'

133

'Go up to your room this minute and wipe off that lipstick.'

'There is no big deal in lipstick—'

'Don't interrupt me when I talk, you should do as you are told. When you finish, you will go to bed. You have school early morning tomorrow.' He snapped.

I nodded sadly. Abednego pulled me closer to him and placed a goodnight kiss on my forehead. Papa patted my head and kissed my cheek. I left the room reluctantly.

CHAPTER EIGHTEEN

SHELDRAKE

Matha left the party, and I tried to remain calm despite my anger with her.

'How dare she appear at a party with makeup on?' I cursed under my breath. I had sudden flashes of the women that visited the Pink Carnations Bar back home. They always wore red lipsticks to attract men at the club. They ended up having beer, cheap cigarettes and babies. I shook my head to get the image of Martha ending up like them disappear.

'Come on. She was looking forward to this day. You don't have to be so hard on her...' Abednego said.

'She is just a child. I wonder where she is learning all this bullshit from?' I gulped my drink.

'But, son, seriously, this is a good day. You need to relax.' Papa tried to calm me down. Just then, Jimmy and the journalist appeared in front of us.

The journalist was a middle-aged woman, who was famous in Nigeria. She was known to be bold in covering her stories, and it always attracted the international community. She was tall, slim and dressed in traditional Yoruba attire. However, rumour had it that her parents were from South Ciskei. She was accompanied by a friend.

'Hey guys, this is Silver the renowned and powerful talk-show host and journalist. She just bought a sports media company as she is the African Oprah. She is proposing to buy exclusive rights to cover all interviews with you guys before the world championship games. I think we should hear her out.' Jimmy said with a broad grin.

'You flatter me, Jimmy, as always. Nice meeting you, Sheldrake. Let's get to business here.'

'Silver, you are always the business woman and so how much are we talking here?' Abednego asked in his business-like tone.

'Two million dollars for two exclusive interviews, which cover a few days before the fight and one after the fight. Also, we want access to cover one day of a live episode of Sheldrake's training.'

'Wow! That's a lot of cash we are talking about here!' Papa exclaimed.

'No, it's not. You have to increase the fee. If the BBC were to cover it with other international television stations, we will get more publicity. And besides, there shouldn't be any interruptions during Sheldrake's training,' Jimmy said.

'So how much are we talking about here? Honestly, I think, it is a fair offer because we are just covering Abednego and not Sheldrake, so ideally there would be no interruptions.'

'I thought this offer was mainly for Sheldrake.' Abednego asked in confusion. 'He is our new brand for boxing. He has a story to tell and sell.'

'We still want you, Abednego,' Silver interjected firmly. 'His time will come. You made him happen.'

This particular crowd in the room fell quiet for a split second at that point, but to end the uncomfortable silence, I spoke up.

'I am the one fighting over there, and I don't get an interview?'

Abednego spoke up. 'Don't worry, buddy. Let's discuss this in the study. Jimmy, Jide and Silver please follow me... You, friend, stay here and enjoy your party.'

Soon, I was left standing alone in the middle of the room as I watched the guests fraternize with each other, with the orchestra of Giacomo Antonio Puccini playing in the background. Half of the room were white people and the other guests were black from prestigious families in Nigeria. It hit me that none of these people were from my world. I observed some of the female attendees pick up glasses of wine from the passing waiters with sophistication, while some of the male guests looked intently at Abednego's family portraits on the wall, conversing in French, English or Spanish, while they smoked their expensive Cuban cigars. I felt that I didn't fit in as I couldn't understand their languages, and then I realised that in reality, nobody was making any effort to talk to me. They had all come to see

Abednego, the British world champion who made this fight possible. I felt like a nobody.

Silently, I made my way to the balcony with half a bottle of champagne and a full glass of Moet. I stared at the stars as I consoled myself with a long gulp. I still felt small in another black-dominated country, regardless of my win that day. I felt the breeze from the wind and chills. I wondered when I would ever feel accepted in this world.

'A penny for your thoughts?' A soft subtle tone distracted me from behind. Dr Nina was standing behind me. She looked completely radiant in a simple cream dress with embellished shoulder straps. The deep line cut of the gown and the silky texture of the chiffon fabric exposed her cleavage. Her beautiful black hair was packed in a bun. She not wearing her glasses, which gave her the professional look. I pulled a frown on my face because I was speechless and confused by her exotic beauty as she continued speaking.

'You should be enjoying your party.'

'Feel out of place here. Doesn't seem to be my party, because I don't know a soul around here... Besides, no one has come to say hello.'

'Your face is not an approachable one.'

'Are you calling me ugly?'

'I am just saying your perception of you 'being out of place' is all in the mind.'

'Then you are calling me mentally ill, doctor?'

'Mental and ugly... I think you have done enough drinking.'

'So I am drunk then?'

'You just got out of the clinic and are still on medication. You shouldn't be drinking.'

'You are not being paid for consultation here, are you, pretty?' I finally found nicer words.

'No! As a matter of fact, I am not. I was invited by Abednego. I normally come for all his sport-affiliated parties.' She replied with a broader smile. She moved closer to me and gently collected the glass of champagne from my hand.

'Did you come here to baby sit me too? I was restless. I felt I was not in control of my emotions in front of this lady. The hardened demeanour I had created for myself over the years fell apart. I felt she could see through me. This made me vulnerable, and I didn't like it.

'Just trying to help my patient, Mr Sheldrake.'

'Why don't you help your fiancé? Word on the street says he is almost eighty years of age; he should be the one needing the looking-after before he kicks the bucket.' I blurted out. She didn't take the comment well. Her face turned red, and the fury in her lungs was palpable. As soon as those words left my mouth, I regretted it. She threw the Champagne at me. My face, body and trouser... everything got wet. She turned around in a fit of rage and walked out on me.

Impulsively, I caught hold of her waist and swiftly turned her around to face me.

'Let go of me!'

I had pinned her against the wall, with her arms above her shoulders and my body resting firmly on her heaving chest. Her feminine fragrance overwhelmed me. It was clear to me at that moment that I wanted her.

'I will let go if you say you forgive me. It was supposed to be a joke.'

'Look, I am sorry.' I added after a pause. 'I don't know what came over me. I swear. I am bad at making jokes, as you see.' I stammered and apologised. I stared into her eyes to see if my words had made any impact. Her eyes were captivating. *Big and brown.* It seemed that in a split second she could read deeper into my soul.

'Let go of me then.' She stopped struggling.

'I just need to be sure I am forgiven. I am usually not like this. I was clearly out of line.'

'Well, if you keep holding me down, I might not be so forgiving.' She challenged me with anger in her eyes. I didn't know what spell came over me at that moment because I felt the tension in the air, the heat from the rise and fall of her chest and the touch of the sensual fabric that covered her perfect breast. She kissed me. I pulled her body closer to my chest and responded to her kisses. Her lips were soft as I held her, captivated, in my arms. I felt her shiver at my touch as she responded to each and every kiss I placed on her lips and neck. I had been waiting for years for someone to soften my heart. I longed for her as I had never for another. Soon, I was pulling up her dress above her knee to her butt line. I slipped down her lace panties while she hurriedly unbuckled my belt. She zipped my pants down and waiting for no further invitation, I entered her. I separated her legs wide apart as her back was placed against the wall while she pulled me closer and I covered her mouth with deep kisses to hinder her from crying out loud, as our bodies moved to the rhythm of the instrumental music coming from the party indoors. I felt the wetness of her thigh as she came. I stopped and watched her catch her breath. I smiled at her. I saw a strand of hair from her perfect hairdo fall to her forehead and I tried to brush it away with my fingers, when she violently pushed me away all of a sudden.

I saw tears and shock in her eyes as she hurriedly pulled up her panties and adjusted her dress.

'What have I done?' She blurted out loud.

'You did nothing wrong, we just responded to how we felt,' I replied calmly zipping up my trousers. I felt hurt, did she suddenly feel I was a mistake? Again, I felt a little wounded by the look in her eyes.

'This isn't right. We just had sex in a fucking balcony, in the open. Jesus Christ, I am your doctor, and I have a fiancé!'

'Hey, please calm down.' I tried to move closer to her but she backed away.

'Please don't touch me.'

'You know you should have thought of this first, before allowing me fuck your brains out,' I blurted out in annoyance.

I was shocked by the response I got: a resounding slap across the face.

She raced out of the balcony. I tried to tell myself that this awkward feeling was because she was the first real lady that I had slept with in comparison to the other trailer trash girls that I had casual sex with in the ghetto. Maybe this eccentric feeling was ignited by something else? I tried to run after her but was interrupted by Uncle Jide, Jimmy and Abednego as they stepped out of the study room that separated me and Dr. Nina. They were done with their meeting with Silver, and they were calling me to a corner to give me feedback on the proposed agreement reached.

CHAPTER NINETEEN

ABEDNEGO

I sat down with Sheldrake, Jimmy and Jide in my study room. Sheldrake looked at me expecting to hear the outcome.

'So, what was the conclusion?' Sheldrake asked. Jimmy looked at me and decided to take the burden from me. He spoke.

'Silver says that the exclusive interview and the reality show have to come from Abednego. She doesn't believe that you have been in the business long enough to have the interview.'

'I just won a goddamn good fight!' Sheldrake responded.

'Let me give it to you straight, I am not into sugar-coating the obvious. It seems to me Abednego or Jide doesn't want to hurt your feelings. I understand, but in this line of business, we see champions come and go. Yes, you defeated the Nigerian champion yesterday. That was fantastic, but you need more than that to go as far as you yearn for.'

'I don't get it.'

'If you really want to be the best, you need to think globally not locally. The fight has gotten you this far, but Silver says the world needs more than a victory story on national fights; they want an international champion.'

'How do I become international then?' he asked.

'We need to arrange a match between the African champion, the Ghanaian and you before the world championship takes place.' I interjected. They all turned around to look at me in astonishment.

'The world championship is in a few weeks. He hasn't fully recovered from his last fight. We shouldn't push our luck,' Jimmy blurted out in annoyance.

'Maybe he's right,' Jide agreed.

'Finally, we agree on something.' Jimmy teased.

'You said you wanted global success, then arrange it, Jimmy. You heard your boss.' Sheldrake interrupted Jimmy.

'You heard the man. Do it. This meeting is over. Let's go back to our guests.' I opened the door for Jimmy and Jide, and then I gently pushed them out of the office door before they could protest and shut the door. I turned around and watched Sheldrake staring outside the window in silence as he sipped on a glass of Jack Daniels.

'Are you sure you want to do another fight now? You haven't totally recovered.' I asked him.

'Back in South Ciskei, the first time I ever saw life differently was the day I set my eyes on your mother, and I believe Mama saw it too. She looked so beautiful because she had this thing in her, which the French chef in the vessel would call "Je ne cequoi..."' He laughed a little before he continued, 'We lived in so much poverty and suffering that when we saw her charisma and looks, I knew Mama wanted Martha to become exactly like her, and she strongly believed education could turn her into that. Wealth makes everything possible, my brother....' he spoke, sounding distant like the words weren't coming from his mouth.

'Come on, man, all that wealth doesn't mean shit. My mother was the most miserable person I know.'

'If I need that fight to set my career on a different plateau, then I am going to do it. Martha needs to walk into a room, and her aura should be felt and respected. I don't want her to feel so out of place like me. She needs that education from a good school. She needs to travel the world, and the only way I can afford her education is through these fights. I believe that's what Mama and Papa would have wanted.'

'I understand.' I walked up to him and collected his glass of whiskey and gulped it. 'Everything is possible, and I believe in you as a fighter. You taught me all I knew. But out here, you just need to know the tricks of international fights. That's more practice and for that, I have to call on Dr Nina to run a full physical test on you again...'

'Well... About that... She might not want to see me.'

'I don't get it.'

'Nothing.'

'I saw her running out of the party when I came out... What is going on man?' I watched his usual frown turn into a sheepish smile. I knew that look. I burst out in laughter. 'I don't believe this; you have fallen for the ice queen doctor.'

'It's crazy, man, because I have never felt like this in a long time... she makes me feel that I have a chance in life to be genuinely happy.'

'No fucking way!'

'But I am just confused. Something tells me she feels the same way...'

'Wooooah, slow down man! Don't you think you are going too fast here? This is not some ordinary woman we are talking about; this is Dr Nina Warmate. Before you get carried away, she's not going to leave her fiancé for you man... They both came together. She adores him.'

'Then why the hell would she have sex with me on the balcony a few minutes ago?' He blurted out in confusion.

'She did what?' I exclaimed in shock. 'Holy shit! In the open? You mean you cracked that ass open. I didn't know she was that kinky. I knew something was wrong with her. How can she choose you over me? I don't get it. You are an ugly motherfucker.' I chuckled. We both began to laugh.

'You know she's a doctor, she probably needs you for an experiment or probably she wants to suture your constant scowling face to a smirk, because, believe me, friend, there is no other explanation to this.' I shook my head as I giggled in amazement. I poured him another glass of whiskey. Somehow, that was another victory for him, a different kind of victory, and I was damn impressed.

'Or probably she might just have strong feelings for me as much I do for her. And she might just be as scared as I am.' He replied quietly. I felt him drifting away. *He really had it bad for Nina.* I studied him for a while before I spoke up in a serious tone.

'You need to take it a step at a time, Brother. In truth, I can't explain how you feel or relate to it. I have never been in love. Don't think it exists from where I am standing. The only person I know that loved someone that much was my mother. It turned her into a wreck because it didn't last. From the little I know of Dr Nina, she is a good doctor, in fact, the best in Nigeria. Getting involved with her would complicate her work. Her job comes first. And as for her fiancé, he made that job possible. She owes him that. People like her never forget. She's that principled.'

'You are always optimistic. Why so different now?' he asked.

'Because Nina reminds me of myself and that's really why I hired her in the first place.'

'Yourself?'

'Let me explain this to you man. My wife might be a certified pain in the ass, but I owe her everything. Gratitude is what my old man lacked. I never want to end up like him. My mother gave her whole world and fortune to him, and he ruined her. I would never leave my wife. That is why I would never remove my wedding ring, no matter how many fantastic women come my way, the ring reminds me of gratitude. So, do you understand what I am saying? Gratitude is a bitch.'

He nodded slowly before talking again.

'Let's get out of here, man. I need another drink. The party awaits us.'

CHAPTER TWENTY

MARTHA

From the window of my room, I watched the car drive out of the gate. I sighed sadly. Brother, Abednego, Jimmy and Papa were on the way to the airport in Ghana for the friendly match with the African World champion. My birthday was in two days. Brother said the fight was important for the family, and he promised to return on my birthday. I felt that there was a probability that he might not return early. Abednego and Papa pleaded with me not to stress or distract my brother's training with my complaints. I had no one to pour my heart to, because I was going to be left alone in the house for two days. Brother had arranged for a private tutor from an agency to come and give me extra tutorials on chemistry to prepare me for the Joint Administration Matriculation Board examination. The teacher was supposed to be arriving in the next few minutes but I was frustrated because I didn't want to study. *I hate my life!*

My thoughts were soon interrupted by the knock from the maid who came into my room to announce that my lesson teacher was here. I nodded. In annoyance, I picked up my books and pen and made my way to the study room downstairs.

I opened the door of the study room and spotted a male figure standing and looking outside the window, his back turned to me. He had not realised that I had stepped in. I walked to the table separating both of us and slammed my books on the table. The sudden sound startled him and he turned around to see me. He was young and hot in an unusual way! I frowned as he walked up to me with a smile on his face. He was dark, with brown eyes, average height with a well-groomed moustache. He was dressed in a white woollen sweater and dark blue stone-washed jeans.

'I am Habib Adissa. You must be Martha?' he stretched out his hand for a handshake, but I ignored it and sat down. He stared at his hanging hand in the air, and he then took his seat, which was directly opposite mine.

'Hey, Habib, I am going to be honest with you. I don't need a lesson teacher because my grades are already perfect. My brother just needs to make sure I get a scholarship. As you can see, I don't need those scholarships because we are going to be rich. Brother is going to be the world boxing champion soon. And at my age, I am supposed to be organising my birthday party and not being stuck in some room with the likes of you.'

I watched him stare at me without saying a word. I was irritated by this. I stood up from my seat, walked to the fridge in the study and took a bottle of coke. I opened it, and I studied him as he got up from his seat and walked up to me. He opened the fridge and pulled out a bottle of Smirnoff ice.

He picked up the bottle opener that was on a table. He then took the coke bottle from my hand and handed me the bottle of Smirnoff ice. I was stunned by his reaction because Smirnoff was an alcoholic drink, and I wasn't allowed to drink it.

'You know this is alcoholic right?' I was puzzled.

'Of course, I do. You have a point. I have looked at your grades, and I believe you are a smart girl. But you can see I am already here so I can as well teach you something.'

'I am not allowed to drink alcohol.' I was shocked and tried to hand him back the bottle.

'There is always a first time.' He smiled. Our eyes met and I smiled back, sipping the content cautiously.

'Not bad,' I said in a flirty tone. We both began to laugh.

'So, tell me what you do for fun. As for me, I give private tutorials to beautiful women like you when I am not studying at the university. I am in my final year.' He pulled out another bottle of Smirnoff for himself.

'I am beautiful? Do you plan to mock me? I am not drunk yet.'

'You are the most beautiful girl I know, and you are all natural. That is what marvels me. The minute I saw you, I was speechless for the first time.'

I smiled again. Soon, I felt the alcohol taking effect. I had finished the bottle already.

'I need another one.'

'You learn quite fast. I am impressed.' He handed me another bottle.

'I have never had fun in my life. I would want to be free for once and go out. I just like what girls do with Abednego.'

'Sorry?' he asked confused.

'Forget I said that, I just want people to see me as a grown-up girl and not a kid.'

'And so, you shall. Tell you what, if we do some further maths together when I come around, then I will take you to SIP, it's the baddest club in town, and you are allowed to bring your girlfriends too.'

'Really, do we seriously have to do further maths?' My eyes sparkled in delight.

'Well, we have to show some reports to your brother and the white dude, don't we?'

I nodded. He suddenly pulled me closer to his chest and held my waist as I staggered. I could perceive his cologne and I liked the smell. He reminded me of Abednego. Impulsively, I drew him closer and kissed him. *My first kiss.* He responded and soon, he was roughly pushing me against the wall and shoving his tongue down my throat, and then his lips moved to the tip of my ears. I gasped at his touch. I felt his hand move swiftly under my dress to my thighs and immediately, I found my sense of reasoning and I pushed him away.

'I must go.' I rushed out of the room and ignored him as he called my name. I ran upstairs, into my room and fell on my bed. I began to quiver. *I have lost it.* I touched my lips and felt them swollen. I loathed Abednego for this at that point. Why couldn't he just see me as a woman? If he did, I wouldn't have let the lesson teacher touch me. I felt the heaviness of my eyes, and I was rapidly drifting away into dreamland.

***

British Lekki International School, Lagos

Next Day

I stepped out of the jaguar that brought me to school and walked into my empty classroom. I was usually punctual at school. I pulled out my literature textbook, The *Gods Are Not to Blame* and was about to read it when a male and two female students walked in. They walked directly to me.

'You must be Martha.' I nodded. 'Great! I have heard so much about you. I read about your famous brother and his hot friend on TV.' One of the girls said dreamily.

'She is Bola. She could talk you to death, 1 am Idris, her unfortunate boyfriend,' he stretched out his hand for a hand shake while Bola and the others giggled. I shook his hand and smiled. He continued. 'My brother says he was at your house yesterday...'

'Your brother?' I asked, confused.

'Yeah, he is the hottie that is giving you private lessons. He used to be my boyfriend before we broke up, and I started dating Emeka here. By the way, I am Ngozi.' The other girl put in with a smile as she clung to the boy in front of me.

'Hey look here, my brother digs you, and he says your birthday is coming up soon. He promises that if we make you come to this crazy party I am holding tonight, he will take us all to the craziest club in Lagos on your birthday.' Idris said.

'I really don't know,' I replied in confusion.

'Why the hesitation?' Bola asked.

'Well because I have to study...'

'We all study love, and besides, Habib says that your grades are pretty good. We have been watching you and believe me, it's not so cool being a loner. You are pretty with a tight ass.' Idris interrupted me.

'Don't go hitting on her.' Bola hit him playfully on his back. He began to laugh.

'So, what do you say?' Ngozi asked.

'I don't know what to wear.'

'Well, leave that to us. We will dress you up.' Bola replied with a broad smile.

Soon the classroom was full because other pupils were walking in along with the teacher. My new friends all returned to their seats and the literature class began.

CHAPTER TWENTY-ONE

SHELDRAKE

I shut my eyes, but I couldn't sleep. We were on a chartered plane to Ghana for the fight coming up the next day. Before we embarked on our journey, Abednego had drilled the shit out of me in the ring. I recalled the lectures he gave me the first night we trained for the amateur tournament. It was so damn long!

'The Basics of Boxing is a very fun sport to study. The skills you learn in boxing can assist you in many ways. Boxing is different from street fighting... It is more elegant because it comes with rules that must be adhered to. You can box at many different levels. To discover the fundamentals of boxing, it is necessary to discuss the basic stance, defensive moves and offensive moves. A great boxer needs an excellent basic stance. The stance depends on whether you are right or left-handed. If you are right-handed, your left foot should be about 12 inches in front of your right leg. If you are left-handed, you should have your right foot in front of your left about 12 inches. The stance you are in decides which hand will be your lead hand. If you are right-handed, your lead hand is your left. If you are left-handed, your lead hand is your right hand. When boxing, you should never bring your feet together and get squared up. If you were to get squared up, it won't take much to knock you down.'

'Jesus Christ! Abednego, I don't need this lecture!'

'Believe me, Brother, you need it. Knowing and understanding the fundamentals and the history of boxing differentiates you from other contenders. It's not all about having the skills, Sheldrake. If you must own this game, then you have to dream it and that means understanding all the technical shit I am saying to you! Believe me, that's how I got this far. And after this lesson, brace up for Dr Nina, she's going to give you some anatomy lessons too.' He winked as he handed me a bottle of water before he continued.

'She says understanding the intricacies of anatomy is the soul for every breathing boxer. If you own your anatomy, you own Dr Gray and every shithole you throw a punch at because you can automatically visualize their weakness.'

'Who the fuck is Gray, and what does Dr Nina have to do with my training?'

'Dr Gray is the author of the best human anatomy book. Nina might be your fucking nightmare but she taught me all about Gray. She is good and right when she said a boxer has an upper hand when he understands the human anatomy….' He paused then continued teaching.

'The defensive side of boxing is essential. Defence will help you steer clear of getting hit and possibly hurt. Blocking is a defensive move that renders your opponent's blow weak with your hands, shoulders or arms. Bobbing and weaving is shifting your body from right to left while your head is almost rotating while you are in and out of a partial crouch. Clinching is a move done when an opponent is about to hit you. What you do here is to grab and hold your opponent, so that they cannot attack. Covering is something that must be done often. That means you must hold your arms in front of your face and body to avert the opponent from getting in a clean shot. Ducking is a straightforward move that is done by bending at the waist to avoid a blow. Offense is a good key skill in boxing. Offense is the punches you throw. The jab is the most important punch...'

Somehow, I found myself envying Abednego for his calm and self-assured mien despite whatever situation he faced. It felt good to be in a private jet for the first time in my life, however, I couldn't experience the thrill properly because my mind was not at ease. I needed to win that fight tomorrow. If I did, my life would be different for good.

I watched the air hostess walk up to Abednego and pour him a glass of white wine. She was bending over funnily so that he could see her exposed cleavage while she filled his glass with the drink. He smiled at her. He would never change. I beamed to myself. My gaze fell on Papa, who was quietly reading his newspaper and then on Jimmy, who was snoring loudly. I turned to the end of the jet and looked at Dr Nina. She was on the phone. My gaze fell on her long-crossed legs and short grey cotton shirt. She looked breath-taking in her corporate outfit, a white plain cotton shirt, grey blazer and knee-length skirt. When we both met at the airport, she was polite towards me but in a cold sort of way. I stood up from my seat and made my way to hers. The seat next to her was empty so I took it without asking her permission. I pulled out a newspaper and pretended to read it while I watched her relaxed composure, while she spoke on the phone. I eavesdropped on her conversation.

'Hey darling, I will be rushing home before you know it. Hope you don't forget to take your medication. I put it on your bedside table. You must take the Co-Diovan and the Lexotan before you sleep. Remember the Lexotan is 1.5 mg nocte and not the 3 mg you normally take. You have to go slow on that sleeping pill, my love.'

'I miss you too, darling. See you soon.'

'Of course, I know that. Love you too.'

She placed her phone. She disregarded me, picked up a medical journal on her lap and began to flip through it.

'Do you seriously love him? Because you sound more like his mother to me.'

'What the hell do you mean by that and by the way, how dare you listen in on my conversations?' She snapped, as she turned to look at me with bloodshot eyes.

'Finally, she speaks to me.'

'What?' she snapped.

'Well, just needed a reaction from you,' I replied with a grin. I watched her scowl slowly turn into a smile. She laughed. Her laughter was intoxicating; I loved the way her head moved while she chuckled, exposing her gapped teeth. I knew I had fallen in love with her.

'You are beautiful.'

As soon as I uttered the words out loud, she stopped laughing and gazed at me. At that instant, it felt like it was just the two of us in that plane. We experienced an unusual rise in the atmospheric temperature, which culminated in a combination of palpable sexual chemistry. The spell was suddenly interrupted by the air hostess who came to inquire if we wanted something to drink. When I turned to speak to her, Nina got up from her seat and hurriedly exited to the restroom. I shook my head to indicate to the hostess that I didn't require anything. I waited for about 15 restless minutes in my seat, and I realised that she intentionally got up and wasn't coming back. I got up from my seat and walked to the restroom. I knocked on the door.

'Who's there? Just give a sec, please.'

'It's me...'

'What do you want?'

'I need to talk to you.'

'There is nothing to talk about. Please go back to your seat.'

'Don't flatter yourself; I also need to use the toilet.'

'Ok. I will be done soon.'

I waited for about a minute and heard the toilet flush. Yet, the door didn't open. I pushed the door and realised it wasn't locked. I stepped in and shut the door. She looked shocked and tried to brush past me to leave the restroom. But it was impossible because I held onto her hand and–shoved her against the closed door.

'What are you doing, let go of me,' she protested through her gritted teeth.

'Why are you hiding here?' I breathed down her neck as I smelled the sweet perfume on her neck, which aroused me.

'I don't know what you mean. I came to use the toilet! Now let me go.'

'You have been here for too long, and we both know you didn't use the toilet.'

'Now you are a psychic...' I didn't let her finish her sentence as I started kissing her. She tried to struggle as usual and then she gave in. Almost immediately, we were lost in a long passionate kiss until we were interrupted by the air hostess, who knocked on the door several times to remind us to take our seats because the pilot had announced that we were about to land at the Accra International airport.

***

Boxing Arena, Accra Ghana

The bell rang again. We were already in our fourth round in the ring. I stepped into the ring after drinking some water. I tried to ignore the cheers coming from the commentators and the audience. I heard Papa screaming from outside the ring.

'Come on! Hit 'im! Hit 'im!

'You're dancing.'

'Holy shit! Give the sucker some action. You're fightin' like a whore.'

After an hour, the bell rang again to indicate another break. I sat near the ring with my left eye swollen as a result of the Ghanaian's jab. My vision was becoming blurred but I couldn't dare talk about it. My head was pounding. Sheldrake swiftly came behind me after my braces were removed by Papa. I knew he realised that my stance was distorted. I seemed frail. *I need to keep moving.* I looked above my shoulder and saw Nina in the front row. She looked tense while she watched me. Our eyes met and she gave me a reassuring nervous grin.

'Water!'

'You feel strong?'

'Absolutely!' I replied.

'Want some advice?'

'Remember what you learnt and your anatomy? Good, then take him in the middle! The thoracic region is the best place to start now. I heard he's got Peptic ulcer and hypertension.'

I nodded.

'That is the epigastrium, the part of the abdomen above the stomach, and this is the apex of the heart, which is located in the fifth left intercostal space of the chest, at the mid clavicular line a sensitive area of the clavicle called the fifth left intercostal space, do you understand what the mid clavicular line is?' I asked.

'Yeah.' He nodded.

I put on my gloves, which I had taken off earlier on, and then knocked my boxing gloves against each other. In a few seconds, I was ready to fight again.

The dark and ferocious-looking Ghanaian was still on his feet when the bell rang again. Immediately, he tried throwing me a jab but I ducked and then danced around him in circles. When I realised he was wearing out, I took my final punch at the delicate place above his stomach. Like magic, he fell face flat. Ironically, my headache stopped immediately. I knew that I had won.

I watched through my battered eyes as the crowd went into a frenzy. Their joy was indescribable. Abednego, Papa and Jimmy had jumped into the ring. The reporters were also in the ring trying to talk to me and Abednego.

'What do you have to say?'

'How do you feel?'

'Who do you owe these undefeatable victories to?'

I tried to respond to them but at the same time, my eyes searched for Nina in the crowd. She stood at the exact position I had last seen her. Our eyes met and from that distance, I could see joy and pride on her face.

'Of course, I owe these victories to my brother Abednego and my anatomy professor.' I responded to the reporter's question, while my gaze was transfixed on Nina. At that moment, I had a flashback of the previous night in my hotel home. Nina and I were lying down together on the carpet while she taught me the anatomy of the body from a textbook called *Gray's Anatomy*.

'Did you learn all of these to be a doctor?'

'Yep.'

'You must be brilliant because this is hard stuff.'

'It's easy when you familiarize yourself with it. Look at it this way, if Abednego knows it, so can you.' She looked up at me and gave me a sheepish smile.

'That's true.' We both burst out laughing.

'You know it would be easier if you showed me the real anatomy of a body instead of pictures.'

'We did use projectors earlier on Sheldrake...or would you rather have a cadaver included in your studies?'

'I meant a living human being, like a woman.'

'Hell no! What happened between us in the restroom shouldn't happen again. I mean it. I am in your room because this fight is important and you need this knowledge to guide you. I would leave the tutorial CDs so you can familiarize yourself with more of the anatomy.'

'Let's make a bet. If I do win this fight, you owe me a lecture on anatomy using a living specimen.'

She hesitated before replying:

'Who would that specimen be?'

'If I win, then I get to pick. You are not the only woman in the world, Doc. Remember that...'

'Then that's fine by me. Anything for a little motivation.'

I pulled out my hand and we sealed the deal with a hand shake.

My thoughts were distracted by Papa. He held onto my hand and whispered proudly to me:

'Welcome to a new world, son.'

CHAPTER TWENTY-TWO

ABEDNEGO

I looked at my wristwatch while I made my way to my suite and at the same time trying to comprehend what Nina was saying to me over the telephone.

'The pilot has been diagnosed with gastroenteritis, Abednego. I doubt if he will be able to fly today.'

'What the hell is that?' I asked.

The other telephone rang and I handed it over to Jimmy, who was by my side.

'It simply means he is down with acute diarrhoea. We would have to stay in Ghana one more night. It's best he gets adequate fluid, Oral Rehydration Therapy and bed rest today. And I looked into international flights. They are all fully booked.'

'What the hell is the cause?'

'Food poisoning, he had some local food at the marketplace. So, the infection is probably coming from there.'

'What the hell are we going to do now?'

I was interrupted by Jimmy, who tried handing me the phone.

'It's Martha, she says she wants to talk with you.'

'Tell her I am busy right now, I will call her later.'

'She's asking if we are coming today. What should I say?'

'Tell her I doubt it.'

I walked into my room and pulled off my jacket with one hand, while I tried to hold the phone with the other hand.

'Hey, are you still on the line, Nina?'

'Do you think we have any other option? Because Sheldrake told me he has to go for his sister's birthday today. This news will kill him.'

'Good lord! I totally forgot!' I replied.

'You know what I think? Silver can arrange something. I heard she came with some diplomats to watch the game.'

'Oh really. That's cool then. Thanks, babes.'

I put down the phone and turned to Jimmy.

'Make a call to Silver, we might just need her help.'

CHAPTER TWENTY-THREE

SHELDRAKE

I stood in the middle of my suite fuming. I had just defeated the Africa heavyweight champion and still, it seemed like I had not accomplished anything. I was pacing the room in anger when my thoughts were interrupted by a knock on the door. I hurried towards the door and opened it, thinking it was Silver again.

'What do you want this time?'

'I am sorry to disturb...' she was about to turn away in embarrassment when I stopped her.

'Sorry, I apologise, I thought it was somebody else.'

'Oh, you were expecting someone.'

'It's a long story.' I was dazzled by her appearance. She looked lovely in short white, silk transparent lingerie, a bottle of champagne and a box of strawberries in her hands. Her hair was let down to touch her prominent and perfect clavicle. I was captivated by her revealing cleavage and long legs.

'Are you going to invite me in? It's freezing out here.' She finally said, breaking the contrived silence.

'Yeah, so... Sorry, please come in. Forgive my manners.' I stammered.

She walked into the room and put down the bottle of champagne on the table. I saw her shocked look at my dishevelled room. I had turned the centre table upside down and smashed the mirror in my rage a few minutes back.

'What happened here?' she asked.

'Just furious before you got here.'

'Please sit down, tell me what happened. Talk to me please, just maybe I can be of help,' she rushed to my side with concern. She led me to the only accommodating sofa, and we both sat down.

'I can't remember when last I lost my cool. It has been like forever. Now I get so easily agitated and this Silver lady is not making anything easier...'

'I don't get it. Please explain.'

'I'll rather not talk about it...' I suddenly started feeling a throbbing headache. I placed my hand on my head.

'What's the matter?' she asked, holding my hand.

'I have this terrible headache.'

'We have to get you to a hospital then. I have to run some tests on you. Where is the phone? I have to call the clinic downstairs.' She began to sound professional. She was about to move away from me and reach for the phone by the bedside when I stopped her by pulling her close to me and kissing her. She didn't try to struggle this time. She responded to every bit of my kisses. She was soon hurriedly helping me take off my singlet and unbutton my pants, leaving me in my briefs while I took off her lingerie and exposed her flawless naked skin. I carried her up as we kissed passionately while leading her to the bed. I soon forgot every pain in my head or what had precipitated my previous outburst. *She was that special.*

Five hours earlier

I watched Abednego come into my room with his usual grin, accompanied by Papa, Jimmy, Silver and a waiter carrying a bucket of chilled 1966 Dom Perignon. Abednego walked up to me and gave me a hug. Jimmy rushed to the mini-bar and pulled out champagne glasses for us all. He handed me the first glass with a broad grin, I had never seen him so energized. He filled my champagne glass while he whistled.

'I have never seen Jimmy so excited before,' Silver said aloud while she giggled.

'Me neither, I am kind of scared with all this excitement he is exhibiting.' Papa chipped in dryly.

'Me too,' I concurred.

We all burst out laughing, while Jimmy ignored our comments and gulped his drink in seconds.

'Let's toast to our everlasting success. I have never seen so much press before out there! This is the right step. I am so proud of my brother Sheldrake. This is the future!' Abednego lifted his glass.

'Cheers!'

All our glasses were clinking in unison.

'So, let's get down to business now. Silver, are you still going to top up your offer on exclusive interviews with me now?' I asked in a business-like tone.

'We didn't come here to talk business, although the fight was brilliant. I came to celebrate and tell you that Abednego called and asked for my help in flying back to Nigeria. Your pilot has gastroenteritis. So, there is only space to accommodate one passenger, which obviously is Abednego.'

'Is this true? The pilot is sick. What about Martha's birthday?'

'Yeah, it's crazy bro, but not to worry, I will be there for her.' Abednego put in a reassuring tone.

'Well, it's settled, we will call Martha. Abednego being there should be okay, son. Martha would understand,' Papa said.

'In that case, you would have to get ready because the plane is taking off soon. You guys don't mind if I keep our champion company here, while you assist Abednego to sort his luggage out?'

'Of course, not. Let's go.' Papa said. I watched all of them exit the room, while Jimmy whistled happily until the door was shut.

'You seem like a smart woman, Silver. Why didn't I get a place on the plane? It's my sister's day today and not his,' I asked calmly.

'Well, if I will be straight with you, Abednego is the world champion; he is a legend because he is comparable to Sugar Ray and Ali. And like Rocky Marciano, he retired from the heavyweight championship undefeated. But for you, who would you be compared with? Because as far as you are under him, he practically overshadows you because he trains you. Besides, he is the white golden boy.'

'You are wrong... I proved everyone wrong today. I will be fighting in the world championship soon, and when I win, my name will never be forgotten.'

'Yeah, maybe you are right. I watched the fight today. I know you are that good. I have been in this business for a long time. That's why I am here today. I see that hunger in your eyes. In fact, I can smell it. But the question is, how far can you possibly go when the presence of a white legend is constantly taking your shine?'

'That's bull and you know it.'

'Do you really think the surprise party thrown for you was actually meant for you? Everyone in that room came to honour Abednego. Look at what is happening at this instance. Who would be on the private plane rolling with the big boys to Nigeria? The diplomats who own the plane wanted to only accommodate Abednego and talk business with him, alongside bringing boxing into their country. You put on a brilliant show but the shine goes to Abednego, because he has the right package, he's white, learned from the family of a diplomat and he breeds little black boys like you to stand up on their feet. You are just a symbol of his victory.'

I clenched my teeth and stiffened my fist in annoyance as she spoke. The words were biting hard.

'I can see you know nothing about my life or his.'

'Believe me; I know all that is necessary. I am the media, remember? And stop all '*he's my brother* shit because as far as the world is concerned, colour-wise, he is white as an angel and you have got the virus tan.'

'What's your angle, Silver?'

'Did you know that on October 26, 1951, with 37 wins and 32 knockouts under Marciano's belt, he faced former heavyweight champion Joe Louis and knocked him out in the eighth round? Louis was his boyhood idol, and Marciano cried in Louis's dressing room after the fight.'

'Don't get your point?'

'I see you are slow… Marciano was Louis's boyhood idol, and he still fought the shit out of him and he won, and then he cried. That shows that he was goddamn hungry for the championship and the perks that come with it.'

'Are you proposing I fight with Abednego?' I asked, confused. She nodded.

'I like you... more than a lot.' She replied with a sassy smile. She took a step forward towards me and ran her fingers down my bare shoulder to my biceps. I took a step backwards to indicate my sign of rejection while her hand fell down to her side. I watched her facial expression turn into a frown.

'You know, if you had a lot of sense, you would jump at my offer, come join my team. I would hook you up with a manager and make sure you get the best publicity you deserve. You don't deserve to be second best.'

'Get the hell out of my room.'

'Sorry?'

'You heard me.'

'This is my card. You would need it for a rainy day. Good luck. You need it. Your naivety won't take you far, love. Au revoir.' She put her card on a coffee table, gave a flaccid smile and left my room. I was livid. I turned around and caught my reflection in the mirror in front of me. Suddenly, I could hear the frightening whispers of Mama's voice.

I walked towards it and threw a punch at my reflection. The mirror shattered to pieces.

***

Five hours later

I lay under the white silk sheet with Nina. She was fast asleep as she wrapped her long legs around my waist. I could smell the freshness of her beautiful hair and skin. I had lost every anger or burden that I carried within me. I felt peaceful anytime she was around me. Her aura was like magic.

'I love you.' I whispered into her ears. Instantaneously, I saw her big brown eyes slowly open. She looked up at me with this panicky demeanour, as I felt my heart skip. I thought she was asleep when I uttered those words. I didn't want to feel any sense of rejection from her.

'You don't have to reply.' I whispered to her. 'Thought you were asleep, go back to bed.'

She pulled me closer to her bosom and kissed me tenderly. I responded fervently and I knew that without her saying the words, she felt the same way too.

CHAPTER TWENTY-FOUR

MARTHA

I walked into the club for the first time as a teenager and I was shocked by the number of people dancing half-naked and the strippers dancing on the poles. I had a flashback of my first experience at the club Pink Carnation. My new friends were already singing and dancing to Femi Kuti's song *'beng beng beng' booming* on the loudspeakers while we were ushered to a reserved table by one of the bouncers. As we made our way to the table, I felt uncomfortable trying to pull down my mini-skirt. It was too short and was almost revealing my pant line. Bola had made me wear a cream skirt and a navy-blue crop top. She said I would look more mature in it and she made my face up with pink lipstick, blue eyeshadow and brown powder. I had frowned at my reflection in the mirror then but when I visualized Abednego drooling at the way I looked, I was encouraged to allow Bola to dress me up further. I recollected trying to talk to Abednego on the phone but he didn't have the time to talk to me, instead, it was that nasty Jimmy who took my call. My brother could not be reached on the phone. Habib had shown up and decided to take me out to have a good time and I agreed. At least, he saw me differently and desired me, like a woman. That sensation made me feel better about myself.

The waiter ushered us to a round table near the strip pool.

'This is the birthday girl, and I want her to have the best alcohol ever!' Habib spoke to the waiter that came to wait at the table.

'No, I don't want alcohol; I'll rather have a glass of orange juice.'

Everyone burst out laughing.

'Orange juice keh, this is a club girl. Better arrange yourself.' Bola said.

'It's your birthday baby, so we would give you a shot of tequila to start up the day.' Habib turned to the waiter and continued, 'A shot of tequila for everyone here but two shots for the birthday girl.'

In a few seconds, the waiter had arrived with the drinks. Habib handed me my glass.

'Go on.' He encouraged me. I sipped it and immediately began to cough. Everyone at the table laughed. They gulped theirs at once.

'Hey, dear, like this.' Habib demonstrated how to drink it. I picked up my glass again, closed my eyes and gulped my first shot of tequila. Everyone began to clap for me. I felt good. I took the glass and gulped it again. Habib handed me a slice of lemon and I sucked into it. I felt excited as my head began to spin.

'Another shot please, I am the birthday girl.' I called a passing waitress. Before you could say Jack, I had another three shots of tequila placed before me. Bola, Habib, Ngozi, Emeka and Idris began to beat the table with their hands in exhilaration.

'Down it! Down it!' They cheered.

I smiled up at Habib, pulled his neck closer and gave him a kiss and turned to the drinks on the table, picked the tequila glasses one after the other with my mouth and gulped them. At my last shot, I already felt like my head was rotating as I began to giggle. I let Habib pull me towards his chest and stick his tongue down my throat; I responded by throwing my arms around his neck. The DJ was at his best dishing out the latest hits. Iyanya's song 'Your Waist' was playing at the moment. I pushed Habib away from me and climbed the table. I began to sing the song as I unbuttoned my blouse, dancing wildly to the song. I didn't realise that most people in the club were staring at me and I began to receive a lot of cheering from the crowd.

'Hey get down,' Bola and Ngozi moved towards the table and tried to bring me down but I pushed them off.

'Let her be, babes. I love where this is heading,' Habib told them. He pulled out a 500 naira note and placed it in between my bra. I smiled at him.

'This is not cool; this is not the plan,' Bola turned to Idris for help.

'Come on girls, live a little!' Idris ignored her as he lustfully stared at me while I took off my skirt. I was now lost in my seductive dance to the melody with only my bra and pants and with my eyes shut. Little did I realize that the party has turned into chaos, with punches and slaps flying in different directions. By the time I opened my blurry eyes, I saw Abednego throw a punch at Habib. Abednego was soon pulling me down from the table.

'What the fuck? I never want to see you in my house again.' He screamed at Habib. He pulled his blazer and was trying to cover my nakedness. I remember trying to struggle with him.

'Let me be, where is Habib? It's my birthday! You are ruining it!' He ignored my protest as he lifted me and carried me out of the club to the car. I began to vomit and soon, I passed out. I woke up on my cosy bed the following morning.

CHAPTER TWENTY FIVE

ABEDNEGO

I watched her sleep peacefully like an innocent child. Indeed, I had always thought she was an innocent child, but still, I couldn't get past the incident that occurred the previous night. I pondered. I had arrived home in a hurry to take her out for dinner but realised she wasn't around. The maid informed me that she had gone out with some friends from school. Somehow, I was comforted that she was now making friends. I didn't want her to emulate my footsteps when I was growing up a loner. I then decided to meet up with the ambassador from Ghana, who had invited me for drinks at the newest and hottest lounge on the Island. I recalled getting there and sitting in the VIP section upstairs overseeing what was happening downstairs, when my eyes fell on a lovely, slender and gorgeous girl that was dancing half-naked and provocatively while making the whole club go wild.

'Who is she?' I had asked the club owner curiously. He said he didn't know her. He was excited to have her too.

'You should bring her here to join us.' The ambassador told the club owner. The owner ordered his manager to send bottles of champagne to her table and invite her over.

A few seconds later, the manager had returned and informed us that her boyfriend was called Habib and he said the girl won't talk to anyone until he was included in the VIP party.

'What's her name?' I asked, curious.

'Martha Sheldrake,' the manager replied.

I was about to take a sip of my drink when I heard her name. I almost choked.

'What the fuck?' I jumped up from my seat and hurried to the dance floor to clear my suspicion. As soon as I saw her from a distance, I realised that it was Martha. I got hold of Habib as he was about to run away when he realised that I was the one approaching him and landed a few solid punches on his face. The whole club broke loose that night, and I made sure the club was shut down that night by my security.

I watched her open her huge brown eyes in a few seconds. She struggled to sit up with a frown on her face.

'Here is a cup of coffee for you. It will help you recover from your last night's atrocity.' I handed over the cup of tea. Inadvertently, her halter neck top exposed her bare breasts as she collected the cup.

'Cover up, would you?' I snapped at her because I felt a sudden rage within me. I angrily left the room and made my way to my office. I walked directly to the bar and poured myself a glass of Jack Daniels. Immediately, my office door flew open. Martha stormed in rage.

'I don't get it, what the hell have I done for you to look and speak to me like I am a disgusting child?'

'Those words sound quite stupid coming from your mouth, Martha, don't you think?'

'I just went out to have fun with my friends for the first time, and you are acting as if I killed the Queen of England!'

'I found you drunk and you were displaying your whole body in public, Martha. I am quite disappointed in you and as far as I know, this discussion ends here. Sheldrake would not know about this because it would kill him. Your lesson teacher is fired, and he won't step foot into this house again,' I replied calmly.

'It was my birthday, and I did nothing wrong. He is my boyfriend; you can't restrict him from coming here.'

'What has come over you, child. I don't understand this sudden display.'

'I am not a child! You have come over me.'

I watched her break down in tears suddenly. I was confused. I put my glass of JD down and walked up to her, I tried to hold her but she aggressively shoved me aside.

'I am in love with you, can't you see? I tried to act like that just to get your attention so that you can look at me differently… like a real woman. Those girls who come home with you every day, this is how they act and dress, isn't it?'

181

'Oh, Martha,' I pulled her closer to me, pulled a handkerchief from my breast pocket and tried to wipe her tears.

'Don't you feel something for me?' she whispered to me. I saw her sad teary eyes expectantly looking up at me. At that instance, I was bemused.

'You are a child, sweetheart; you don't know what you want now. It's sort of normal for you to have these feelings. It's called a crush. It will go away with time, and you will fall in love with someone your age.'

'I am not a child! I am a woman! Look at me,' she let her robe slip down the floor at that instance, revealing her nakedness. Staring back at me invitingly were full pointed breasts and slender hips, succulent skin and a lusciously hairy vagina concealed by black lacy panties. She was beautiful. *What's wrong with me?*

'Good God, Martha! Cover up. Please leave this instant, I need to get some work done,' I replied harshly as I turned away from her and moved towards the window. But it looked like she sensed the weakness in my voice. I heard her soft footsteps approach me from behind. I tensed up as she came closer to me and put her arms around my waist. She began to place kisses on my neck. My knees grew weak because I could feel the softness of her bare skin on my body.

'Please don't.' I turned around to face her to stop her from coming any closer to me. She took advantage of my reaction and threw her arms around my shoulder and placed kisses on my lip while she continued sobbing and whispering to me at the same time '*make love to me.*'

'Stop this child,' I tried to gently shove her away, but she was relentless. She began unbuttoning my shirt, shivering and kissing me at the same time. At that instance, I was lost. I knew I had to stop her but I couldn't. Women were poison and definitely my downfall. Instead, I picked her from her feet and carried her towards the long settee in the office while I lustfully responded to her kisses. Soon I was ripping out the remaining layers of her lace fabric and making ravenous, fiery love to her.

CHAPTER TWENTY-SIX

ABEDNEGO

I poured myself a third glass of cognac and emptied it in a single gulp. I was perplexed and I loathed myself. I couldn't believe I had just made love to Martha. I tried to erase all the memories of the previous night but it was impossible. When she had come on to me, I knew that I had to stop her because she was just a kid, but yesterday, she felt like a woman. I couldn't resist her any longer. Curiously, she wasn't in my bed when I woke up in the early hours of the morning. I thought I was dreaming but it became so real when I stared down at the white silk bed sheets and realised that it was stained with blood. *I had busted the cherry!*

I hurried downstairs to the breakfast room to see if I could catch up with her, but the room was empty and the maid explained that Martha had gone to school. I was more confused than ever because most girls I spent the night with always wanted to cuddle after sex. But, interestingly, little Martha had woken up early and had gone to school without disturbing me. *I have to stay away from her.*

I was about to take my fourth glass of cognac when Sheldrake opened the door of my office, accompanied by Jide and Jimmy.

'Hey, bro, how are you doing?' he walked up to me, and we embraced.

'Did I just catch you drinking in the morning?' Jimmy asked.

'Yeah. Just have a nagging headache.'

'You should take an aspirin for that, son.' Jide said.

'Down to the business of the day. I just got a call from NTA Network news. They want an interview with Sheldrake. That's fantastic publicity because the Lagos State Governor is a guest too. That means we have to go through a few pointers with you and then do our routine training today.' Jimmy added, at the same time, handing him over a paper with his detailed schedule for the day.

'This is a long schedule. Men, I thought I could have a few days off to spend time with Martha. It was her birthday and my not being here killed me....' Sheldrake replied.

'You will have that spare time with your sister when you become a millionaire with some goddamn universal popularity, after you win the world championship.'

'Give the guy a break, man. Besides, today is Martha's PTA meeting at her school at 2 pm and I think he should go.' I quietly imposed.

'The live interview starts at 2.30 pm; I can't make that PTA meeting. You have to go for it instead,' Sheldrake replied as he glanced through his schedule.

'Hell no! I am damn well not going to Martha's school. You are her brother, and you better find a way to juggle your damn responsibilities!' I exploded.

'Jesus Christ, man. What's gotten into you? You know all I do is for my sister.'

'That means you bloody well can call the NTA network and reschedule the appointment, you could be an hour late. You have gone this far already in boxing, then you better learn to call the shots and demand some respect. Cause I sure have my own problems, and none of it involves going to babysit Martha!'

As the words came out of my mouth, I saw all three of them staring at me in astonishment. They look astonished at my outbursts. I was usually the one who would opt to look after Martha whenever situations like this arise. Why the sudden change, nobody knew.

'Are you okay, man? Seriously? Because you need to take that aspirin badly, I am going to the car.' Sheldrake looked hurt as he walked out of the office. Jimmy followed him. I was left alone with Jide, who had a worried expression on his face. I poured myself another glass of Cognac.

'Did Martha do something to you?' He asked thoughtfully. My heart skipped a beat. It appeared that I was giving myself away with my unexpected outbursts.

'Why would you say that?'

'Your reaction.'

'No, Jide, she didn't. Just have a few problems with my wife, which I promise I will resolve soon. Forgive my juvenile reaction.'

I put my glass down and walked up to him. I tried to keep a straight face.

'Ok, anything that I can help you with?'

'No, it's all good.'

'Then try not to say things like this to Sheldrake again. He lives to fight for that girl. If he begins to feel like a failure in her matter, it could distract him entirely from his training. We both know that, son.'

I nodded.

'I will speak to him when he comes back home.'

'Thanks, child.' Jide smiled at me and left the study room.

CHAPTER TWENTY-SEVEN

MARTHA

I walked into the auditorium with gaiety and confidence, whistling a tune. *I was a real woman now.* I spotted Bola and Emeka at the extreme end of the hall and took a seat beside them. I recalled every minute of my night with Abednego as I rode to school. I could hardly wait to see him at the PTA meeting today.

'What the hell happened to you? We were so worried sick. Did you get into a lot of trouble?' Emeka was worried.

'Habib was so fired! God, I hope your uncle doesn't say anything to my parents today. Is he the one coming for the meeting?' Bola asked, distraught.

'Yes, he is, but really my friend. Do I look like I got into trouble? On the other hand, whatever happened yesterday was the best thing ever.' I grinned in delight. At that moment, I felt everything I ever wanted was falling into place. I had the man of my dreams and famous friends. I felt beautiful.

'I don't get it. Getting caught almost naked on a bar table was a blessing?' Bola asked, mystified.

'Yup!'

'I hope you haven't started taking that crack that Habib normally uses?' Emeka butted in.

'Nope, no crack, dear. He just pulled me out because he was jealous.' I corrected her.

'Jealous?' They both asked in unison.

'Abednego is in love with me!'

I watched them exchange glances before bursting into laughter.

'Be serious, girl, and don't play with us. This is some deep shit we are involved in. If my mother finds out that I was in a club, I will be grounded for life. So cut this love crap.'

'We made love yesterday. That's why I am telling you that he won't say a word.'

'What?' they both exclaimed.

'Come on, girl, don't mess around. You don't know shit about love-making.'

'Am I not glowing?'

'In a weird way you are... You look different,' Emeka was now accessing my face.

'So, you see, he won't want to get me into trouble.'

'But, wait a minute, he is married, and isn't he meant to be like your brother?' Bola asked, still astonished.

189

'He definitely will leave his wife; I know he would never hurt me. Last night proved it all. He doesn't love her, and he obviously would marry me when the time is right.'

'Good lord, girl. I am so confused.'

'But wait, what about Habib?'

'What about him?' I replied nonchalantly.

'He's crazy about you, and besides, he told me that he is coming here today to see you.'

'He shouldn't....'

'Speak of the devil,' Bola said pointing behind me.

I turned to see Habib approaching us. I frowned. He walked to me with a grin.

'What are you doing here? You are not allowed in here. These sorts of meetings are for parents, teachers and students only.' I bluntly told him, before he even got close to me.

'Well, I came in with my aunt, Emeka's mom. I told her I wanted to see how Emeka is doing in school...' he pointed to a lady that was being ushered to her seat by a teacher. I realised that the lady was Silver, the woman with the bad haircut.

'Well, you shouldn't have come.'

'Wait a minute; it sounds like you are not happy to see me.'

'Look, I have to go, and I don't want you getting me into extra trouble.'

'Hey, my love...'

'Look, Habib, it's over, whatever happened between us. Please excuse me.'

I didn't want Abednego coming into the hall and seeing both of us together. I brushed past him before he could argue any further and made my way to the front roll. I knew he would not chase me, because I took a seat beside Mrs Silver. From the angle I sat, I could still see him conversing with Bola and Emeka. He had a morose look.

'Morning, ma'am.' I greeted Mrs Silver. She lifted her head from the newspaper she was reading and looked up at me.

'Don't I know you?'

'Yes, you do, I saw you at my house the other day. I am Sheldrake's little sister.'

I impatiently tapped on the table in front of me as I spoke to her. I was looking at the entrance-waiting for Abednego to arrive. I missed him already. But instead, I saw my brother walk into the hall. Abednego wasn't with him. At that moment my heart skipped a beat. *Did my brother know? No, it couldn't be.* My fear disappeared when my brother spotted me with Mrs Silver and his smile broadened. *He wouldn't smile that way if he knew that I had slept with Abednego.*

'Hey, my little princess' He pulled me closer to his chest and placed a kiss on my forehead.

'Welcome, Brother, where is Abednego?' I asked, still searching around the room and hoping that he would appear soon.

'Hey, you don't sound too pleased to see me? Don't tell me Abednego has replaced my sister's affection for me,' he frowned at me.

I gave a soft chuckle and smiled back.

'Of course not, Brother, I am happy. Just that I am not used to you coming here to check up on me. You are always busy. It's just more of Abednego's thing to worry about my school activities.'

'Well, that's going to change very soon. I apologise for not being there as I always promised that I would... Things are shaping up now, so I can have that time for you, pumpkin.'

'Oh, so affectionate, it's true what the media says. The vulture does have a heart when it comes to his hawks...'

We both turned around to see Mrs Silver observing us both with an amused look.

'I beg your pardon,' Brother said.

'Pardon? His vocabulary too has improved... Looks like Abednego has done a hell lot of a job on you both.' I heard her say it in a sarcastic tone. I watched my brother's face harden. He was about to say something when we were interrupted by my gym instructor, who cordially ushered my brother to his seat. The meeting was about to begin. The principal soon came in and instructed the students to go and wait in the lobby while they had the meeting with the parents. I made my way to the lobby and then to the vending machine to get a coke. I was thirsty and confused. *Why didn't Abednego come to see me in school? Was something wrong?* The way he caressed me last night after we made love was amazing, I reminisced on how I watched his face light up to mine while he held me close to his bosom. *He couldn't have played with my heart. He loves me.* Emeka's voice interrupted my thought. Bola and Habib were with him.

'So, what happened? I haven't seen Abednego?' Emeka anxiously asked me.

'He is not coming; my brother said he had to sort out work stuff.'

'Can I talk to you in private?' Habib spoke up in a harsh tone.

'I already said I don't think we should talk. Talking isn't very necessary.'

'Fucking yes, it is!'

'Don't raise your voice here, bro.' Emeka tried to hush him down.

'I will raise it more than this if Martha doesn't come with me now,' he said.

'I am not going anywhere with you...' I challenged him.

'I have nothing to lose, remember? I have already lost my job. Let's see what your brother is going to say when he hears that you have started fucking his best friend.'

'You told him that?' I turned to face Bola and Emeka.

'He is my cousin; he just wanted to know why you were tripping. I am sorry.'

'Well, this cousin of yours is going to get all of us into trouble if he doesn't shut his mouth.'

'Please, Martha, just let him talk to you.' Bola pleaded 'My mother is the principal remember, I would be killed at home, if this gets out.'

I reluctantly walked with Habib to the far corner of the hallway, where we had privacy.

'Hey, baby, I know you probably made that story up about having sex with Abednego and even if you allowed him to burst that cherry of yours, I am sure it was just to save my arse and those of your friends. Well, I am here for you now baby.... I am all yours,' he moved closer to me at the same time, caressing my hand. I pulled my hands away from his and backed out. He saw the spite on my face.

'What the fuck is going on? Few days ago, you were all over me and now...'

'And now, I don't want you. Abednego told me that you wanted to trade me off for a VIP pass in the club. You disgust me. I will repeat myself, so please listen carefully... Whatever we had is over. Please excuse me and stay away from me.' I was about to walk away but he held on tightly to me.

'Who do you think you are to dump me?'

'You are hurting me... let go.' I struggled to move away from him but it was futile because his grip was too tight.

'See this pikin wey no know anything before, now your mouth dey sharp now abi...wen I don groom you. Now u think say you fit dump me for a white man? You don see white preek? And now e com fire me sef so that he go get free time to fuck you abi?'

'Let go, Habib, I swear I would scream out loud if you don't let go,' I threatened through my gritted teeth.

'Scream now, I dare you. Let everyone know that you are a whore.'

I struck him with my free hand on his cheek. He was taken aback, and I had the chance to pull myself free of his grip. As I was about to flee, I experienced a sudden excruciating pain in my head. He had grabbed hold of the ponytail on my hair. I tried not to scream as tears ran down my cheek.

'Where do you think you are going, you bitch?'

'Let her go, Habib! What the hell is going on here?'

He instantly let go of my hair when we both heard the stern tone of Mrs Silver's voice from behind us. I turned around and kicked his crotch. He squealed like a pig and hit the ground holding his thing. I turned around and fled, leaving a dazed Mrs Silver behind. I sprinted down the stairs of the hallway, which was now empty, and made my way to the car park where I spotted my brother's vehicle. I told the driver to open the door. I ran in and shut the door behind me, bending down it the back seat to prevent Habib from seeing me. I waited impatiently for Brother to arrive, hoping for the damn PTA meeting to come to an end.

CHAPTER TWENTY-EIGHT

SHELDRAKE

I walked out of the classroom with a broad grin on my face. I was a proud brother because I had spoken to Martha's teachers, and they all had lovely things to say about her academic performance. The principal had said that she was an 'A' student and that if she kept it up, she could obtain the Shell scholarship to study in America. At that moment, I felt fulfilled because I knew that Mama would be smiling wherever she is. That was the only thing she always wanted. She constantly alleged that acquiring an education was the finest way to any accomplishment in life. I spotted my car at the car park and soon was making my way towards it.

My smirk soon disappeared when I spotted Silver approaching me at the parking lot. She had a scowl on her ugly face as usual.

'Can I talk to you, Sheldrake?'

'Don't have that time for your nonsense, Silver. I have an appointment.'

'It will just take a minute.'

Reluctantly, I waited. 'Go on, woman'

'Have you considered what I discussed with you?'

'If that is what you stopped me for, then bluntly speaking, the answer is NO. I don't have time for this game you are playing. I did a little bit of digging about you, and it appears you and your husband are trying to open a boxing agency... and it's so ironic that your husband is white because you are trying so damn hard to turn me against the only loyal white man I know.'

'Loyal?' I watched her laugh before she continued. 'Look here, Sheldrake, before you speak on strong words such as *loyalty*', you should scrutinize your newly found English vocabulary well because those words are really big and dangerous. I am definitely sure loyalty means a lot to you...'

'I don't have time for these trivialities....' I cut her short. As I made to pass her, she grabbed onto my arm and looked me up straight in the face with bloodshot eyes.

'Abednego is not as loyal to you as it may seem. I know this because a white man just can't be! They only appear to give with one hand, and on the other hand, they take back in two folds.'

'You know nothing about suffering or the white man.' I calmly challenged her.

'Believe me, I do. I have covered stories and witnessed the massacre of babies, fathers, husbands and mothers. As a black woman married to a white Ambassador husband, it was an intentional choice. It was the only ticket to my present life of riches and fame. I know all his whores, whom he shares with Abednego at their so-called luncheon, and I don't give a rat's ass! Why? Because I know where I am and where I am heading. I know what I want, but the question is Sheldrake, do you know what you really want?'

I pulled my arm away from hers and tried to speak to her as calmly as I could.

'You only cover other people's stories. You didn't live it. I am sorry I can't be a scapegoat for your supposed lived experiences. I am in a better place right now. I know that I am going to be the world heavyweight champion at the right time.'

She chuckled and gave me a devilish smile before replying:

'The easiest and quickest way to begin that is to go into the ring with Abednego. You have all the cards laid down in your palms and it takes a black man not to notice them. You definitely are not hungry enough for the power and success that comes with it... you remind me of a pathetic wounded dog.'

'It's funny because you also remind me of a wounded and pathetic reject on heat.'

She forced a smile before continuing, 'It seems that I will be seeing you soon. You need me but you don't know it just yet.' She ran her fingers down my biceps seductively.

'Excuse me.'

I walked up to my car, infuriated by the old hag. I found Martha seated at the back of the seat, looking agitated.

'Are you okay, Brother? Did that lady bother you?' she asked.

'She is saying nothing important, child. Don't let that trouble you. You are doing well in school, and I am so proud of you and I am sure Mama would be. I know I haven't been there for you as much as I should be, but I promise, soon everything will be fine.' I pulled her closer and gave her a huge kiss on her forehead. I watched her brighten up, and I was happy.

In a while, the driver had dropped Martha at home, and I made my way to the TV station and later, to the hospital. I had an appointment with Nina.

***

May-Weather Reddington Hospital

I knocked on Nina's consulting room door, and she invited me in. I opened the door and found her sitting across her desk, with her eyes buried in a medical textbook. She didn't look up.

'Hey baby.'

I expected her to acknowledge me when she saw the bunch of flowers in my hands, but instead, she frowned.

'You shouldn't do this, Sheldrake'

'Why?' I walked closer to her table.

'You are practically late for your appointment. I had to refer my patients to other doctors because of you. We have to talk about your test results. I am a professional, damn it. I don't appreciate sitting in my office for thirty minutes waiting for you to show up for a necessary appointment...'

I cut her words short when I pulled her close to my chest and covered her mouth with my kisses. After our invigorating ten minute-kiss, I let her go. She was breathless, and then I handed the flowers over to her with a huge grin.

'They are beautiful.' She smiled.

'You are beautiful,' I responded.

'Shut the door.'

'Sorry?' I was confused

'You heard me. Close the door.'

'Okay' I walked up to the door and obediently locked it with the key. When I turned around, I saw that Nina had taken off her blouse. She stood in front of me exposed in her lacy white bra and half-unzipped pencil skirt. I stood for a few seconds to assess her in amused shock.

'Waiting for you to properly unzip me. I have patients waiting. Hurry up, please.' She had her hands placed on her hips.

'Yes, ma'am.' I responded submissively. I hurriedly walked up to her. I lifted her up and placed her on her desk. I tenderly placed kisses on her navel, while my fingers unzipped her skirt exposing her white underwear, I then used my teeth to unravel the knots of her panties. Slowly, I started to place exotic kisses on her thighs and gently worked my tongue to her vagina. Her moaning increased until she squirted on my face.

CHAPTER TWENTY-NINE

ABEDNEGO

7 days later

I intentionally stayed out of the house for about a week and afterwards, and consistently returned home late at night to avoid running into Martha. This very Saturday night, I tip-toed to my room while I passed Martha's room. I didn't want to make a sound. I had gone dancing with some female reporters that Silver's husband had introduced me to. Jimmy had previously discussed with me that our financial turnovers had been increasing since Sheldrake joined our team. He had positive reviews on all multinational television stations and a lot of endorsements from sports companies. My father-in-law finally had the balls to pick up the phone one day to congratulate me because my success in Nigeria was having a positive impact on his campaign ratings too.

I staggered into my room. In the dark, while I was pulling off my shirt, attempting to find the light switch on the wall, I smelled the funny smell of weed. When I finally found the switch and turned the light on, I was shocked at the sight in front of me. I found Martha sitting down in my bed. She had only my t-shirt on with her hair freely let down her shoulders. She had a lighted wrap of weed in her hand.

'Jesus Christ!'

'Hello Abednego, you didn't expect to see me here, did you?'

'No, I didn't... are you smoking?' I stammered.

'What does it look like?' She appeared so calm and relaxed that I became confused.

'When the fuck did you start doing this? I hope you are not associating yourself with that bastard again,' I blurted out, walking towards her, and forcefully took the weed from her.

'I already smoked two packs while waiting for you. Look at the packs over there...' she pointed to them. I saw her watering red eyes and it felt like a knife was piercing through my heart. 'I know it's crazy what I am doing. But one ends up doing crazy things when you have your heart smashed into pieces. Like almost allowing a total stranger I met at the beach when I went to buy this joint, to have sex with me...'

'What?' I was shocked.

'Don't worry. We didn't go far, I just gave him an ordinary blow job...'

'Jesus Christ, Martha, what have I done to you?'

'Smoking is one of the added habits you pick up too. Your whores smoke, don't they? And besides, you come back smelling like the whores you fuck. Were they better than me in bed?' She walked up to me and looked me straight in the eyes. I realised that she was drunk too. *What have I done to her?!*

'Look, child, I am so sorry, what happened between us was a mistake...' I couldn't complete my sentence because she had struck me hard on my face.

'You call me child and call us a mistake? You made love to me because you love me. I know it because I felt it and you dare stand in front of me and call it a mistake?'

She kept on slapping my face and when I didn't react, she started hitting me while she cursed me in Xhosatan, as tears trickled down her eyes. I tried holding her down to stop her from hitting me any further but she kept struggling with me. While we struggled, we both fell on my bed. I pinned her body down on the bed by holding both hands and her legs with mine. Also, I realised too late that pinning her down was a huge mistake as I was soon caught in the charm of her beautiful large brown eyes. Her eyes were challenging and fierce. It gave away a flicker of sexual arousal when I felt the softness of her body beneath her fabric. She took advantage of my weakness by opening her legs and wrapping them around me. My eye quickly drifted and ran through the rise and fall of her heaving chest. I noticed the irresistible beauty of her smooth and naked dark thighs and was captivated. I swore under my breath that very moment because I immediately disregarded all the promises I had earlier made to myself: *I was never going to touch her again.*

'Kiss me,' she whispered to me.

I let go of her hand and slowly took off her shirt and pulled her closer. Soon, we were kissing each other like raving dogs in the heat. We made passionate love.

***

One hour later

I made my way down the stairs to my study. Immediately, I got in and went directly to the bar and poured myself a glass of whisky. I emptied my first glass and then poured myself another glass again. I was drained because of emotions. For once in my life, I didn't know what I was doing and that scared me. I was always in control of my life, but Martha had taken over my power of discretion. I tried not to think of what would happen if Sheldrake found out. I remembered that there was only one person that could straighten me out. I sat across my desk and made a direct call to my grandmother in Yorkshire. I sipped my drink while I anxiously waited for her to pick up the ringing phone. My grandmother was eighty-five, but she was still as sharp as a bat. She had seen me struggle since I was a child. I ended up always calling her anytime I felt like a broken man.

'Hello, son.'

I was silent for a few seconds when I heard her voice because I suddenly realised that I was at a loss for words.

'Abednego, is that you? I can see your number here.'

'Yes, Grandma.'

'It's three in the morning, is everything alright son?'

'I didn't know who to talk to, sorry, Grandma.'

'What have you done this time? The last time I got this kind of call from you, it was when you heard about your father's death back then in the boarding house. So, speak to me.'

'You know when Father died; I swore to myself that I would never be like him. Oh! How I hated the bastard. He made Mother suffer till she died and didn't give a damn after that. He didn't even try reaching out to me. I was his son, and she was his wife. He lost every penny she had inherited. Now, I am stuck in a loveless marriage because of him. He was cruel. Now I look at myself every day and I realise that I am not only a splitting image of him but I am him!'

'I don't understand, son?'

'In every action or decision that I make now, I just keep being him.'

'Is it a woman, son?'

'You know me too well, Grandma,' I chuckled bitterly as I drained my glass.

'That was your father's poison, especially with the coloured ones. So, is she coloured?'

'Yes and just a child. I am worse than him, it seems.'

'Then you know what my advice would be. You might not love your wife, but you are married to a woman who is on your pedigree. She has kept the family's financial status solid after your father squandered all of it. She has given you that opportunity to be successful in boxing, and now, her family is running for a suitable place in politics. I am old now, but you are my blood and I would tell you for free that we royals don't do well without money. I know her well enough to assure you that she would take every penny you have in court. So, stop that drinking and remember where you come from. What you are experiencing now is a mistake because it is a distraction and you can always obliterate a mistake. You understand, son?'

'Yes, Grandma, I understand.'

'Good. Goodnight, son, it's late.'

'Night, Grandma.'

I heard the phone click, and I replaced the receiver. Sheldrake walked in then. He was still dressed in his bow tie and tuxedo from the night's ball.

'There you are. I was looking for you.'

'You were looking for me?' I calmly asked. I had left Martha sleeping on my bed in my room naked beneath the sheets because I had not expected him home today. Since he hit stardom, he had been spending a lot of time outside our home with Nina. My mind began to quickly race as I spoke to him.

'Yeah. I had second thoughts and decided to have an early night since I wanted to be up early to take Martha to school tomorrow. As you said the other day, I need to take some responsibility about my sister, man. She's just a little girl, and her teachers at the PTA meeting say she is growing and would need more family time.'

'Yeah, they are right.'

'I went to her room to check on her when I got in, and I realised she wasn't there. I saw the housekeeper when I was about to leave and she said that you were down here. Strange... thought she would be here with you.'

'Yeah, right, she's sleeping in my room.'

'Your room, how come?'

'You know, Martha. She woke me up and said she had a bad dream about your mother and South Ciskei. Had to watch her fall asleep, and then I came downstairs.' I lied.

'Oh my God, thanks, man. That is one of my biggest fears. I pray every day that she doesn't remember those terrible days. I too have tried to block it out of my memory.' I watched him fall silent.

'Come on, man. That is the past. I am sure she is okay. It's just a nightmare.'

'I know. Thank you, Brother, I really don't know what I would have done without you.' He patted me on the shoulder 'I will go upstairs and check on her.'

'She's my little sister too. Don't mention it. Come on, let's have a drink together, don't bother her.'

'Thanks man, but will pass. I have an early start, and really need to check up on her.'

As soon as he walked out, I began to fidget, and I quickly picked up the phone and dialled the land phone in my room.

Pick up. Pick up, damn it. I listened to the phone ring for a few seconds and I panicked because I remembered she was naked when I left her. I didn't want Sheldrake to see her lying down in my room butt naked and besides, my clothes were left lying carelessly on the floor. I was about to hang up when finally, I heard her sleepy voice.

'Hello.'

'Martha! Sheldrake is coming to my room now. Dress up, and pick up my clothes lying on the floor and pretend to be sleeping.'

'What?' she stammered.

'Do it now!' I heard the line click. I hurriedly made my way to the stairs and the hallway.

CHAPTER THIRTY

MARTHA

As soon as I received that call from Abednego, I panicked. I jumped out the bed and dashed to wear my night shirt and picked up Abednego's clothes on the floor and tossed them under the bed. At the same moment, I heard footsteps approaching the door. I swiftly jumped into the bed and covered myself with the duvet. Almost immediately, the door opened, and I shut my eyes.

I could hear his familiar footsteps as he walked towards my bed and sat next to me. He then spoke softly to me in Xhosatan. There was sadness in his voice.

'Sheldrake said you had a nightmare. I am so sorry that I have been away, and I couldn't be there when you needed me the most. Every day, when I wake up, I pray to the Virgin Mary that she intercedes and makes you a happy child because as much as I try, I cannot see myself being happy. Too much memory from South Ciskei wakes me up at night too. I love you, sis, and I promise you, just as I promised Mama: you will have the best in life.' He went silent for a few seconds and then planted a warm kiss on my forehead. He walked out of the room. I opened my eyes and exhaled.

***

Fourteen days later

I walked into my classroom after the driver had dropped me off and took my seat next to Bola. The literature teacher was already in class

'You are late, Martha. You know that I don't tolerate lateness in my class.'

'I am sorry, ma.'

'You ought to be, because this is your first time, and that is why I am sparing you.'

'Thank you, ma.'

I couldn't wait for the class to finish that day because I wasn't feeling too good. That day I vomited twice in between lectures. The literature teacher instructed Bola and Emeka to accompany me to the Sick Bay.

'What is going on with you?'

'I don't know because my stomach is hurting badly... and this morning, I vomited at home, and the worst part of it is that for the past few days I have been eating too much and my nose is always irritated by some sort of smell.' I complained to her as we made our way to the clinic.

'When did you last have your period, Martha?' She asked quietly.

'I can't remember, why?'

Immediately, they stopped walking and turned to look at me alarmed.

'Martha, I don't think we should go to Sick Bay again.'

'Why?'

'Martha, when you slept with Abednego, did you guys wear a condom?' Emeka asked.

'Condom?' I naively asked.

'Yeah, for sexual protection?' Bola added.

'I can't remember. My head hurts.'

'Jesus! Martha, you should know these things. How naive can you be! You might be pregnant.'

I froze. I vomited again. It sounded like my whole world was crumbling.

'No, it can't be. Don't be silly.' I argued.

'Okay, I am going to ask you again, Martha, and you must remember, when did you last see your period?'

'Yeah, saw it a few weeks ago,' I replied.

'Well thank God then. It might be malaria. So don't panic yet.' Bola heaved a sigh of relief.

We made our way to the clinic and the nurses took me to the ward. Moments later, the doctor came in and examined me while she set up an IV line for me. Later, the phlebotomist came in and took blood from my vein. The doctor explained that it was to carry out a routine test. After she collected a detailed history from me, she asked me if I have had any sexual intercourse before, and I remembered keeping a straight face while I lied. She nodded and a few minutes after that, she left me alone in the room to sleep.

I can't remember how long I slept because when I woke up, I noticed that Bola and Emeka were sitting beside my bed.

'Sleeping beauty awakes,' Emeka teased. I responded with a smile.

'I just spoke to Habib. He is worried sick about you. Told him you were in here.'

'That is nice of him, but I would rather he stays away from me.' I responded. Before Emeka could respond to my comment, the doctor had come into the room. She told Emeka and Bola to excuse her and they left the room. Then she looked at me and calmly spoke.

'Your test results would be out in a bit; however, I spoke to your teacher while you were asleep, and I wanted to find out about your guardian...'

'You mean Brother?'

'Yeah, but he isn't around. He went to the final championship match in America.'

'Okay, if he isn't around then who takes care of you?'

'Abednego, he's like another brother to me.'

'Ok, I remember Abednego. Can I get in touch with him?'

'He isn't around; he had to leave with Brother for the tournament too.'

'Ok then, who is responsible for you now?'

'Hmmm, Brother's Doctor, Miss Nina. He gave instructions that she should check up on me while they were gone.'

'Okay then. Do you have her number?'

I nodded and called out the number for her. She wrote it down and then she asked finally:

'You told me you never had sexual intercourse before; I need to know again if you had.'

'No, doctor, I haven't.' I lied again. She nodded as I watched her pick up her cell phone to call Nina. When she hung up the phone, she looked down at me and forced a smile.

'Doctor Nina's office is around the corner; she will be here in a few minutes.' Soon, a nurse came in with my hospital file. She told the doctor that my results were ready. I studied her face as she scanned through the results. Her reaction did not give away anything. She closed the file and looked sadly down at me and said:

'The test results show that you are pregnant, Martha'

At that moment, it seemed as if my whole world had stopped. I began to have palpitations.

'No. It can't be. I saw my period a few weeks ago.'

'When exactly did you see your period again, and how long was the duration of the flow?'

'On Oct 21st. I remember noticing it after I had slept with...'

'After you slept with whom?'

'No one.' Tears trickled down my eyes.

'How long was the flow?'

'Just that day.'

'That was after the sexual intercourse?' she asked firmly.

I nodded.

'Was that your first time?'

'Yes.'

'That blood stain may have occurred because you were a virgin. The hymen was broken, which has nothing to do with your menstruation.'

Nina walked into the room. The doctor told her they needed to discuss it in her office. She placed a kiss on my forehead before following the doctor. As soon as the door was shut, I began to cry. I was distraught because Abednego had not picked up my calls after he travelled with Brother, and before then, he had avoided me after our last sexual escapade. I assumed that he was worried because Brother almost caught us and Bola had encouraged me that he just needed some time to think.

I placed my hands on my stomach and thought again. Maybe this pregnancy wasn't so bad after all, because if Abednego knew I was expecting his child, he would leave his wife and marry me. I thought he loved me that much.

CHAPTER THIRTY-ONE

SHELDRAKE

New-York City, USA

I stared at my opponent on the floor and realised I had just knocked down the former United States champion. The referee lifted my hands and declared me the winner. I had just become the new world heavyweight champion.

I began to experience rapid flickering of the eyes and a recurring headache in my temporal region. I closed my eyes for support because my head began to spin in circles, which made it difficult to hear the screams of triumph from the audience and my team. I opened my eyes when I heard Abednego screaming 'Victory!' and raising my hand. The referee handed me the championship belt, while the commentators screamed that I was the new world champion.

I caught Papa staring up at me with a huge grin and teary eyes as he marvelled at my victory, knowing that this road to conquest had been a long one. I smiled back at him only to realise that the cameramen from the media were already in the ring and were focusing the cameras on Abednego as he spoke to them about my training routines.

'So how often did you train him, Abednego?'

'Was Sheldrake's success entirely up to you?'

'Is your wife coming to Nigeria soon?'

'Is the rumour true that her new charity gala would focus on sea cadets and African boxing?'

I immediately felt empty seeing the reactions of the media once more. I realised I was becoming agitated because, from the position I stood in on that day, I could spot Silver in the crowd as she smiled sheepishly at me, indicating that she was right about Abednego. Her phone rang, and she picked it up after she winked at me. My vision became hazy as I saw a lady that looked exactly like Mama standing next to Silver. She was dressed in her maid's uniform from the past. She was staring straight at me with a poignant look as she shook her head in disappointment before turning away and disappearing into the crowd. *I must be losing my mind.* Immediately, I experienced another severe throbbing headache. I looked around and realised that the media men had forgotten all about me. *Was Mama disappointed? Was my victory all about Abednego and him being a white man? Was Silver Right?*

I recalled letting go of my championship belt at that very instance as it fell off my grip. I screamed out loud and then smiled as the echo of my voice overwhelmed the boxing arena. As I did that, the camera crew stopped filming Abednego and focused on me. I could see the shocked expressions on most people's faces and especially Abednego,

Jimmy and Papa. I walked up to the reporter that was initially talking to Abednego and snatched the microphone from her.

'I am the world champion now. I deserve all the respect that I can get. My brother is here...' I tapped Abednego's shoulder, 'He did assist me in the training and all... well because he is my manager and coach, regardless of all of that, I did the winning and all. So, what did I say Mrs Reporter?' I pulled up her chin and forced a smile at her.

'You said you did it all,' she repeated nervously with shocked eyes.

'Bien.' I smiled genuinely now and then handed back her microphone. This made the cameramen follow me with their lenses now as I left the stage infuriated, ignoring commentaries coming from the reporters and commentators that followed me.

'*What the hell?*'

'*What was that all about?*'

'*Seems something is going on here that the outside world is oblivious of?*'

I made my way to my changing room without waiting to respond to Papa and Jimmy, who called after me. As soon as I got into the room, I walked to my locker and forcefully pulled it open. I saw my reflection in the mirror. I flinched. My lips were half engorged, and my left eye was half closed because of the swelling around my orbital region. I spotted blood dripping down my nose. These were preceded by flashes of light and severe body pains, while I saw Mama's image reflected in the mirror before me. She had a disappointed look on her face again. At that moment, I recalled losing my senses because I screamed aloud and at the same time, I threw a punch at the mirror and watched it shatter to pieces. Papa and Jimmy rushed inside and shut the door against the media men who were trying to get in. Papa hastened towards me as I kept on punching the locker. I recalled him speaking sternly in our native dialect.

'What the devil has gotten into you, my son? This is the beginning of your victory. You are a Sheldrake. Compose yourself.'

That instant, I stopped throwing punches and panted heavily. I turned to stare at him in confusion. He embraced me.

CHAPTER THIRTY-TWO

ABEDNEGO

I was confused by the sound of Sheldrake's cry from inside the changing room. Everything happened so fast that day. I recalled that one moment we were all excited and I was talking to the reporters in the ring and the next moment, Sheldrake caused a scene. I followed the press alongside Jimmy and Jide to find out what the hell that stunt was all about and the next thing I was distracted by my vibrating phone.

'Hello, who is this?'

'Hi, it's Nina....'

At that very moment, I heard Sheldrake's roar, followed by the murmuring of the media men.

'What the fuck! Nina, I can't talk right now, you have to call back...'

'Wait, Abednego... Martha is pregnant.'

As soon as I heard those words, I believe my heart stopped beating for a few seconds, followed by sudden palpitations.

I stopped walking towards the changing room amid the crowd. I fell silent.

'Are you there?'

'What did you just say, Nina?'

'Martha is pregnant, and she has been expelled from school.'

I put my hands on my head to comprehend what I had just been told.

'And the father?'

'Don't play dumb with me. She told me everything. She is a mess right now.'

'Did you tell Sheldrake?'

'No, I haven't. It's not my place to. You need to come home right away. I will stay with her till you get here.'

'Thanks, Nina.'

I hung up and immediately made a call to Jimmy. I instructed him to meet me up in my private plane and that he should tell Jide and Sheldrake that it was an emergency. He tried to argue with me that leaving Sheldrake right now in the middle of his meltdown was bad publicity. I yelled at him and told him that I pay his damn salary and that I didn't need his advice. We were silent almost throughout the entire flight back to Lagos. I was sitting in agitation at the window seat, while I unconsciously gazed out of the window.

'It's been over six hours, and I have watched you look lost while you stare out of the window. What the fuck is going on?' I heard Jimmy's voice, interrupting my thoughts. He was standing close to my seat.

'It's nothing, Jim.' I dismissed him.

'I have known you for too long, man, and besides, we have come too far to see what we are trying to build crumble.'

'Crumble? We just won the fucking world championship.'

'Besides winning championships, we both know that the aim for this organisation is holistic capacity building for young men, and that's why we receive funds from the United Nations and NGOs from England, which your wife's family is involved with...'

'I know all that please! This is not the right time to tell me about a business I engineered,' I snapped at him.

'But it is the right time to tell you that your friend and your best fighter just had an emotional meltdown and you dashed off... What the fuck is going on here? I moved my life to Africa for a dream you believed in and when I see a gap or stumbling block in that dream it's my duty to caution you.'

'Well, some things are more important than a meltdown right now?'

'Like what?'

'Like Martha getting pregnant,' I blurted out.

'Holyshit! That slimy girl! I knew she was not naive at all...
but wait! Does Sheldrake know? Is that what happened to
him?'

'He has no clue, but the thing with Sheldrake is that his
unconscious bond with his sister is very strong. Back home
in South Ciskei, I used to hear stories of how bonds are made
by spiritual attachments by African people. I believe that he
felt something. It's more of a spiritual attachment to his
sister.'

'Then I don't get you, man. You made us leave an important
event for the news that Martha is pregnant. We would have
sorted that out when we got back... That's not your priority.'

'I am the father, damn it!'

I watched him sit down in astonishment. He looked up at
me in revulsion for the first time. He said in the most
composed way he could muster, 'You just ruined a man's
life.'

'What?'

'What the fuck don't you get? That little girl is Sheldrake's
Achilles heel. She is all he got. Before every fight, I did my
research and would talk to him about the life he can give
Martha. That's how I made sure he won all those goddamn
fights. She was our card to success. He fought his way to the
top because of her.'

'And you think I don't know that!'

'No! You fucking don't! Because if you did, you would have kept your thing in check! I may not have wanted this move to Africa and not have accepted this 'bro' bond you have formed with Sheldrake, but I sure know when to stop. She is a child! Any conscientious person saw how she worshipped you. Just by her look, I knew that she had a crush on you. But I never said anything because I thought that you would be man enough to never go that route. I watched you fuck all those women while you had a wife, and I didn't give a shit because it didn't affect the business or your sense of reasoning. But this is the most fucked up thing ever! This affects everything we have worked for over a year in Africa. This affects everyone, especially your father-in-law's career and our major sponsorships. I can't believe I gave up my life in England for a minor's pussy. I believed in you, goddamn it!'

'I don't need your lecture.'

'But you have got to hear it! Because we both know you are never gonna leave your wife! Jesus Christ, Abednego! You can never fix this! As soon as we get out of this plane, I am done with all of your crap. I am walking away.'

'Then that's fine, you walk! You think I planned this? I am in a mess right now, and for the first time in my life, I don't know what to do! So don't preach to me about you giving up your fucking career or life for me, you were fucking paid!' I yelled back at him. He was about to reply when the voice of the pilot and air hostesses interrupted us. The plane was about to land.

CHAPTER THIRTY-THREE

MARTHA

It was difficult to regain consciousness of my surroundings that very day, but slowly, I tried to open up my eyes as I heard whispers from familiar voices around me. I was not sure whom the voices belonged to initially, but I soon realised the owners. I shut my eyes and pretended to still be asleep while I listened to the heated dialogue between Nina and Abednego. *They were discussing me.*

'Are you trying to tell me that you don't want her to have that baby?'

'It's not a matter of what I want. She has no option, Nina, she just can't have it.'

'Why again, if I may ask?'

'I already told you that having this baby would ruin her life.'

'You mean your life? She has already been expelled from school. She has no life for now.'

Nina I am expected to donate a huge amount for an important project for that school, her expulsion is not a problem. Things can be arranged. She can go back to school. All I ask now is that you help me take care of the baby she is carrying… you can always say it was a false positive result from the lab in the school.'

'Jesus Christ! Don't ask that of me. You are talking about the integrity of my career here.'

'She would be ruined if she had that child, and we have not even begun to talk about my wife and her family. And spare me the details about your career because we both know that you are having an affair with your patient and that is not ethical…'

'Jesus Christ, Abednego… Don't make me feel bad about that. That's not fair, and you know it.'

'Come on…. I apologise, but I am desperate here. Look here, most importantly what do you think Sheldrake's reaction will be when he finds out? All I am asking, Nina, is that things can be sorted out my way without Sheldrake ever knowing and any other person getting involved in this mess.'

'I am sorry, Abednego. I care too much about Sheldrake to get involved in your mess…'

'For the love of God, this issue can be solved, I have a wife, goddamn it! I owe her that much, I can't leave her.'

I couldn't bear the thought of what I assumed he was proposing to Nina at that point. Silently, I began to cry as I slowly opened my eyes. I began to sniff. They realised that I was conscious, and I saw them dash to my bedside. I recognised my environment and became conscious. I was lying down in my room.

My head was throbbing as I tried to recall the last event that happened that morning when the school principal summoned me to her office at lunch-time and unsympathetically gave me my due punishment: *Expulsion.* As soon as I came out of her office in tears, I saw Habib chitchatting with Emeka and Bola in the hallway, which was directly opposite the principal's office. I realised that the door of the office was left ajar and I began to ponder. *Did he hear anything? Did he know?* Our eyes met, as chills ran through my body as he walked up to me.

'What are you doing here?' I asked in tears. I saw the burning hatred in his eyes, which was followed by a smirk. He handed me his mobile phone as he coldly spoke to me.

'Came here for a job interview. By the way, you should watch this. It's gone viral.'

In the video, I saw myself standing in front of the principal while she confirmed I was pregnant.–As she was about to utter the words 'expulsion', I let go of his phone and it crashed on the floor. Chills ran through my spine as I realised that the world would soon find out that I was pregnant. I fainted. However, the dialogue between Nina and Abednego indicated that they had no inkling that a recording ever took place of the ill-timed incident.

'What happened to me? Where am I?' I sniffled, staring around my surroundings.

'You fainted in school. But you are okay now, love.' Nina consoled me while she stroked my hair.

'And the baby?' I murmured as I turned to Abednego, who stood there staring blankly at me.

'The baby is fine, love,' she assured me. I smiled at her as I put my hand on my abdomen. Seeing that, Abednego stiffened, then walked out of the room. As soon as I heard the slamming of the door, I couldn't control my tears and anguish any longer. I began to wail out loud.

'He doesn't want the baby, Aunty Nina? Why does he look at me like he does not want me now?'

'Ssssssh, don't talk now love. He will come around.' She kept on stroking my hair as she reassured me.

CHAPTER THIRTY-FOUR

SHELDRAKE

JFK Airport

I walked into the private lounge wearing my lazy black stripe tracksuit, earphones and Ray-Ban sunglasses. I deliberately needed to conceal my puffy eyes from the constant flashes of camera light of the media, who anxiously waited to take my pictures as I departed from my hotel room at the Ritz Carlton that day. I ignored the various comments from the reporters as the bodyguards and Uncle Jide steered me into the waiting limousine.

'What instigated your meltdown, Sheldrake?'

'Are the rumours true that you are having a dispute now with Abednego?'

'Why did Abednego leave New York without you?'

I had not slept well from the previous night, and I was knackered! I recalled that I had paced up and down my room that dark night when we got back to the hotel. I was on the edge which was ignited by the preceding events. I didn't feel the excitement of victory that I was supposed to be experiencing at that moment. We had escaped the press using the back exit door, an idea suggested by Jimmy after he dashed off from the room to answer Abednego. I couldn't comprehend why they had to leave America so abruptly. Papa interrupted my chain of thoughts when he came into the room with a sombre look.

'Take a seat son. We need to talk.'

'Talk about what?' I stopped pacing and sat down and then lit a cigarette.

'All your life, I watched you grow, I watched you turn into a man without experiencing the joy of childhood. You had to cater for me and your sister...'

'Where is this going?'

'Don't interrupt me, boy.' He snapped. 'We never spoke about what happened during the Apartheid and it's my fault...'

'Uncle...'

'Let me speak. You watched your mother get violated and die. You killed a man to save her when you were just a child. These things mess with people's minds and change people. It did change you. I hoped and prayed that when we escape this route of poverty, we would all forget these past events in our lives. But I was wrong. I say this because I am like a father to you, and I failed in my duties for not trying to get you to a doctor to talk about these things...'

'You mean a shrink? You think I am crazy?'

'No, son, I mean a doctor like Nina. Speaking to a doctor would have helped. The white man's ways are not as negative as we always thought. If this was done earlier, maybe you would not have been so aggressive and angry at life, although it forces you to achieve so much all the time, it is dangerous to your mind and health. You have to let go, son. Be happy, you have come this far in life and it's time to let go. Your mother would be proud of you when you decide to live a little and let your sister live a little too. She's a good kid. I am so proud of you. So, stop this attitude of trying to get more than what you have got. Abednego loves you like a brother, and you should never forget that.'

I looked up at him and nodded. I put off my cigarette and we both embraced.

I took off my sunglasses and sat next to Papa at the JFK airport the next day . The waiter walked up to me and handed me a menu list and I ordered a glass of cold lemonade. After a few drinks, Papa excused himself to go to the restroom, and I saw Silver approaching. She was as usual sophisticatedly dressed in a white vintage fur coat. I made a face. Regardless, she pulled out a seat next to mine and gave me a flaccid look.

'Your invariable nasty look towards me is like a broken record now,' she said freely and sat down. The waiter arrived with a glass of lemonade in a tray for me but she picked it up and sipped it, ignoring my demonstration.

'This is frosty, but you need a lot of this now with the news I am about to break to you.'

'Look, I am not in the mood for your bullshit.'

'Of course, you can't be in the mood after your display of global meltdown... Not so good for business,' she tossed the daily sun newspaper on my table. The headlines were boldly written *New World boxing champion meltdown?*'

'They have to write something to get paid. Who cares? I like the *World Champion* part,' I calmly replied. I collected the glass of lemonade from her and tasted it. I suspected that my calm reaction threw her off balance. I had come to terms with the fact that she was one great part of my life that stimulated negative thoughts about Abednego in my head. Uncle Jide's discussion with me the previous night made me want to go easy on life and give myself a pat on the back once for what I had achieved. I couldn't wait to go back to Nigeria and apologize to Abednego and embrace Martha. I was at long last going to permit her to throw the biggest birthday party she had always sought. Uncle Jide was right. She was a good kid and Mama would have been proud. Also, I was going to talk to Nina. I was going to ask her to marry me. I didn't know the logistics of getting a fancy ring, but I had decided to let her pick it when she had agreed to my proposal. I knew she loved me and I couldn't wait to see her take off the champagne diamond engagement ring of her old-looking fiancé in exchange for my own ring. I thought I had life all planned out that day. *Only if I knew...*

'Cheers,' I continued. Suddenly I watched her frown turn into a smile.

'You amaze me sometimes, Sheldrake, but I am sorry. I have to let you know that my offer still stands open when you hear this...'

'Humour me, madam...' I didn't finish my statement because we were interrupted by Uncle Jide.

'Haven't you tried to do enough harm by poisoning his mind against Abednego? He doesn't want to come to work with you. I would appreciate it if you go back to your husband. Leave us alone.'

He pulled up a seat next to me, which was opposite her and then folded his hands. I thought at that point in our lives he felt a sudden need to protect me from her. He had a distressing look on his face.

'Poison his mind? He is a big boy, Jide.'

'Don't worry, Uncle. She is about to leave.'

'No! Actually, I am not going anywhere, I have just started...'

'Leave now, Silver, before you provoke me to call security. You are harassing us, ma'am,' he sternly interrupted her.

'Security for me? Harassment?'

'I said get up now and keep walking. You don't need the embarrassment, ma'am, because I am sure big shots like you can't take it.'

I turned to Jide and was thrown back by his surprisingly harsh attitude. His hardened jaw with a cold and warning tone alongside his bloodshot eyes revealed that he meant everything he said. I remember that day so vividly because, at that second, Silva got up from her seat with poise. We watched her turn around to leave and then stopped and turned back to look at Uncle Jide with a forced grin.

'Come to think of it... following your profile...you are the calmer, older and wiser one amongst this bunch. Your reaction at this instance towards me gives away two things... you know, and you know that I know too.' I watched Uncle Jide uncomfortably nudge his shoulders, and his silence made her smile because she realised that she had hit a nail.

I was confused by what just transpired between them.

'Leave, Silver,' he ordered calmly.

'He should know, Jide.'

'Know what? What the hell is going on here?' I asked, perplexed.

'Obviously, you haven't heard the news yet...'

'Don't, Silver...' Uncle now had a pleading and tired tone.

'He is a big boy, Jide. You shouldn't protect him from the truth.'

'What truth?' I spoke up.

'I think you should watch the news more often. I mean, YouTube channel.' She walked towards me and handed me her phone after opening YouTube channel. On the tiny screen, I saw Martha in front of her principal. The principal told Martha she was expelled because she was pregnant, and a few seconds after that, Habib appeared on the screen saying:

'Here is the school of the little and dear sister of the African Champion... Martha. She has been expelled from school because it has been confirmed that she is pregnant...'

'What is this?!' I couldn't bear to listen anymore at that point. I smashed the phone on the floor.

'How far can you go with this? Don't you ever bring my sister into one of these sick games!' At that instance, I saw an image of Mama standing behind Silver. She had tears and sorrow in her eyes and just like that, she disappeared. I felt I had disappointed her once again. I grabbed onto Sliver's neck with one hand in anger and slammed her on the wall. I lost it. I began to strangle her as she coughed. I ignored Papa's pleas, the cries of frightened children and women as well as the approaching footsteps of the airport security operatives.

'Ma'am, are you okay?'

'Back away, sir!'

'Let her go, sir!'

I was oblivious to the comments or reactions towards me. I was filled with so much rage that I could barely hear Uncle Jide's voice trying to tell me to back down. I ignored the frightening looks of the previously enchanted female fans as they stared at me in revulsion.

'Let go of me. You are weak and slow,' Silver spoke with gritted teeth. At that point, the cops had come to hold me.

'Don't you ever come close to me or my family again.' I warned her amidst bloodshot eyes and protruding facial veins. However, to my wildest dismay, she looked quite composed. She straightened her ruffled dress and gave an irritating grin.

'It's okay, officer.' She said. 'He is just having another of his famous meltdowns.' Right after she said those words, the volume of the TV in the lounge became louder, and appearing on a large TV screen was Fox breaking news, which featured the exact clip that Silver had just shown me. I felt my inner spirit leave me that instant; it was replaced by an empty void, which made my hands tremble. I tried to make it stop trembling, but I couldn't control it, and neither could I sustain the turn of events that very day as I turned around to stare at Uncle Jide, who looked distraught. He too must have known about it. *That means this might be true?* Silver witnessed my raging anger turn into despair and took advantage of it.

'By the way, you must know that the father of her baby is your devoted friend Abednego. Don't forget to watch that part.'

I placed my hands on my chest to stop the piercing pain and tightness of my chest that was accompanied by a crushing sensation of defeat, failure and betrayal. *It couldn't be!*

'Now you know where to find me,' she turned around and walked away.

CHAPTER THIRTY-FIVE

ABEDNEGO

I decided to lock myself up in the study that day and drink myself into a stupor while I listened to the miserable and loud melodies by Johann Strauss's orchestra. I instructed the staff not to let anyone into the study. I felt lost and confused. So, my options were either to drink myself to sleep or take charge of the situation, which included speaking to Martha and trying to convince her about the negative consequences of having the baby. That day, I chose the latter option. I had downed about three glasses of Dalmore 62 Single Hiland Malt Scotch.

I heard the banging of the door. I ignored it as my drunken mind began to flashback to South Ciskei when I was a little boy. It felt like I was in a trance because the music playing in the background at my father's mansion was still the same melodies from Johann Strauss's orchestra. It was the very same day that my father was throwing a welcome party for me and mother because it was our first visit to South Ciskei. I recall hearing moans from my bedroom that day after Mama had tucked me in bed. The noises distracted me from the sweet melodies from Strauss, so I decided to get up and trail the noise. After a few silent steps, I found myself in front of a door ajar, and Sheldrake's mother was sitting on my father's lap half-naked as they had sex, while Sheldrake stood dumbfounded at the entrance of the door in between me and them. I had screamed out loud in confusion and more, in an attempt to distract them and help avoid a scenario where Mama would walk on them. It was that very day I felt this hatred for my father for the first time. *How could he do this to my mother and me?*

Again, my mind travelled to England, and I could still hear the same music playing because it was my mother's favourite. I had arrived from school and rushed upstairs because I was distracted by the wailing coming from the next room. It was my mother's room and the screams sounded like Grandma's. I saw Grandma holding onto the lifeless body of Mother on the floor, while grandfather was fidgeting on the phone trying to call the ambulance service. I stood lifeless in the doorway as my heart began to beat fast; it gradually began to break into pieces as my eyes caught the empty bottle of prescription pills on the floor next to my mother. *She killed herself.*

The banging on the door increased, as I felt my eyes shut down and my head fall on the office desk. Almost immediately, I felt someone's hands on my shoulder.

'Go away!' I lashed out as I opened my eyes. Martha was standing in front of me. She looked morose as she stared down at me. *She has turned me into a father now.*

'I gave instructions that I should be left alone. Don't you get it?' I lashed out.

'Does my pregnancy affect you so much that you want to drink to death? I have been banging on that door for over thirty minutes,' she asked as tears poured out of her eyes.

'What for? I thought Nina gave you some drugs to sleep.'

'I didn't take it; I sneaked out of my room when she was answering a call from her fiancé...' she gives a sarcastic giggle and said, 'I thought she was Brother's girlfriend? She practically has a husband.'

'Well, that is what your brother and I do. Fuck the wrong women.'

'Don't say that... We love each other and we are expecting a baby.' She moved towards the table and tried to touch my cheek, but I backed away. I saw the hurt in her eyes, but I didn't care, because I needed her to see reason.

'There is no us, Martha... and there has never been, you need to get rid of that child.'

'You love me. I know you do.'

'You are a child. What do you know about love? You have to stop this!'

'No! You don't kiss somebody... or make love to someone as you did to me and not love them!'

'Jesus Christ, Martha! I am married and I am never going to leave my wife! You need to understand. It's my fault; I should have been firm with you right from the start and controlled my urges when you approached me. You are just a child. This was a mistake and you are about to ruin your life, mine, Sheldrake's and the life of that little child if you decide to bring it into this world.' I felt a piercing pain slice through my heart as I uttered those words, but I ignored my feelings.

'What are you trying to say, then?' she asked in anguish as she clinched onto the neckline of her night robe and cried.

'We need to quietly terminate the pregnancy before it ruins everything we have laboured for.' As soon as I uttered those words, the door of the study room flung open and I saw Sheldrake standing in front of the door, with Uncle Jide behind him. He looked straight at me with an expression I have hardly seen before. *He couldn't have known. Jimmy would never tell him.*

'Terminate what?' he uttered as he walked into the room. He looked from me to Martha, who immediately started fidgeting.

'Terminate what?' he asked calmly again but this time, looking straight at Martha.

'We were just discussing terminating Habib's appointment...' I tried to explain, but he interrupted me by pointing a finger at me.

'Shut up. I am talking to my sister,' he said calmly. Then he continued, 'I have two questions for you Martha and then one for you Abednego.' My head was racing because I had no clue he knew; I interpreted his mannerism as his usual mood swings. He took a few steps forward and stood directly in front of Martha.

'Martha... were you expelled from school, and are you pregnant?' I was shocked. I saw tears pour down Martha's eyes as she trembled. She nodded, and Sheldrake's eyes immediately became watery. My heart immediately became heavy as I realised the gravity of my fuck-up. He knelt in front of her and cupped her face into his hands tenderly.

'Were you raped? You can tell me. I am your brother. Mama was too, you know. I would understand!'

She shook her head in reply and wailed, 'I am sorry, Brother!'

He wiped off his tears with the sleeves of his shirt and stood up. I could see his chest rising as he began panting in fury.

'So, Abednego, do tell me, who is the father of this baby?'

I became speechless because I had just received a bolt from the blue. *He knew.*

'Speak up, man! Who the hell is responsible for violating my sister?' he screamed as he stared at me. I could see his protruding jugular veins pop out of his neck.

'I am, but it's not how it sounds—'

I couldn't finish my sentence because I was interrupted by a blow on my face. The impact of the punch threw me down across the room. Blood splashed out of my mouth. I tried to stand up but was thrown off guard by Sheldrake's imminent reaction; he jumped on my body, and I fell right back on the floor. He began to hit my face with his fist in rage. I tried not to retaliate and let him hit me, covering my face to block the punches.

I could hear Martha wailing as she screamed, 'Get off him,' and she tried to push Sheldrake off me, but Sheldrake shoved her away with his other hand. She landed on the floor crying. I could hear Jimmy's and Jide's call out for security. Soon, security men arrived, and with immense difficulty, they pulled Sheldrake off me while other guards' assisted me to stand up from the floor. My eyes were swollen, and I caught the reflection of my battered image on the opposite wall mirror and instantly I lost my composure. *My face, which was my vanity, was everything!* He had known that that's why he targeted my face. I could still hear his outbursts.

'Let go of me. Let me tear your damn face apart! You bloody pervert! You raped and ruined an innocent child I left in your care! Now tell me? What is the difference between you, your father or your uncle Jefferson!'

'Enough! You better shut the fuck up! I didn't rape Martha, and you know it! If you were around to accept responsibility for being a proper guardian, instead of feeling sorry for yourself about the past or running after a woman that clearly would never be yours, you would have damn well noticed that Martha's reputation was already close to being ruined! If I hadn't knocked her up, believe me, somebody else would have had!' I couldn't take the insult anymore. My pride would never allow him to disgrace me in front of my staff.

'What did you just say?' he stammered as my statement caught him off guard. I could see his body stiffen and unruffled. He looked straight at me, like a stranger for the very first time.

'Order your guards to let go of me,' he uttered calmly but firmly. I gave them a nod and my bodyguards complied. As soon as they released him, he stared at Martha, who had her head buried in Uncle Jide's chest.

'Pack your bags. We are all leaving this place. We are done with Abednego. Silver was right about you all along. How could I be so stupid? You just used me to get away from your miserable life in England and ahead in your long career? I gave you the credibility and famous headlines an aristocrat like you always wanted. *The white hero who comes to Africa to rescue the niggers by boxing.* Silver has been right all along. I am slow and weak'. He chuckled bitterly before continuing, 'What kind of man watches his father die at the hands of a white man and his mother forced to sleep with the boss to put food on the table and still gets raped and killed by the same family? What kind of man experiences and knows all of these things and yet still blindly leaves his sister to the care of a person from that same family? A negro. I must have been the joke of the town.'

'You need to stop saying those things son… you are hurting yourself' Jide tried to interrupt him, but he wasn't having it.

'One last question. The night I came home looking for Martha, she was in your room sleeping. Did you have sex with her?' he suddenly asked calmly.

'Yes, I did.' I replied calmly. I was tired of lying. I watched the disgust on his face.

'Your family was always cursed... like father, like son... and like uncle. Now, look how you repay me, by once again violating my family.'

'Stop it. I am not my father!'

'You are right. You are not. He was more honourable. He was more direct and never pretended to be a snake. At least he was not a paedophile...that's what you whites call it, isn't it?'

'I picked you up from the gutters and put you in my home because I loved you as family. That doesn't give you the right to insult me. What happened between me and Martha was a mistake!'

'And, from that gutter, I am going to reap all that glory from you.' He challenged me.

'You think I don't know that Silver has been approaching you? I always knew you were too thirsty for power, and now, you want to use this as an avenue to wrestle me. So now you want to leave and work with her? We have a contract, Sheldrake; things don't damn work that way.'

'You did pick me from the gutter, and I learnt a lot from you. At least the pitiful monkey wasn't that slow to pick up some legal terms. Cancel that contract if you don't want a lawsuit. Martha is a minor. I am sure that your name and your wife's in England means everything to you.' I didn't reply because I was exhausted, and I knew that he got me by the balls already. I watched him walk out of the room, with Martha following him. Soon the room was empty, after I had screamed at the rest of the staff to get the fuck out.

I remember that day vividly because I felt my heart crushed into smithereens after I was left alone in the room; that lonely feeling suddenly crept up on me again after all these years. The silence of the room accompanied by the droplets of blood from my wounded hand and the site of scattered furniture with broken scotch glasses left me distraught. *I am alone.* I ignored the distracting ringtones from the land phone. It was my wife calling. I wasn't in the mood for her nagging. I walked to the window of the study, when I heard the sound of car engines. I watched through the open windows as Abednego, Jide and Martha's suitcases were lifted into the cars outside my house. I watched them get into the back of the vehicle and I exhaled. My attention was soon diverted by the knock on the study door. I turned around as Jide walked in. He looked at me with disappointment in his eyes.

'I forgot my diary while the fight was going on.' He walked to the bookshelf beside me and reached for his diary in the middle of the shelf and then attempted to turn around to leave.

'Jide, at least say something to me.'

He stopped walking and then turned around to face me.

'I know I fucked up.... I didn't mean a word of those things I said to Sheldrake. He hurt my pride just by saying that I am like my father... I just need all this to go away.' Tears suddenly dripped down my eyes.

'I know you didn't mean them. But what I do know is that you slept with a lost child, who he thought was like a baby sister to you, and now you want her to terminate the pregnancy. Do you know what psychological trauma an abortion can have on a woman of Martha's age?'

'What I do know is having a child who feels lost, and doesn't experience love in this world is worse than death.'

'You white people...' He shook his head and continued, 'You know nothing about death in comparison to life... every child has a right to life. Do you love Martha?'

I paused and looked at him in confusion because I never expected that question from him.

'What does it matter? I can't leave my wife.'

'It does matter... I am a tired old man and I have seen a lot. I have known you since you were a kid and what I do know is that beneath that arrogance of yours, you would never have slept with Martha if you didn't feel something for her. Family means a lot to you. It is something you should think about. Goodbye, son.'

He walked away, and I was left alone once more standing in the middle of an empty room.

CHAPTER THIRTY SIX

SHELDRAKE

I remember being silent throughout the drive to the hotel. I ignored the irritating sobs coming from Martha and the conversation Uncle Jide was now having on the telephone with Jimmy, who was trying to persuade him to talk me out of the termination of the contract with Abednego. I understood then that despite Jimmy's attitude towards me; he was a good man. He told Jide that he had quit working for Abednego, but somehow, he loved his job and still cared for Abednego so much that he was willing to stick around and resolve the mess before going back to England. He claimed he knew Abednego was a lost soul.

As soon as we had pulled up in front of the hotel where Silver was lodging, on the Island, we saw her already waiting for us at the entrance of the lobby. She was quick to make reservations for us after I had called her and informed her about the preceding events.

'I made sure I booked you guys into the master suite.'

We walked into the hotel. I ignored her gestures and replied sarcastically, 'I didn't expect to see you here, I thought you already had people to do this kind of work.' She ignored my comments and instructed the concierge to give her the keys and told the bell boy to carry our suitcase. Moments later, we had taken the elevator and were shown into the executive suite.

'Martha, dear, hope you are okay. I understand the shame you had to endure because of Abednego,' she turned around to speak to Martha, who was still sobbing.

'He didn't do anything I didn't want, so why don't you just get out of here and leave us alone?' Martha screamed at her and hurriedly walked into a room and slammed the door.

'Woooah, that's very touchy and unexpected,' she commented.

'I will talk to her,' Jide cut in as he followed Martha to her room.

'Thank you, Silver, I really think we need to settle down now. It's been a long day.'

'Yeah, of course, you are doing the right thing, sweetheart. I have always known that.'

'There's something I have wanted to show you. But I waited for the right time. My instinct never failed me.' She handed me a picture. It was an old picture of an elderly man in a familiar house in South Ciskei.

'Do you remember him? His name is Minschini,' she asked calmly.

I recognised him immediately. That was a picture of Mr Minschini from my past in South Ciskei.

'Yes. How did you get a picture of him?'

'He was my father. He stole some money from the mine to send my mother and me to Nigeria after he was fired. I watched Jefferson beat him up to death for stealing. I saw you that day with Sheldrake's father sitting and watching him die.'

'You are Minschini's child?' I was shocked by the revelation. I had a flashback of Jefferson flogging Minschini and the woman I saw behind the straws.

'Yeah, I am. The police arrested my mother too for stealing. I took my brothers and made it to Nigeria alive. Then I promised myself I would never be broke again. So, I learnt white men's way of studying media. We will never be their friends if we are poor. Now the world has changed, and they want to help the black vulnerable and displaced people. But guess what? They made us vulnerable by taking everything from us. That is why I tell you for free, Abednego is not your family. He shares the same blood as his dad and uncle.' I was startled by her revelation. She smiled.

'You knew my story all along?'

'I have always known everything. I knew a day like this would come. I waited patiently for Abednego to let you down…'

'Anyway, see you tomorrow.' She seductively stroked my biceps and then cat walked out of the room after she instructed the servants to leave the room. As soon as she left, I stormed into Martha's room. She was talking to Uncle Jide.

'What was that impertinence all about and that the remark you made? *He didn't do anything I didn't want?*'

'It means exactly what it means, Brother... the truth. And by the way, congratulations! Seems-Silver is teaching you new words, Brother... impertinence?'

'What?' I was startled. Was she getting mad as well?

'I am not a child!' She challenged me.

'Have you gone mad, or it's the pregnancy hormones?'

Enough of that, Brother, Abednego did nothing to me! I was the one who chased him like a lovesick puppy! His crime was only falling for my body and loving me.'

'Loving you? You are stupid. He wants neither you nor your baby.'

'He will... He just needs time. He loves me, Brother.'

'Have you finally lost it, child? Or did he brainwash you too?'

'It's Mrs Silver who has brainwashed you. Abednego is right, Brother. You have been so intoxicated with the money and fame that you are getting from boxing that you won't stop until you get it all. Now, you want to use my misfortune to fight against him. He delivered us from poverty. We couldn't even afford a bottle of coke but still, I was happy back then because you were around, but now we have all this and you were never there. I needed my brother and a friend. He was there for me when I needed you the most...'

'He pretended to be there because he is a sick pervert, just like his father. He wanted to take advantage of you.'

'Why won't you get this, Brother? I am no longer the sweet little girl you think I was. I wanted him to fuck me, he did, and I loved every minute of it.'

I slapped her, then choked her until Uncle Jide jumped between both of us to separate us. I let go and watched her let out a wail as she fell to the floor. Uncle Jide tried to hold her. I stared at her in disgust because I couldn't believe the words that came out of her mouth. She acted like she was being possessed by the evil spirit Mama used to talk about. I looked at my quivering hands. I could never have believed I was capable of hitting my baby sister. Everything I held dearly seemed to fall apart at that moment. It came along with the sudden feeling of emptiness and failure. Then I understood the phrase that Mama usually made 'all that glitters is not gold'. Martha seemed to fit right into that picture and the feeling broke my heart.

I stormed out of the room and walked to the bar in the next room. I pulled a bottle of Jack Daniels from the shelf and gulped it straight from the bottle. I shut my eyes and tried to block out the abrupt flashes of light and severe temporal headaches that accompanied the images of Abednego having sex with Martha. I tried to quench my anger with liquor as memories of overlooked events began to add up. I had flashbacks of my time with Abednego when he would stay at home with Martha while I went for training. The memory of the night I had gone looking for her in her room and later finding her lying in her pyjamas in his room made me feel like a fool for trusting him because he had lied that she had nightmares. In raging anger, I smashed the bottle of liquor on the wall.

The noise of the broken bottle attracted Uncle Jide, and soon, he rushed into my room.

'What the hell is going on?'

'I need to be alone, Uncle.'

'What you need to do is to listen to me... Son, you are going about this whole thing the wrong way...'

'What do you mean?'

'Strangling your sister or fighting Abednego is not the answer.'

'Then tell me, Uncle, what is the solution?!' I screamed at him with bloodshot eyes.

'If I told you I knew right now, I would be lying... but the reality is Martha is expecting a child, and she needs her family, that is, her brother and the father of that child to be united.'

'Tell me, Uncle, are you saying that it is okay for her to bring a bastard into the world? Wake up and smell the coffee, Uncle. That baby's daddy is a married, racist prick and wants nothing to do with that Negro baby. He is a British royalty. Is that justifiable?'

'That's not what I am saying…'

'Then agree with me that taking what he loves the most, that is the image of him being the undefeated world champion is the right thing to do… and don't tell me otherwise.'

He shook his head in disagreement and continued, 'You may fail to believe this but the championship is not really what Abednego cherishes the most, son.'

'And what is it?'

'Family, you and Martha. You both leaving the house is enough punishment for him.'

I burst out laughing.

'Uncle, you are still living in an illusion. That monster stood in front of me and claimed he delivered us from poverty after he defiled my sister! He looked me straight in the eyes and told me I wasn't good enough for Nina… it seems he always wants to be on top.'

'It was in the heat of the moment. You called him his father… That is what he has dreaded to be called all his whole life… He made a mistake. Let it go. We can all work it out together. Silver is not the solution.'

'No, Silver is the solution. It is funny because sometimes I still feel you are still living in the era of Apartheid. It is not okay for a white man to feel he is king after having sex with a child! That shit doesn't fly anymore. I am fighting him and that's final.'

'How about if you lose... have you ever considered that defeat could just take you into a much darker place?'

'I won't.'

He paused before saying, 'You know, you, I or Martha, whom you love so dearly would never have made it alive if Abednego didn't give us the tickets or 100 rands to sail across the sea. However, my deepest fear in all of this... is that you are the one wanting this championship so bad that you just can't see it. I won't be there to support this fight...'

'You don't have to. Just shut my door and leave.'

I turned and walked into the bathroom. I heard the outer door shut. I walked into the shower and let the water run for some time before stepping into the hot shower. As the warm water poured on my skin, I felt lost in the shower. I shut my eyes and realised that I wasn't alone. I felt the calming touch of her hands on my chest. I opened my eyes and saw Nina standing before me naked. She threw her arms over my neck and began to kiss me. I was so swept away by her touch and the warmth of her lips. I felt my anger subside and in delight, I picked her up in my arms and carried her into the bedroom.

Two hours later

I opened my eyes. I saw Nina sleeping next to me. She looked beautiful wrapped in my bed sheets. I thought to myself, *this is the only thing that makes me sane right now.*

'You are staring at me,' she whispered to me with a smile while her eyes remained shut.

'Just watching you sleep and thinking about how you make me happy despite all of this mess.'

She opened her eyes and pulled me closer to her and kissed me gently. She stroked my head and spoke, 'I am so sorry, baby. I know how you must feel. I just wish I could do something to make you feel better.'

'Marry me.'

'Wh..a..t?' I watched her stammer and her eyes looked away from mine in shock.

'You heard me. Marry me.' I pulled her chin towards mine, as I poured my heart out to her. 'There is one thing I have learnt from all of this madness. I love you. You are my reality in this fucked-up world. I want to spend the rest of my life with you. You make me happy and content. I know I would make you the happiest woman in this world if you would let me.' I watched as she began to silently cry.

'I can't...' she replied.

'Sorry?'

'I can't marry you, Sheldrake,' she tried to touch my face but I pulled away. I got up from the bed and put on my trousers.

'Don't go cold on me. Talk to me.'

'What the hell do you want me to say? I just poured out my heart to you and asked you to be my wife and you rejected me.'

'I have a man that I am getting married to in a few weeks you know that... Please don't make me feel worse than I already am,' she got up from bed and walked towards me.

'Do you love me, Nina?'

'What?' she tried to back away, realising that my question caught her off guard, but I held onto her arm.

'You heard me. Damn it! Answer me.'

'What difference does it make?' she tried to pull away.

'Do you love me?'

'I do love you… but…'

'But nothing... If you can admit that you love me, why can't you be mine?' I let go of her arm, now fully content with her response.

'Because you knew what the terms were before we started... Please try to understand. My fiancé is a good man. He has taken me this far in life... my family had nothing...'

'Then I will pay him back every dime he has spent on you.'

'He loves me...'

'And I love you more.'

'I am so… sorry I can't bring myself to hurt him. It won't be right.'

Tears poured down her eyes but for once in my life, I was not moved by it. I realised that Abednego was right; she was never going to leave an aristocratic white man for a black boxer from the ghetto.

'The white man always wins... I think you should leave.' I walked to the door and opened it.

'Don't do this. Let's talk about this.'

'Talk about what? That I am good enough to fuck, but not good enough to marry. I guess I am not that white enough for you.'

'Please...' she tried to touch my face again, and I turned my back on her.

'Get dressed and get the fuck out of my life. We are done.' I walked out of the room and out of the hotel, ignoring her tears.

CHAPTER THIRTY-SEVEN

MARTHA

Six weeks later

I lay on the couch in front of the obstetrician as she examined my abdomen with a digital ultrasound. She told me she could detect the baby's heartbeat, but I was lost in thoughts. The past few weeks were one of the most challenging times of my life. Brother had buried himself in training for the upcoming fight with Abednego in a few days. He hardly came home. The few times I ran into him at the hotel, he was engaged in discussion with Mrs Silva and his new coach and manager. He would completely ignore me. He looked at me repulsively when our eyes met, especially on days that I carelessly came into the living room with a tan top which exposed my protruding stomach.

Meanwhile, Uncle Jide grew paler and older by the day because he appeared worried about my brother and my situation. It seemed that brother and Nina had fallen apart because he had forbidden me from associating with her, and he refused to pick up any of her calls. He encouraged me to register in a clinic that Aunty Nina had recommended.

During this period, I never actually saw or heard from Abednego. The only time I saw him was when I caught a glimpse of him from the newspaper clips that Papa would read and hide away from me or on the television. I remember crying to sleep all night because I sat in front of the land phone every morning and waited to receive a call from Abednego, but it never happened.

The analysis of the boxing match was trending in every social media, and my anticipation grew. Silver had arranged a lot of interviews and publicity for my brother. It seemed she was a damn good Public relations officer. Brother appeared to be pleasantly overwhelmed by his increasing popularity because he had many important guests coming into the hotel now to see him. However, his relationship with Papa had deteriorated.

'Do you want a scanned picture of the first baby's heartbeat?' I realized the Doctor was speaking to me.

'No doctor.' I answered.

Soon Papa and I left the Doctor's room and were walking down the hospital hallway when we ran into Miss Nina. She had a worried expression on her face.

'Good to see you, Mr Jide and Martha' She said with a broad smile. She kissed my cheeks and Papas.

'Good to see you, Doctor.' Papa replied.

'How's the doctor's appointment going?'

'Not bad. Thanks for the recommendation. We are most grateful.'

'I have been trying to get a hold of Sheldrake for a while now... I tried calling both of you, but your phones were unreachable.'

'Brother took away my phone, so I haven't been able to call anyone.' I answered.

'Been so distracted by the family feud. Sorry didn't remember to return your call. Getting old, I guess' Papa put in.

'I must reach him... he is not picking up my calls. Can you tell me how?'

'We all have seen your wedding in the newspaper. It's the same day as Sheldrake's fight. Maybe it's best if you let him be Doc Nina'.

'Mr Jide, I understand you have hesitations for practical reasons, but we must see...please.'

Her pleas touched me, and I knew Papa was not going to speak up about Sheldrake's whereabouts, so I broke the ice.

'Brother trains at Mrs Silver's private gym in Ikoyi at 2 pm. You can reach him there.'

'Silver won't let you in...She watches him now like a sick puppy even if you can find the place,' Papa interjected.

'She's attending a gala with her husband by 3 pm. So you can get in.' I overheard her conversation with my brother yesterday.

'Thank you, Dr Nina kissed my forehead and hurriedly dashed off, only to be left with Papa and the disapproving look on his face.

CHAPTER THIRTY-EIGHT

SHELDRAKE

Without any company, I trained in the ring at Silver's clandestine apartment and kept throwing aggressive punches at the punching bags. I stopped for a second and picked up a bottle of water from the fridge outside the ring. I pulled off my boxing gloves and stopped to look at the television news. It was a caption of Nina in the arms of her fiancé' with Abednego at Nina's elaborate engagement party. The reporter was commenting about Nina's chic Valentino floral dress. I threw the water bottle against the T.V. screen and hopped back into the ring with a renewed determination to break every bone on Abednego's body.

I was so preoccupied with throwing straight and front-circle punches at the punching bags that I failed to hear the sound of Nina's approaching footsteps. However, her familiar fragrance and voice sound gave away her presence. I turned around and saw her standing a few inches away from the ring. I wanted to hate every bone in her body, but her beauty's simplicity still captured me. I held myself not to give away any inch of my longing towards her. I frowned at her.

'What do you want? Who the hell let you in?' I continued boxing.

'I need to talk to you.'

'We have nothing to talk about, Nina.'

'Please, this is important... Please read this. I have been trying to get hold of you for weeks...' I ignored her and kept doing a straight punch-circle punch combination, alternating between the right and left fists. Then I moved my feet and swivelled my hips.

'Please!'

The reverberations of her plea made me stop and, again, turn around to her. She looked different. She appeared distressed and paled in her cream cotton tunic dress. I got down from the ring and walked up to her. She handed me a brown envelope. I calmly collected it.

'What is this?' I asked calmly while opening it. She didn't reply. I pulled out a paper from the large envelope and saw that it had a scanned image of a brain and below the picture were written interpretations of the central nervous system, which I clearly couldn't comprehend. The only thing I recognized was my bio-data written boldly on the top of the scan.

'What is this, Nina?' I asked once more.

'It's the test results of the M.R.I. we carried out a few months ago on you. Your Uncle contacted me a few weeks ago,-the last time I was at your place. He was concerned about some of your attitudes, like mood swings and hallucinations. So I decided to take a second look at the scan. I sent them to a neurologist in England when I detected something the radiologist had missed in Nigeria. The results just got back to me a few weeks ago....'

'What the fuck are you saying, Nina?'

'You have Glioma, a tumour in the brain, Sheldrake. It is precipitated by the trauma you get while boxing. You can't fight Abednego!'

On hearing the news, I burst into hysterical laughter. I watched her stare at me in confusion as if I had gone mad.

'My love, please listen to me...' she began to tremble while she attempted to touch my arms, but I shoved her hands away.

'How dare you come in here to tell me this shit?. You tell me my Uncle called you about my health the day you screwed me. So, what was that, a messy fuck?'

'Don't say that!'

'I will speak as it is. To tell me I have cancer so I could drop out of the fight? Did Abednego put you up to this? Is your white boy suddenly developing cold feet?' I grabbed her arms and began to shake her violently.

'You are hurting me! Please stop!'

'Tell me the truth!'

'You know my practice is my life! I would never defy it!'

I observed her eyes water in agony as I let her go. I believed her. Despite the hatred I felt for her at that moment, I knew deep inside that she loved me, but she was willing to give that up for a man she didn't love just because he assisted her in getting her medical degree. I exhaled and tried to give away no sign of anguish.

'Explain this condition to me?' I asked coolly.

'It is called Glioma, glioblastoma multiforme, grade four astrocytoma. It presents with symptoms such as occasional behavioural changes, hallucinations, epistasis, head tilting, nystagmus (rapid flicking of the eyes), difficulty swallowing and unsteady walking. Your condition is most likely caused by exacted pressure on the spinal cord by boxing or previous history of trauma.

As she listed each symptom, I suddenly began to have flashbacks. When she mentioned epistasis, I recalled my fight with Abednego and the incident when I had fallen on the floor and hit my head at club carnation after catching Mama sleeping with the Mayor. I vividly remembered the bleeding, flashes of light and pain that began afterwards.

I remembered the visions of Mama's face when she mentioned hallucinations. I also remembered my temper tantrum in the U.S.A after she said the 'behavioural changes'. Suddenly, every sign and symptom I experienced as a child and adult seemed to add up. I felt defeated again by life but didn't dare reveal any sign of weakness. *Weaknesses are for pussies.*

'What is the prognosis of this disease?' I interrupted her harshly but calmly.

'Poor… If you get on that ring, Sheldrake, it wouldn't be a good one. Your chances of survival will be minimal. But if you let go of boxing, it could be managed.'

'Who else knows about this?'

'Nobody.'

'So, I still have my doctor-patient confidentiality, as you educated people call it?'

'Yes, you do, but….'

'Good. You are not to tell anyone. The fight continues.'

'Jesus Christ, Sheldrake! I will not let you get into that ring and die!'

'You would do exactly as I ask. Now, please leave.'

'I love you...with all my being... I wouldn't live without you. Please let me help you.' Tears trickle down her cheek. At that moment, I didn't care for anything anymore. I didn't give a damn about how she felt towards me. Her reciprocated feelings came too late.

'You would say nothing to anyone Nina. If I hear whispers from even the pigeons about my health, I will let the whole damn world know that you screw your patients while treating them.' I coldly spoke up to her.

I saw the horror in her eyes.

'I mean every damn word I say. I will ruin your precious career, Nina. Now, get the hell out of here, Seyi!' I got back into the ring and watched the security guards escort Nina out as she subbed.

I walked to the room's window and watched her slowly walk to her car. Immediately, I saw Silver's car pull up the driveway. She got out, and Nina spoke to her. I watched them both enter the house again. I knew they were both going to Silver's study because that was where she entertained her business meetings. I made my way there.

I stood in front of the door and eavesdropped on their conversation.

'So why did you want to talk with me?' I heard Silver ask.

'Sheldrake can't fight. What I tell you is confidential, but I have no choice.' Nina replied.

'Why? Because he has Glioma.' I heard Silver speak up coldly.

Immediately I was shocked that she knew and had never mentioned my condition to me. Nina's face looked shocked too.

'You knew? How?'

'Before I bet on any player, I do my research. Without my homework, I will not support someone with erratic behaviours in the ring. I had a doctor pull up his medical report years ago. His illness was confirmed as we reran other medical check-ups. You missed checking on the report of his C.T scan when you started screwing him.'

'You didn't tell him?' Nina's voice was weak as she trembled.

'No.'

'How could you? He might not make it if he goes into that ring, and we both know it.'

'It is going to be the fight of the century, and I have invested a lot in it. So, Dr Nina, I am not calling it off.'

'You bitch. You care more about money than Sheldrake's life. He is a good man.'

'So good, but you are going to marry someone else? You are just like me, sweetheart…cold.'

'I am not like you, and my relationship has nothing to do with this…. I am going to tell Abednego…'

'No, you would do no such thing. You seem to forget that this tumour had been there for a while. You, as his Doctor, should have noticed it. But you preferred to screw the world champion than attend to his medical needs. That's how the cover page of my international sports magazine would cover it, Dr Nina. Anyway, you see it, your life is screwed, and your license to practice will be gone. So I would advise you to marry your little white husband and live happily in a house by the lake or something. Just stay away from matters that don't concern you. Because I promise you, I will ruin you if you mess with my job, so don't you dare mess with me.'

'If he dies?'

'Then Abednego has it on his conscience for the rest of his life... who knows? He might even be charged with abetting Sheldrake's death if a report shows that he knew Sheldrake was ill all along. Who knows, he might end up like his mother and take his own life.'

'You witch.'

'Yes, I am a witch. The kind that makes damn sure that the father's sins fall on their children. Abednego's family was no saint, and he is not escaping this one. Now get the fuck out of my premises, Cinderella'

I had heard enough. I realized that Silver herself was damaged goods too. Her childhood had been damaged by the white man, too. She cared more about defeating the family that took her father's life away than saving my own. But at that point, I couldn't care less about her intention because I only cared about taking away Abednego's pride, even if I had to die fighting. I slowly walked upstairs to the gym room, into the ring and continued training.

CHAPTER THIRTY-NINE

ABEDNEGO

I kept working on the treadmill for three hours before taking a break. I went into my study room and sat down. I needed a smoke. The quiet nature of the house sort of disheartened me. My gaze fell on the newspaper and magazine clippings on my desk. It was filled with all captures of Sheldrake and Silver. I frowned as my eyes fell on another magazine of Nina's engagement party. I wondered how Sheldrake was taking the news. *Poor bastard. I did warn him.*

Jimmy walked into the study room.

'The loneliness in this house sucks,' I said carefreely.

'Yeah, it does. Fix this. It would suck more when I leave for England after the fight, but you still got time to talk to Sheldrake'.

'Look at all these damn clippings, man; he loves this. He has always wanted to be king. The fame has intoxicated him.'

'Well, he might have wanted this all right... but he would never have conformed to this if you hadn't messed with Martha'

We both fell silent for a moment before I spoke up.

'What do you propose I do, man?'

'Call him. You owe him that much.'

I picked up the phone and called, but he never picked up my call.

CHAPTER FORTY

MARTHA 13:00, ABUJA, TWO WEEKS LATER

At a snail's pace, I squeezed myself through the crowd and tried to saunter towards the front of the sizeable T.V. screen at the swarm and rowdy pub, which was two kilometres from the Yar'adua Boxing Arena in Abuja. I was still in my first trimester but the messed up physiological changes of pregnancy were now telling on me. My stomach had protruded, and I had put on an additional 10 kg. I placed my hand on my stomach as I felt uncomfortable. I tried to talk to the waiter who stood beside me to get me a glass of water, but he ignored me; he, too, was engrossed in the live match.I couldn't blame him. It was the hottest boxing match of the century and nobody wanted to miss any minute of the game—nobody but me.

I suddenly felt dizzy. I wished the game could stop, as it was my entire fault. This brawl was never meant to occur, but my ignited passion and love for Abednego seemed to have ruined everyone's lives. The adoration, friendship and respect that brother, Papa or Abednego ever had felt towards me, and each other had painfully come to an abrupt halt. If I had known better, I would have avoided throwing my body at him numerous times, but I didn't. I was wantonly, emotionally and crazily spellbound to Abednego for too long, and now there was no turning back. Luckily for me, the waitress behind the cocktail bar noticed the agonizing look on my face and in concern, she asked if I was okay.

'Please, can I have a glass of water with lime?' I calmly requested.

'Sure. Sorry, this match is what we have been waiting for, for ages. Our services are a lot better than this,' she smiled apologetically before going to get my drink. After about twenty seconds, she returned with my cold glass of water with a slice of lime.

'Hope you don't start labour any time soon.' She joked. I forced a smile in return. I handed her a 100 naira bill. I was not in the mood for dry jokes; she got the message. She collected her money and turned around to attend to another customer while I concentrated on my drink. No sooner had I started drinking than I heard an uproar in the pub, making me almost choke on the water.

'Oh shit!' I heard the crowd scream.

I was forced to look up at the T.V screen before me, and what did I see? I watched as Abednego threw a hook punch at Sheldrake. It was a semi-circular punch thrown with the lead hand to the side of Sheldrake's head. Abednego drew his fist from the guard position to protect his jaw and chin from the opponent. He was firmly rooted to the ground as he confidently threw a free brilliant punch against Sheldrake.

It was a hook that troubled Sheldrake because he did not expect it. Blood gushed out of Shedrake's nose as he fell flat face down on the floor of the ring. The referee began to count; the crowd was cheering wildly. Abednego looked weak, and he was sweating profusely. His left eye was half closed, and his temple was swollen. He finally stood up. It was as if he dared Sheldrake to stand up. I soon began to have palpitations as I heard the commentator count to five.

'Sheldrake is standing up. Is he truly the undefeated world champion? That can defeat the legend of our time.'

Sheldrake, too fully stood up on his feet. His eyes were inflamed, and saliva flowed freely from his battered lips down to his chest. Despite my concerns, the referee motioned for the fight to continue. I felt a rush of chill go through my body as my eyes were fixed on Sheldrake. There appeared to be no life left in him. He was staggering alongside Abednego. I noticed the cold stare he gave Abednego as they stood, ready to continue. Sheldrake began to bounce around Abednego. Abednego started throwing jabs at Sheldrake. The crowd began to roar, and the commentator asserted:

'Oh my God... That's Abednego's, the former undefeated World Champion giving his signature and deadly knockout punch which no one has survived!'

Sheldrake staggered backwards a little after the punch was thrown at him, but to everyone's greatest surprise, he didn't fall. He stumbled back a bit as blood splashed down his mouth despite the mouthguard. The mouthguard was halfway out of his mouth, almost ready to fall. Sheldrake used his gloved hand to place it in its correct position.

It all happened so fast. Immediately he replaced the mouthguard; Abednego looked like he was cut off guard because Sheldrake hadn't fallen to his deadly punch. Sheldrake took this shock to his advantage, and before Abednego could recover, he had reciprocated the blow with a similar technique. That was Abednego's signature punch on his jaw. Abednego fell backwards through the ropes, and his body lay motionless on the ring apron in a few seconds.

I watched Abednego fall on the boxing floor alongside the world that day in apprehension. The referee began to count as the commentators continued chattering:

'This is unbelievable because it looks like Abednego is not getting up......'

Suddenly, the whole shout in the pub seemed to be gone or did it just rescind to the background? I felt a sudden sharp pain in my heart. I couldn't hear anymore. But I could see, and all I saw was my brother, pacing menacingly over the fallen champion, Abednego. The referee lifted my brother's hand as he had won. I was numb. Something was not right because I still couldn't hear the crowd scream. I just kept on watching my brother's odd facial expression. He was given the belt. His new manager and Silver had come into the ring and were screaming aloud in victory.

'I knew this was the real champ.'

'An African and the first migrated Nigerian world champion in Nigeria! This is unbelievable...'

Abednego was getting up now with the help of Jimmy. I observed Jimmy talk with him as he gradually stood up from the floor. The championship belt slowly fell from my brother's grip. I put my hands on my chest as my heart raced. Before we knew what was happening, my brother had fallen flat on his face. The crowd looked confused and shocked. The referee rushed to him and tried checking his pulse, but it looked like he wasn't moving. Blood flowed freely from his nose as his eyes remained shut. His new manager kneeled next to him and tried to sit him up. Abednego was now by his side, too, frantically trying to bring him to consciousness. He took my brother's wrist and tried to get the pulse. The next thing I heard was his screams.

'Where's *the damn paramedic! Can somebody help!'*

The paramedics were now in the ring. The commentators continued, *'This looks like a serious situation up here...'*

I didn't wait to listen to it all. I rushed out of the pub like a crazy woman, racing towards the direction of the taxi park and hoping to get to the boxing arena on time

CHAPTER FORTY-ONE

SUN INTERNATIONAL HOTEL, 12:00 PM

The Oriental hotel penthouse suite was playing host to about ten bridesmaids, makeup artists and a couple of wedding photographers from top soft-sell magazines in the country as they competed to take pictures of the bridesmaids in her magnificent Vera Wang. It was a combination of both long and short styles: short strapless tulle dresses with a bubble hemline and long elegant, crinkled chiffon column dresses with asymmetrical draping. The colour of the day was fusion pink. The ambience in the room was lit up with Asa's song 'Mr Jailer'. Everyone sang harmoniously and danced.

Nina opened the door and walked into the room's open admiration. She was dressed in a vintage wedding dress with a clean geometric line, open back and sleek silhouette in bold black and white. Her hair complemented her look, which was neatly rolled up into a bun, exposing her bare shoulders. Her sister accompanied her.

'You look magnificent!' the French lead photographer screamed out loud.

'Thank you Monsieur Lafi,' she replied with a forced smile. She cleared her throat before speaking aloud. She whispered to her sister to turn off the CD playing. She did, and immediately the room fell silent.

'Everyone, please excuse me, I am so sorry to be the one to stop the music, but you can see I am the bride...' Everyone smiled. She smiled back and continued. '....You girls look stunning, and I know the photographers would make them look more heavenly when this event is featured in *Vogue, Genevieve and Ovation Magazine*. I just wanted to thank you all for being here before the big moment starts, which is about now. So if you don't mind, I would like everyone to excuse me for some time. I need to talk to my sister for a bit. Thank you.'

Soon she and her sister were left in the large room.

'I don't know if I can do this, Caroline...' Nina suddenly broke down in tears. Caroline, her sister, was shocked but quickly gathered herself to console her sister. She pulled out an armchair and a tissue from the tissue box placed next to her. She handed it over to Nina.

'Is this cold foot? Because I read that it happens to all brides.'

'No, it's not...' Nina snapped

'It's about Sheldrake then... isn't it?'

'Yes.' Nina nodded in agreement.

Caroline exhaled before speaking. 'I knew there was something always going on between you two. You were always lousy in trying to hide anything...'

'Am I?' Nina asked with half a smile as she lifted her face and looked up at her baby sister.

'Yep. Ever since you met Sheldrake, I noticed that you became different. You became happy. It's been a while since I heard you laugh so often. You love him don't you?'

'With my entire heart, sister....'

'But love is not enough, sister. That's what you have always told me. Tim paid for your studies at Harvard and a fellowship at Yale, making you the best Neurosurgeon. He paid for my music school at Brown ever since Papa died. He has cared for us because he loves you. You can't throw that all away. He made it possible for you to have that education that allowed you to meet Sheldrake. You owe him. We owe him.'

'But my heart's breaking,' tears began to drop down her cheek.

'With time, it would be amended. You would live, sis.' Caroline replied in a firm tone. She handed her a handkerchief and watched Nina clean her cheek.

'... Now don't ruin that gorgeous Shomya makeup. The wedding is in a few hours.

She kissed her sister's cheek and then walked to the door, pulled it open, and called out the bridesmaids waiting in the lobby.

***

SAINT DOMINIC CATHOLIC CHURCH

13:00

Nina slowly walked into the church as the church orchestra began to play the wedding march song by Mendelssohn. She smiled as her elderly Uncle held her hand while they walked down the aisle. She stared straight ahead at her groom. He was beaming with smiles, looking proud in his grey Armani suit, cravat and tuxedo. *He is a good man.* She reminded herself, and these thoughts kept her going. She wanted to cry again but knew she had to be strong. Her Uncle had traditionally handed her hand to him and took his seat. Nina saw his eyes glitter as he lifted the veil that covered the magnificent features of her dark brown eyes. The ceremony began, and he whispered sweetly in her ear: 'I am a lucky man' She smiled.

'We are all gathered here today to witness this holy matrimony....'

Nina was already lost in thoughts. She had acted against her medical ethics when she dropped off an anonymous letter that revealed Abendego's condition for Jimmy in his home. She hoped the letter got to him in time and he had read the note before the fight commenced. She was worried sick as she deliberated on the outcome of the match between Sheldrake and Abednego if Jimmy never got the letter.

'Darling...'

'Nina? Are you okay? You are gazing into space'.

Soon her thoughts were interrupted when she realized that the priest and Tim were simultaneously calling out her name. She became conscious and noticed the looks of agitation on the faces of the concerned congregation.

'Sorry, baby. I am okay. What did he say?' She asked.

'Are you sure?'

She nodded. She stroked his face with her fingers and smiled.

'Please continue.'

'Do you take Tim as your lawfully wedded husband, in sickness and health, for richer or poorer? Till death do you apart?' the priest repeated.

'I do.' She replied. She looked up and saw Tim's eyes lit up, and he exhaled with relief.

The exchange of vows went on for the next thirty minutes, and finally, the wedding rings were exchanged.

As the church wall clock struck 13.00, Tim put the wedding ring on Nina's finger, and Sheldrake's hand was lifted as the new world heavyweight champion. Concurrently, Martha was placing her hand on her chest as she experienced a sudden awkward feeling while Papa Jide had taken off his eyeglasses and slowly sat down on his sofa in front of the T.V in his hotel room. Like a movie script, it all played out simultaneously now: Sheldrake fell flat on the ground and closed his eyes in the ring just as the wedding ring slipped down Nina's trembling finger. Nina stared down at her wedding band on the floor with sudden weird intensity as she felt a piercing pain go through her heart. She knew instantly what had occurred because she felt it. Her heart had stopped beating. She bent down to pick up the ring on the carpeted floor, just as her groom made for it, but he was faster than she was. He picked it up and looked up at her. He realized that tears were pouring down her cheek. Her eyes were shut and she gripped her chest. He held onto her hand and assisted her as they stood together. He misinterpreted her tears of sadness for tears of joy. She forced a smile, and the ceremony continued.

CHAPTER FORTY-TWO

St Nicholas hospital, Lagos

The ambulance sped into the hospital, and the medical team wheeled out Sheldrake, accompanied by Abednego, standing next to him. An oxygen mask was fixed on Sheldrake's face. The accident and emergency doctors and the Neurosurgeon were already in front of the A and E unit. They were waiting for him to disembark. The media men were not left out, taking pictures of every detail they could capture. This occurrence was covered live by all the broadcasting news television in Africa. Abednego looked confused as he ran alongside the doctors when they rushed Sheldrake inside the hospital with the stretcher. He was holding onto Sheldrake's hand. *'Stay with me.'*

They wheeled him into the theatre. Abednego ran his fingers through his damp hair.

Jimmy soon arrived at the waiting area in the hospital and looked apprehensive. He had forgotten the bruises and arching pain the fight had left on his body. He knew something was wrong. Jimmy had felt that he had a faint pulse when he abruptly appeared and jumped into the ring.

'What's going on, Jimmy? Talk to me.' Abednego said to him. 'What did the paramedic mean that there was faint pulse reading and why did they use defibrillators in the ambulance…' Jimmy handed him a letter. It was a copy of the summary of the medical report Nina had slipped under his office door.

'What is this?' Abednego read it slowly.

Mister Sheldrake Mandiva/ male/ Hospital Number 12014

The patient named above is diagnosed with Glioma, glioblastoma multiforme-(grade 4 astrocytoma) precipitated by exacted pressure on the spinal cord by boxing. He presents with occasional behavioural changes, hallucinations, epistasis, head tilting, nystagmus (rapid flicking of the eyes), difficulty swallowing and unsteady walking. The patient has failed to adhere to recommended medical advice....

Abednego stopped reading the note halfway and looked up at Jimmy.

'What is this...? I don't understand.'

'This seems like a photocopy of his medical report from St. Nicholas hospital... it was slipped under your office door. I tried to get to you before the fight began, but it was too late.'

'What the fuck is a glioma?'

'It's a malignant brain tumour...'

As if suddenly realizing the mess he was into, Abednego knelt on the floor and began to weep.

'This can't be? No... he wanted everything I had. He always wanted to be the world champion!' He turned towards Jimmy with a fierce look for reassurance.

'The weird behaviour, sudden change, aggressiveness for wanting it all, his agitations, and midnight screaming when he said he hears his mother... this note explains it all, Abednego.'

Abednego had stopped listening. He had wanted to wrestle with him. He began to have flashbacks of his first fight with Sheldrake at the Club Carnation years ago.

'You white bastard, don't you dare talk about my ma' like that. Your father raped her! I will kill you.' He recalled that Sheldrake had bounced on him with bloodshot eyes and given him a blow to his head. Also, he had violently bitten him on his hand like an estranged dog.

Then he recollected another moment. He was with his mother behind the Rolls Royce the day they were finally leaving South Ciskei. His mother's face was dazed when she read the caption of a tabloid the driver had just presented to her. At that instance, the Mayor rushed outside the house and tried to stop the moving car from passing the gate. He jumped in front of the moving vehicle to plead with his mother. However, he had only succeeded in stopping the car. He remembered his mother's rage when this incident occurred. She stormed out of the car and walked up to his dad.

'How dare you try and stop me. I am taking my son out of this ungodly country to be far away from you and those savages. Because of you, my son is exposed to your barbaric lover's son who has violently cut off your brother's head in cold blood!' she threw the newspaper at him.

His mind travelled to a conversation with Abednego after he had won the first Nigerian professional championship game.

'What keeps you going, bro? I feel frightened sometimes, man. You were like an animal in the ring. I thought you were finished at a point during the fight until I saw that rage in your eyes.' He asked Sheldrake.

'It's like Mama was there. I might have been in a trance. I might sound crazy, but she whispered to me when I was down to get up. I see that stern look she gives me when I am on the verge of losing'. He had replied.

'Might have been that blow to your head. You better keep on seeing your Mama because it sure worked...'

He shook his head in disagreement.

'This can't be.' He said. 'Every child who experienced what Sheldrake had during those periods in South Ciskei might have reacted that way and even worse. He had a bad life, man.'

'He did. You said so. But it is what it is. I think this is from Nina. She knew and was trying to tell us something, but it was too late...'

'No! Where the hell are the doctors!' Abednego's eyes became misty. He tried to talk to the Doctor. He noticed a doctor in scrubs coming from the Intensive Care Unit. He was one of the surgeons who assisted in wheeling Sheldrake into the Intensive Care Unit.

'Be patient, sir.' He said and hurriedly left his side.

Again he turned for assistance from the nurses coming from the Intensive Care Unit. But again, they were not responsive. Abednego became frantic.

He walked to the window and looked down at the reporters standing outside. He lit a cigarette. His cell phone began to ring. He stared down at it and saw a call coming from his wife. He ignored it and then his father-in-law. *Could it be that the whole world knows?*

Jimmy came up to him and handed him his cell phone.

'Turn that cigarette off, man. It's Jide on the line. You are in the hospital, don't make matters worse.'

He handed the cigarette to Jimmy, collected the phone and exhaled.

'Hello.'

'What Jimmy says, is it true? How's he looking?' he heard Jide ask in a fragile tone.

'Jide....'

'Talk to me. I'm about to have a cardiac arrest. I am too old for this suspense shit! Is he going to make it?'

'Don't know. I haven't heard from the doctors yet.'

There was a period of dead silence on the other end of the phone.

'Did you know he was sick?' Abednego asked, breaking the silence.

'I knew he became different. For God's sake, he has always been different.... but not brain tumour different.' Abednego heard silent sobs coming from Jide's end.

'Where are you?'

'In a car trying to look for Martha....' he sniffed.

'Have you heard from her?'

'No. The driver said he took her to a pub. I need to find her before she hears any of this from outside. It might kill her and the baby, and if anything happens to that girl, that might kill Sheldrake faster than a brain tumour. She's his life. Stay by his side till we get there. Got to go,' he hung up.

'Martha', He whispered her name after hanging up the phone. He had forgotten about her during this ordeal. He initially blamed her for their crisis and didn't want to see her again, but now the only thing that came to his mind was self-hatred. He suddenly realized that he had gone too far and might be too late to turn back the clock. At that moment, the Neurosurgeon appeared in his scrub.

'Family of Sheldrake?' The Doctor called.

Abednego walked up to him, together with Jimmy.

'Mr Abednego, you were in the ring with him today.' He said when Abednego stepped forward, unsure of his statement. '...I watched that fight. I need his family to discuss his medical condition....'

'I am his family.' Abednego assured him. 'His sister and father aren't here yet.'

'Well, it would be difficult to give you details or authorize you to see him now....'

'What the fuck do you mean? I am his family! How is he?' Abednego yelled. He gripped the Doctor by the throat. Jimmy tried to pull him off the Doctor, together with the security and other Doctors present.

'I am sorry. Please forgive me.' He apologized. He let go of the elderly Doctor's shirt and then tried to straighten the man's rumbled clothes.

'I understand.' The Doctor coughed after recovering from the shock he had just experienced.

'Please, if he's awake, tell him I am here. He would want to see me. I know that.' He pleaded.

'He is awake. Would tell him and let you know when he is more stable.'

'Thank you.' He sat down on the sofa in the waiting room in dismay as the Doctor left.

A few seconds later, a nurse arrived back with a smile on her face.

'He calls for you, sir.'

Abednego sprang up from his seat and was led to the room by the nurse. However, Jimmy was not allowed to accompany him into the private ward. *Family only.*

CHAPTER FORTY-THREE

SHELDRAKE

I opened my eyes. I felt awful. *Where the fuck am I?* My memory was blank. I looked up and saw Abednego standing at the door of my strange room. I couldn't budge. I could barely breathe. I had on nasal cannula wrapped around my nose and an O2 pulse-oximeter placed on my thumb, which made my thumb uncomfortable. My other hand held the excruciating discomfort of a pink cannula inserted in it from a drip stand beside my bed. I tried to turn my neck to observe the cardiac monitoring devices positioned around me. Then, I attempted to sit on the bed, but Abednego hurried to my side and gently pushed me back to relax my head on the pillow.

'You can't move. You shouldn't move.' I heard him say in a concerned tone.

'Looks like I collapsed again.' I struggled to speak while I coughed. I was tired of fighting at this point. I knew I had to let go.

'Don't speak. It's okay. You will be okay.' He reassured me.

'Why are you looking like shit,' I asked with a strained beam.

'We were in the ring together, remember? We had the fight of the century.'

The events of the previous night rushed back to my memory. I recollected his hook punch that knocked me down cold flat. At the moment, I thought the contest was over. I was about to give up when I could not rise from the floor. I could hear voices from the commentator and the crowd, but simultaneously I couldn't comprehend what the voices said. At that instance, I felt a chill go down my spine. I realized my vision was blurred because I couldn't see things around me. However, I could trace a familiar face despite my poor eyesight. *It was Mama again. I could hear her soothing voice.* She looked so beautiful in her maid's uniform. Her hair was rolled up in her favourite bun. I tried to reach out to her, to touch her and feel her with my arms stretched wide open, but I couldn't. My knees felt numb. I smiled up at her, but she didn't return the smile. Her look was bland. *Was she disappointed in me? I Failed her. Martha was pregnant now and hadn't completed her education.* I began to cry. I lay on the floor when she majestically walked past me. She stopped beside me, stooped and then whispered in my ear.

'You are a Sheldrake, and we don't cry... So the next time I see you shed a tear, I will hunt you down for the rest of your life. You are going to get your sister...You are going to keep her alive... and get her a damn good education and make her grow into a fine lady...'

Also, at that exact moment, I saw my father standing at the other end of the ring. He wore his black afro haircut, his favourite skinny jeans and a body-hugging v-neck shirt. He appeared ageless, just as he was back then in the Pink

Carnations club. He walked towards me without leaping or using his walking stick. He stood next to Mama and whispered in my other ear.

'You think before acting, boy, that's what a Sheldrake does. Now, that separates you from all the black people the damn whites call savages, boy.' At that time, I summoned courage, got up, and won the fight.

'Yeah, I remember, and I beat you like shit.'

We both laughed for a moment. Almost immediately, I felt a sharp pain in my chest, yet still, I tried to smile as I closed my eyes in annoyance. I remembered every detail of the incident.

'Are you okay?' Abednego asked in concern.

'Yes,' I struggled to reply. I began to cough, and I was feeling breathless. I knew it was time for the pain to go away finally.

'I need to call the doctor....' he was about to rush out of the room.

I grabbed his hand that was placed on the bed and stopped him from moving.

'No, don't leave. Where is Martha?'

'She's on her way here... Jide is bringing her here.'

'You must promise me that she will go back to school... you will take care of her baby...'

295

'It's my fucking kid, man... of course. I will look after him. Enough of this nonsense talk, so let go of me and let me call the Doctor.'

'Promise me.'

'I promise.' He replied.

I then let go of him and smirked.

'You look like shit.' He said.

'Was never the prettiest boy. I couldn't compete with you for that,' I replied. At that moment, I began to experience a sudden relief because the antagonizing pain seemed to disappear gradually. I felt a sense of freedom. I lifted my eyes to the hospital room's ceiling and smiled because, abruptly, my environment appeared familiar. I was lying in the middle of the ring in the Carnations bar. I saw the names of all the great and deceased boxing heroes from South Ciskei written boldly on the ceiling. I saw my dad's name written in red. It was strange because my name was also written boldly in black next to his. I lifted my hand and pointed to the writing with a broader grin.

'Can you see it?'

'See what?' Abednego asked with panic in his voice

'My name, it's written next to Papa's in the Carnation's ring.'

'Fucking crap man, you are in the hospital in Nigeria. You don't see those names because they are all dead people.' He grabbed onto my hand and began to scream aloud. I felt cold. I knew he felt my temperature drop. It scared him.

'Doctor! Doctor!' can someone come in here?

Now I knew it was all over. *I should rest.*

CHAPTER FORTY-FOUR

ABEDNEGO

I watched the doctors put away the defibrillator. The cardiac monitoring machine went static.

'I am sorry. He's gone.' The Doctor said.

I nodded. I couldn't speak. I walked towards the exit door. It was there that I saw her coming. She looked pale and fragile; her face and eyes were swollen, her unkempt hair flying in the air as she raced down the hospital hallway towards me. She had added much weight because of the pregnancy. I realized I hadn't seen her for a while; I wanted nothing more in the world but to protect her from this sudden pain she was about to experience. I also noticed Jide trying his best to catch up with her pace from behind while he limped with his walking stick. My legs weakened as I stood at the door entrance and tried to impede her from going into the room where Sheldrake's lifeless body quietly lay.

'Martha, don't...'

'What do you mean?' she asked, bemused.

'Don't go in. Let's go home,' I softly whispered to her.

'I have no home. Let me through Abednego,' she firmly protested with gritted teeth. She was determined. Resignedly, I stepped out of her way. I followed her as she made for the bed.

'Why isn't he moving...his eyes are closed?' She looked up to me for answers in disorientation.

She touched his arm.

'Why does he feel so cold? Talk to me, brother. Scold me! Open your eyes, please!' she began to shake Sheldrake's body in search of a response as tears flowed down her cheeks. I tried to hold her. I needed her to be calm for the baby. She shoved me aside, and then she fiercely began to hit Sheldrake on the chest.

'Wake up, damn it! I am sorry I failed you. I am sorry... but please wake up. I promise I will abort the baby. Please don't leave me. Come back to me!' she began to hit her stomach as she cried aloud. She wanted the baby dead. It was then that I forcefully held onto her arms. I pulled her close to my chest as she slowly rested her head in submission.

'Please tell him to open his eyes. He promised he would never leave me alone. I will give the baby away and go back to school. I promise.'

'Shsssss.' I pulled her closer to my bosom as she sank helplessly onto the floor. I tried to calm her.

I wrapped my arms around her to comfort her as she wailed. I lifted my head and saw Jide and Jimmy at the door's entrance. Jide had taken off his hat and held it to his chest as a sign of respect - tears flowed down his cheek. I saw Jimmy wearing a distraught look for the first time as he sniffed. His swollen eyes indicated that he had been weeping all along. Jide silently turned away and began to walk towards the approaching doctors down the hallway.

I heard him articulate in a painful tone to the doctors, 'Please take my son away. He's resting now.'

CHAPTER FORTY-FIVE

Jimmy handed the microphone to Jide after introducing him to the congregation.

Jide was surprised at the impressive number of parishioners at the church when he finished his speech. He would never have thought that his nephew's death could attract the whole world.

He was a legend. The church was packed, and most people present cried from the depth of their hearts. His nephew was a good man. *Only if he was alive to see what he had finally achieved.* His gaze drifted to Martha. He couldn't see her face because her huge sunglasses concealed her sad eyes. Her Nanny was sitting next to her. She was holding her baby. The baby was a beautiful baby boy who bore a striking resemblance with Sheldrake, except that he inherited Abednego's curly hair and blue eyes. She named him Sheldrake. She had gone into labour a day after Sheldrake's death. She didn't want to see the baby when he was born initially. Abednego had been in the theatre with her, and she had cursed him throughout the labour process. He remembered he had picked up the baby from the incubator because he was born premature, and when the little one looked at him straight into his eyes, he had fallen in love with him. He held onto the baby and took him to Martha. She had shut her eyes and protested against seeing her child. But he was firm about it and had persisted against her wishes. When she finally opened her eyes and held him. She had broken down in tears.

'He looks like Sheldrake. He has his frown,' she had whispered to her child, and she had finally smiled at him for the first time.

The sermon was now over. They slowly formed a procession, and each congregation member walked up to the open coffin to say farewell to Sheldrake, who lay peacefully in it. Soon, everyone departed from the church leaving behind Martha, Abednego, Jimmy and Jide. They all fell silent as they stared down at the coffin.

'Please take the baby to the car, Emem.' Martha turned around to instruct her Nanny, who carried the baby.

'I will come with you,' Jide said. He walked the Nanny to the car, accompanied by Jimmy.

Martha and Abednego were left alone and fell into deep thoughts.

'I am happy he got the pink incarnations he wanted. He would never have dreamt that his end would be like this. He made history. Mama should be proud,' Martha finally said, breaking the silence. She was looking at the beautiful floral arrangement on his coffin.

'Yeah, she would.' He added in agreement.' The flowers are beautiful' They began to hear footsteps approaching them.

They both turned around, and Martha saw a sophisticated-looking white lady dressed in plain black.

'Hello, baby. I came in this morning...had to pay my duties as a wife,' she kissed Abednego's lips. He looked shocked to see her.

'This must be Martha. I have heard so much about you. I am Shelly. Abednego's wife.' She stretched out her hand for a handshake, wearing a cosmetic smile. She continued, 'the baby I just saw must be yours....'

'Nice to meet you,' Martha responded, shaking her hand.

'Yes, that's my baby, and he looks so much like his Uncle and takes his complexion from his Father,' she boldly replied. She watched the smile vanish immediately from her face.

'I must leave you two. Excuse me.' Martha added calmly

'Martha...' Abednego tried to stop her.

'Please stay with your wife; she has come all the way.' She interrupted him in a cold, firm and gentle tone. He watched her leave as he stared helplessly at her backside. She had grown up suddenly to become a woman of steel.

'I got a letter for you from your grandmother. I think the lady is finally going senile. She says some piece of paper with kind words from her would help you sort yourself out. Winning the election would sort you out and clear our name.' She handed him the newspaper, which boldly had the headline' former heavyweight champion Abednego exploits African boxers to make money. She continued, 'It is so embarrassing that this is all over the news, that you knew your black friend was sick, but you still extorted his ignorance and naivety by allowing him to fight to get different deals.

We must win this lawsuit and get away from this country. It has so much heat and bad roads and inadequate electricity supply. I will be waiting for you in the car outside.' She said calmly, ignoring the statement Martha had made.

She decided to exit and then hesitated, turned around and continued in her usual icy tone.

'We have a reputation to protect, and no illegitimate child of yours or this temporary setback which you created would stop daddy from winning the election. That's the only reason I am here.'

'Do you think this would easily go away?' Abednego asked calmly.

'This is Africa. Dad says the plan is simple. Money talks and bullshit walks. They say their accessors sold them for a goddamn mirror or a bottle of coke. Now put your big boy pants on. Let's get out of this shithole. I am waiting for you in the car,' She handed him the letter from his grandmother with a cold stare and majestically walked out of the church.

Abednego was left alone. He was mentally drained; the premature wrinkle on his forehead was prominent. He stared at the open casket again and closed his eyes. He looked intently at the letter. He studied the paper he pulled out of the envelope. It was old. The handwriting looked familiar; he opened the letter and began reading aloud.

My dear son,

This is the seventh letter I will write to you this year. I don't know if you ever got my previous mails or if you do get them and are ignoring me. If you are receiving my letters and have decided not to reply, I understand and humbly apologize for any misfortune I have brought upon you, son. I respect your decision like the man I know you have grown to become.

Again, kindly accept my sincere act of contrition for being a lousy father. My parents never showed me love so it has been difficult for me to show that too. However, I take full responsibility for whatever drastic actions your mother took by taking you away from South Ciskei and me. I deserve it. I love this African land and culture in so many ways that your mother, grandparents, or you might never understand. I found peace here mainly because I met a woman, Miriam, your friend's mother. She is buried here, which prevents me from going back to England to look for you. For the fear that I may never return to South Ciskei because your mother might-insist that I stay back. I can't leave without the memory of Miriam.

I remember the horrific experience you witnessed back then in my room with Miriam. I must confess that she wasn't just a fling. Your mother always knew about her. I wrote to her a few months before you and your mother showed up at the African ranch. I told your mother that I had fallen in love with someone else and that was Miriam. I loved her from the first day I saw her, regardless of her husband being present. But your mother or her family would never accept my decision, and they planned to take away the funding for my electoral campaign. Besides, I was such a coward to fight your mother's family and openly admit to the public about my love affair with a negro.

Miriam was everything I had always wanted in a woman. She was bold, hardworking, had a positive spirit and was such an upright woman. She had a beautiful heart. We both knew your Uncle killed her late husband at the mine because he had set up the explosives. I coincidently came to the mine that day, and she hated me for that. Her husband tried to save me that night. I felt terrible that he died. But glad to have Miriam. She never wanted to give in to my declaration of love for her. She tried severally to separate herself from me, but I wouldn't allow it. Only her smile could light up a room. It felt like a breath of fresh air, and for once in my life, I thought I could be a better person.

I was a racist…and thought you would turn out like me, to be a white supremacist, but here I am pouring my whole heart down on a piece of paper to my son about how I feel about a coloured woman. I know you must think ill of me that I am inhumane to write such hurtful words after your mother has been kind to me. But when you grow up, my boy, you will understand that love comes in places where you would never dream.

As I write this letter, Miriam is dead now, and I can't find her children to protect them. I made sure I gave her a befitting burial. I am lost because I feel that I have failed her. In addition, the electoral campaign is over, and I didn't win. Your mother made sure of that. I have turned to alcohol to overcome my sorrow, but it seems this antagonizing pain never heals. I have to admit I have lost everything. But my son, it's better to have loved once than never have loved before. I will write to you again soon.

Love,

Your father.

The letter slipped off Abednego's hand as he finished reading, and tears began to drop from his eyes. He wept. He always thought that his father was a bastard, but now he realized that he was only being human. *If only Sheldrake had been alive to read this letter.* Just maybe everything would have been different. He wouldn't have gone through life being so bitter. His father had been looking for Sheldrake and Martha to protect and not harm them. In addition, it meant that his father had been trying to communicate with him throughout these years, and his grandparents had never allowed it.

He picked up the letter and dropped it in the open casket on Sheldrake's chest. Sheldrake was clothed in his native attire. He was always a proud African man, and finally, he looked peaceful; all the signs of his constant frown had disappeared.

'I hope you heard this, brother. My father loved your mother. You were always right, and I guess I am just like him. We don't know how to express ourselves when we are in love,' He spoke aloud. 'Goodbye, my friend. I will make this right.' He promised.

Abednego finally pulled himself together. He felt a heavy burden lifted off his chest as, for once in his life, he accepted he was like his dad. He turned around and slowly made his way to the cathedral's exit door. He put on his sunglasses to hide away his swollen eyes and the flashes of the camera lights from the media men and their outpouring questions.

'What do you have to say about the accusations that you knew sheldrake was ill and you exploited his skills to make money?'

'Is it true your father was a broke politician and a racist?'

'Was it sheldrake that trained you on boxing years ago?'

'Did you come to Africa because you were financially broke and to use our people?' He could hear the venom in their questions

'This morning, your name was removed from the Hollywood walk of fame. What do you have to say about this?'

He realized that the whole world was still waiting for his answers and reactions. He spotted Silver in her Mercedes Benz as she watched him in the back seat of her car outside the church. He could feel her resentment behind her dark glasses. He had learnt that she was the mastermind behind the backlashes from the media. He couldn't blame her. His family had done her dirty. However, she was never going to see him break. He smiled genuinely at the camera for the first time before getting into his awaiting limousine, protected by his bodyguards. His smile was sole because he suddenly knew where to find happiness, and he was finally going to take that chance against all odds. He took off his wedding ring.

The End.

www.ingramcontent.com/pod-product-compliance
Lightning Source LLC
Chambersburg PA
CBHW020842020726
47497CB00005B/1222